LAWR
AND HIS IRRESIS
ARC

"A suspense writer who knows how to mix chuckles with thrills." — *The Wall Street Journal*

"Archy McNally is a raffish combination of Dashiell Hammett's Nick Charles and P. G. Wodehouse's Bertie Wooster." — *The New York Times Book Review*

"Sanders is a huge talent, a writer of smooth, silky prose who can spin a yarn and snare a reader. . . ." — *Mystery Scene*

"You never know what that scamp Archy will get himself into." — *San Antonio Express-News*

"It's a sin not to enjoy Sanders!" — *The Columbia (SC) State*

"Sanders has made Archy, darn it, endearing." — *The Miami Herald*

"Here's Lawrence Sanders, writing with a light touch reminiscent of Dorothy Sayers. Archy McNally is as amusing and rich as Sayers's great creation, Lord Peter Wimsey." — *Cosmopolitan*

"Breezy mystery, with Palm Beach as the posh backdrop . . . Sanders obviously had fun!" — *The Virginian-Pilot*

"McNally is the Nick Charles of the '90s." — *Ocala (FL) Star-Banner*

"As crisp as a gin and tonic." — *St. Petersburg Times*

"An enduring character." — *The Indianapolis Star*

"McNally is a charmer." — *The Orlando Sentinel*

Turn the page for rave reviews of
Lawrence Sanders's bestselling McNally thrillers...

MCNALLY'S FOLLY
An Archy McNally novel by Vincent Lardo

In a play filled with murderers, Archy must separate the actors from the genuine article....

"A frothy caper ... involving an eclectic cast of richniks ... If you've liked previous McNallys, you'll enjoy this one."
— *Fort Worth Star-Telegram*

MCNALLY'S DILEMMA
An Archy McNally novel by Vincent Lardo

A Palm Beach crime passionnel puts Archy in a compromising position....

"The detection is as insouciant as the detective himself ... to be effortlessly enjoyed." — *The Boston Globe*

MCNALLY'S GAMBLE
Archy basks in the sun and sin of Palm Beach— where the rich count their schemes before they're hatched....

"Lawrence Sanders has honed a voice for Archy McNally that is wonderfully infectious. You can't help falling for him!"
— *The Washington Times*

MCNALLY'S PUZZLE

All the pieces fit in McNally's latest case– money, sex, and murder. . . .

"Sanders's novel is easy reading, partly because of the amusing one-liners that McNally delivers throughout the chase."
– The Associated Press

"Should please Sanders's many readers."
– *The Newark Star-Ledger*

"Fun, enjoyable, witty." – *San Antonio Express-News*

MCNALLY'S TRIAL

Archy– and his new sidekick, Binky– investigate the death-styles of the rich and famous. . . .

"Passion, greed, murder, and wit– they are Sanders's stock in trade, and McNally is his most delightful character."
– *Chicago Tribune*

"Archy acts like a character out of Agatha Christie or Dorothy Sayers, and dazzles us with his quick humor and witty analyses of what he finds." – *Pittsburgh Post-Gazette*

continued . . .

McNally's Caper
Archy is lured into a Palm Beach mansion as mysterious as the House of Usher– but twice as twisted. . . .

"Sibling rivalries and passions . . ."   – *The Orlando Sentinel*

"Humorous . . . suspenseful . . . Murder and lust keep Palm Beach hot."   – *The Detroit News*

"Sanders scores with another winner."
                     – *The Wichita Falls Times Record News*

McNally's Risk
The freewheeling McNally is seduced by the very temptress he's been hired to investigate. . . .

"Loads of fun."   – *The San Diego Union-Tribune*

"A real romp."   – *The Sunday Oklahoman*

"Keeps the reader guessing . . . relax and enjoy."
                     – *The Virginian-Pilot*

THE McNALLY NOVELS

Lawrence Sanders McNally's Chance
An Archy McNally novel by Vincent Lardo

Lawrence Sanders McNally's Folly
An Archy McNally novel by Vincent Lardo

Lawrence Sanders McNally's Dilemma
An Archy McNally novel by Vincent Lardo

McNally's Gamble • McNally's Puzzle • McNally's Trial
McNally's Caper • McNally's Risk • McNally's Luck • McNally's Secret

TITLES BY LAWRENCE SANDERS

Guilty Pleasures
The Seventh Commandment
Sullivan's Sting
Capital Crimes
Timothy's Game
The Timothy Files
Caper
The Eighth Commandment
The Fourth Deadly Sin
The Passion of Molly T.
The Seduction of Peter S.
The Case of Lucy Bending
The Third Deadly Sin
The Tenth Commandment
The Sixth Commandment
The Tangent Factor
The Second Deadly Sin
The Marlow Chronicles
The Tangent Objective
The Tomorrow File
The First Deadly Sin
Love Songs
The Pleasures of Helen
The Anderson Tapes
Private Pleasures
Stolen Blessings
The Loves of Harry Dancer
The Dream Lover

THE MCNALLY NOVELS

LAWRENCE
SANDERS

MᶜNALLY'S
CHANCE

*An
Archy MᶜNally Novel
by Vincent Lardo*

BERKLEY BOOKS, NEW YORK

The publisher and the estate of Lawrence Sanders have chosen Vincent Lardo to create this novel based on Lawrence Sanders's beloved character Archy McNally and his fictional world.

MCNALLY'S CHANCE

A Berkley Book / published by arrangement with
the author

PRINTING HISTORY
G. P. Putnam's Sons hardcover edition / July 2001
Berkley mass-market edition / August 2002

Visit our website at
www.penguinputnam.com

ISBN: 0-425-18570-2

BERKLEY®
Berkley Books are published by The Berkley Publishing Group,
a division of Penguin Putnam Inc.,
375 Hudson Street, New York, New York 10014.
BERKLEY and the "B" design
are trademarks belonging to Penguin Putnam Inc.

PRINTED IN THE UNITED STATES OF AMERICA

10 9 8 7 6 5 4 3 2 1

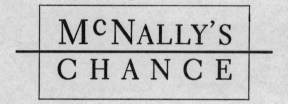

McNally's
CHANCE

ONE

Sabrina Wright.

She was perched on a faux leather stool at Bar Anticipation looking exactly as she did in her author photo on the jacket of her latest bestseller, *Desperate Desire*. Her ebony hair was drawn back so severely from her scalp as to render her startled at what e'er she looked upon and, I suspect, served as a do-it-yourself face-lift. Her eyes were like two shiny black olives; her complexion was one that had never felt the sun's warmth; and her lips, painted the color of a fine Bordeaux, were pursed in an elongated moue reminiscent of the late actress Joan Crawford. She wore a smart white linen suit and black-and-white sling-back pumps that drew just enough attention to her well-turned ankles and calves. Before her was a frothy concoction in a stemmed glass known, I believe, as a Pink Lady.

Sabrina Wright's novels are bodice-rippers *par excellence*. Her first, *Darling Desire* (Darling being the heroine's given name), enjoyed fifty-two weeks on the *New York Times* bestseller list, usurped, finally, by her second blockbuster, *Dangerous Desire*. She subsequently penned such memorable classics as *Deceptive Desire, Dark Desire, Demanding Desire, Devious Desire,* and *Delicious Desire,* as well as this year's sensation, *Desperate Desire*.

Collectively known as the *Books of Desire,* they had been released as a Moroccan-leather boxed set, illustrated in full color, and translated into thirty languages, including Swahili. For the visually challenged they were available in large print as well as Braille. Sabrina Wright's oeuvre had spawned films, miniseries, and a long-running evening soap.

Needless to say, I approached with caution.

"Ms. Wright, I presume."

She turned, startled. "Mr. McNally. How good of you to come." The voice was deep– if she sang she would be an alto– and pure New York. The delivery announced her point of origin with neither pride nor shame, but as a matter of fact.

I moved in closer but avoided mounting the empty stool next to her. "Are you aware, Ms. Wright, that you are sitting in the most infamous bar in South Florida?"

Her dark eyes scanned me, from head to size-eleven white bucks, as her claret lips curved into a condescending smile. "My readers wouldn't have it any other way, Mr. McNally. In Chapter One, my heroine is hustling drinks in a dive like this. In Chapter Five, she owns the joint, and by the final page she's waltzing down the aisle with a title, be it corporate or of the blood."

So the lady had not only borrowed Joan Crawford's lips, she had also borrowed Joan's film plots. As B. Brecht had so aptly put it, "From new transmitters come the old stupidities." Pointing to the empty stool, she invited me to sit. Gray sharkskin merged with Naugahyde as I accepted the offer, saying, "Have you ever considered altering the plots?"

"If it's not broke, Mr. McNally, why fix it?"

Why indeed? "May I ask how you got my name, Ms. Wright?"

"From the Yellow Pages."

"I'm not in the Yellow Pages."

"Precisely. If you were, I would not have called. One cannot be discreet and in the Yellow Pages. That would be an oxymoron."

She referred, no doubt, to my position as sole employee of a section of the law firm McNally & Son, Attorney-at-Law, yclept Discreet Inquiries. My father is the Attorney, I am the Son, who left New Haven after being expelled from Yale Law. Upon my return in disgrace to Palm Beach, my father provided me with gainful employment as a Discreet Inquirer. If our rich clients should find themselves in a compromising position, they may come to me rather than seek help from law enforcement agencies because they do not wish to see their problems headlined in tabloids for their housekeepers to peruse while waiting in the checkout line at Publix.

I tell people I was tossed out of Yale Law for streaking across the stage, naked except for a Richard Nixon mask, during a performance by the New York Philharmonic of Shostakovich's Symphony No. 9 in E-flat major. If you choose to believe that, fine. If not, I will give you a hint that is closer to the truth. It wasn't a Richard Nixon mask and it wasn't Shostakovich's Symphony No. 9.

I WAS IN my office, located in the McNally Building on Royal Palm Way, when Sabrina Wright's call came through. My office is a windowless affair originally intended, I believe, to be a storage closet, albeit a very small storage closet. My father, the venerable Prescott McNally, took pity on me one sweltering August several years back and ordered our maintenance crew to install an air-conditioning duct. This act of kindness made the room's ambiance more amiable not only for me, but for penguins, should they care to stop by. If you think *mon père* is chagrined over my misunderstanding with the authorities at Yale, you are correct.

"This is Sabrina Wright," she announced in the manner of a grande dame on the intercom with her kitchen help. I confess, when I ran the name Sabrina Wright through my mental Rolodex I came up with zilch. However, I found it impossible to say no to a sultry female voice imploring me to meet her in a low-life hangout at high noon. Had I refused, I would have had to turn in my Mickey Spillane decoding ring as well as my gumshoes.

One of the resources of a good law firm is its library. At McNally & Son we are doubly blessed with our librarian, Sofia Richmond. Sofia is a superbly qualified librarian, a computer whiz, and a researcher nonpareil. In addition, she not only keeps abreast of all the Palm Beach gossip but, with a little coaxing, will impart what she knows. Reluctantly, I sought Sofia's help in identifying Sabrina Wright. I say "reluctantly" because I am celebrating one year of *almost* being a nonsmoker. Sofia puffs away happily and will die, I am sure, at the age of one hundred and one with the healthiest pair of lungs in captivity. Leaving my English Ovals behind, I headed for the library.

I found Sofia at her computer, surrounded by intimidating tomes, legal briefs, and an ashtray the size of a flying saucer. Looking at me through her horn-rimmed glasses she tossed out, along with a cloud of smoke, "You look cute."

In my dove-gray sharkskin suit, blue cambric shirt *sans* cravat, and white bucks left over from my preppy days, I must say I had to admire her keen perception and wished I could return the compliment. But, alas, with her thick spectacles, tight French braid, sturdy oxfords, and two-piece denim dress, I couldn't bring myself to respond in kind. I have often imagined Sofia leaving work, arriving at her apartment, removing her glasses, letting down her hair, and donning a strapless sheath in shimmering ice-blue satin, after which she heads for a supper club in Boca where she is the headlined chanteuse. Her signature song? "Let's See What the Boys in the Back Room Will Have."

Lest you think I am off my rocker, I give you the sage words of M. de Sade: "Imagination is the only reality."

"If you fed the name Sabrina Wright into that machine, what would it spew back?" I asked.

"You're kidding," she responded.

"No. Why should I be?"

"You don't know who Sabrina Wright is, Archy?"

"If I did, I wouldn't be here, ingesting secondhand smoke when I could be contracting pneumonia in my minuscule igloo. Who is she, Sofia?"

"Don't you read novels?" she prodded.

"One a week, so help me Marcel Proust."

"And what was the last novel you read?" With those

glasses and that hair, I could swear I was being questioned by Miss Lowenstein, my tenth-grade English teacher.

"All Quiet on the Western Front." It's what I would have reported to Miss Lowenstein, bringing tears to her eyes. All I got from Sofia Richmond was a shrug and a cheeky retort.

"Well, Archy, times have changed since the Big War. Sabrina Wright's been leading the charge on behalf of the sexual revolution."

"An occidental *Kama Sutra*?" I ventured.

Sofia trashed her cigarette in the flying saucer. "Archy, this lady makes the *Kama Sutra* read like the Girl Scouts' handbook." It was at this point that I was given a précis of the works of Sabrina Wright, from desire to desire.

"How old is she?" I asked Sofia when she had finished lecturing.

Shaking her head from side to side as if counting the years, Sofia guessed, "Near fifty, I would say, but you couldn't tell by looking at her." She reached into her bottom desk drawer and brought out a copy of *Desperate Desire*. "See for yourself," she said, handing me the book with Sabrina Wright's photograph on the book's back jacket. After viewing Sabrina, I took a quick glance at the cover art which depicted a blond Amazon being ravished by a young man in football garb, sporting a film of manly perspiration and a torn jersey that bared his torso. Looking deep into the blonde's blue eyes, the jock appeared to be saying, "My chest is bigger than yours."

"You read this stuff?" I chided Sofia.

"It's my job, Archy," she said, retrieving the novel. "I have to keep my finger on the pulse of the nation." With that, she lit another cigarette.

And if the nation were attempting to keep pace with the

Amazon and the jock, we would be on the verge of a cardiac-arrest epidemic any moment.

"The lady is in town," Sofia was saying.

Had Sofia, too, been invited to Bar Anticipation this afternoon? "How do you know that?"

"There was a note in Lolly Spindrift's column yesterday, and I quote: 'That anticipated July heat wave hit town yesterday in the form of novelist *extraordinaire* Sabrina Wright. Here on a fact-finding mission for your next novel, Sabrina, or looking for the man that got away dot, dot, dot?' unquote."

Lolly Spindrift is the gossip columnist for our local gazette, who favors the dot, dot, dot school of journalism in memory of the school's founding father, Walter Winchell. "What do you suppose that means?" I asked Sofia.

"Beats me, Archy. Ask Lolly."

"I'll do better than that, Sofia. I'll ask Sabrina Wright."

I didn't wait for the smoke to clear, so I have no idea of Sofia's reaction to my parting shot.

"WELL," I QUESTIONED the novelist *extraordinaire,* "who gave you my name?"

"A former client who wishes to remain anonymous."

Given the ana of my clientele, that did not narrow the field, but before I could insist on a more concrete reference, the bartender was before us. He was a young man with a lot of attitude, the required demeanor for the adolescents who linger in Palm Beach after the close of the season wondering why they had failed to attract a rich patron of either sex in January. Hope sprung eternal in the less frenetic dog days of mid-July.

"A drink, Mr. McNally?" my hostess offered.

My drink of choice in the summer months is a frozen daiquiri, but in this venue I thought it best to stick to the basics. "What brand vodka do you pour?" I inquired of the failed Lothario.

"The brand that comes in a bottle and looks like water."

My companion found this amusing. I didn't, but to take issue would only serve to validate the wisecrack. Besides, he was twenty years younger than yrs. truly and all muscled P&V. "I'll have one with tonic and lemon, not lime."

"And I'll have another Pink Lady," Sabrina ordered, confirming my suspicions.

Looking around I noted that the place was doing a lively business for so early in the day and assayed the crowd as a mixture of the haves, the have-nots, and wannabes– heavy on the wannabes. The one cocktail waitress did not show promise of ever owning the joint or waltzing down the aisle with a guy boasting any title other than Mister.

In a move that I assumed was meant to rile me, Sabrina whispered, "What do you think of the bartender, Mr. McNally?"

"Not much. Why?"

"He has a common face and a noble derriere. A lethal combination. I shall call him Chauncey and immortalize him in my next novel–   and remember, you heard it here first."

How could I forget it?

Unaware that he had been short-listed for immortality, Chauncey served our drinks and treated us to a bowl of salted peanuts.

"Cheers, Mr. McNally," Sabrina Wright toasted.

I gestured with my drink in the time-honored manner

and continued to try to learn why I had been summoned into her presence. "If you won't tell me who recommended me, Ms. Wright, will you tell me why you invited me here?"

Her dark eyes darted somewhat theatrically from left to right before she confided, "I want you to find my husband."

"I don't take domestic cases, Ms. Wright."

She reared her head and snapped, "This is not a domestic case."

"Your husband took a powder and you want me to find him. Where I come from, that constitutes a domestic case."

Her Joan Crawford lips smiled, or grimaced, I'm not sure which, and finally opened so she could intone, "He did not take a powder, Mr. McNally. My daughter ran off. I sent my husband to find her and now I seem to have lost him, too."

Lost both her daughter and husband? How careless, I thought. However it did enlighten me on the meaning of Lolly's dot, dot, dot item. But if Sabrina Wright was speaking to me in confidence, as I assumed she was, how did Lolly know she had misplaced her husband? Of course I would ask him, and he would stoically refuse to name his source, claiming reporter/informer confidentiality, but blab it fast enough over dinner at Cafe L'Europe, ordering Krug with his beluga, at my expense. Such are the priorities of gossip columnists.

I sipped my vodka and tonic while trying to decide my next move. As Sofia had told me, Sabrina Wright was no spring chicken, despite her trim figure and porcelain complexion. Therefore it would be very unlikely that she had a daughter young enough to be considered a runaway. I munched a peanut as she observed Chauncey, though I'm not certain if it was his head or his tail that kept her captive. To rescue her from prurient thoughts, I asked, "How old is your daughter, Ms. Wright?"

She turned her attention to me, more startled than ever, and answered, "Nearing thirty."

My mind shouted, "How near?" but what came out of my mouth was, "A woman nearing thirty cannot be said to have run off in the manner of a minor child . . ."

"Gillian did," she cut me off.

"She has the right to come and go as she pleases," I continued. "If you suspect foul play, I suggest you contact the police. And husbands have been known to run out for a pack of cigarettes, never to return– however, I believe he has more of a legal obligation to you than does your daughter." Here it occurred to me that the husband could be in cahoots with Gillian, both harboring a desire to flee the dubious family blessing of fame and fortune. Sabrina Wright wouldn't be the first successful woman to rule her roost with an iron hand and a short leash.

But was Sabrina's husband Gillian's father? Here comes the plot twist worthy of a Sabrina Wright novel. A stepfather with a roving eye and his stepdaughter living in the shadow of a successful and, perhaps, overbearing mother. Daughter flees and stepdaddy goes in hot pursuit, literally as well as figuratively. Either the escapade was planned or the daughter, having taken the first step, enjoined stepfather to hop aboard the liberation train when he caught up with her. Had he, or Gillian, made a dent in Sabrina's bank account recently? Doubtful, as I imagine Sabrina Wright kept the exchequer under lock and key, penuriously doling out the walking-around cash.

Gently, I probed, "Is your husband Gillian's father?"

Again the smile, or grimace, and, "I know what you're

thinking, Mr. McNally, and how delightfully naughty of you. Do you write?"

"I keep a journal and am told my expense account shows promise of a creative genius reminiscent of Fitzgerald in his youth."

She flashed me a genuine smile this time and almost, but not quite, let down her guard. "Very cleverly put. We're going to get along just fine, Mr. McNally."

"I told you, I don't take domestic cases."

"And I told you, this is not a domestic case."

I had finished my drink but refrained from signaling Chauncey. I thought a quick retreat rather than involvement in a family squabble the better part of valor. But, like a good mystery you hate to abandon without knowing who done it, I wanted an answer to my question.

"Is Gillian your husband's daughter?" I repeated.

This time I got the phony smile, which was wearing thin. "He is not, Mr. McNally, but unlike a Sabrina Wright novel, Gillian and Robert, my husband, did not flee in tandem, so to speak. She ran off with a young man of her own of whom I do not approve."

And there was the case, a domestic one to be sure, in the proverbial nutshell. "She eloped," I stated.

"She did not," the lady insisted.

"Then why did she leave home?"

"Why?" Sabrina Wright echoed. "Because I told her I was her mother. That's why."

TWO

THE EXPLANATION, DIRECT and to the point as was the lady's style, prompted not only another question but another drink with which to wash it down. As I awaited both, I became uncomfortably aware that Sabrina and I were being observed by the patrons of Bar Anticipation, like a couple of germs on the stage of a mad scientist's microscope. Someone had obviously recognized Sabrina Wright and the gallery was abuzz with sibilant whispers. The fact that these early-afternoon imbibers were bending elbows with a bona fide celebrity had them pickled tink.

Chauncey, who had been paying more attention to his manicure than to Sabrina and me, was suddenly all over us like a cheap suit. When he replenished my drink, he also whisked away our dish of peanuts and replaced it with one of macadamias and shelled pistachios. Such are the rewards of celebrityhood.

Picking up the scent but lacking a tail full of colorful feathers to unfurl for her audience, Sabrina reached into her purse and pulled out an onyx cigarette holder into which she fitted a black-tipped, king-size cigarette. The result was a pipe slightly shorter than the span of the Golden Gate Bridge. The ever-hovering Chauncey struck a match for Sabrina, and as the pair made eye contact over the flickering flame, I fought the temptation of lighting an English Oval– and lost.

As Sabrina basked in the glow of recognition, I recalled that my only previous encounter with the literary set was with the poet Roderick Gillsworth whose book, *The Joy of Flatulence,* was ignored by the reading public and therefore lauded by the critics. Our relationship was cut short when Mrs. Gillsworth was murdered and I fingered Roderick for the crime.

Enthusiastically indulging our vices, Sabrina told me her story, which, was old and trite, but, as she stated, "It's new when it happens to you." What happened was a brief encounter with a college boy when Sabrina was eighteen, resulting in the birth of Gillian some nine months later. Once again borrowing from Hollywood royalty, Sabrina put her baby girl in an orphanage and then legally adopted the infant.

"And the father?" I questioned.

"The father was the scion of American nobility, their coat of arms consisting of crossed oil wells over a sea of gilt-edged securities. To form an alliance with the likes of me would have been his ruin. Besides which, he was engaged to a young lady who was Main Line Philadelphia or

Back Bay Boston, I forget which, but I do know it was rumored that her family kept in their safe-deposit box a splinter from the deck of the *Mayflower*.

"He paid me handsomely to keep a low profile. Very handsomely, Mr. McNally. I was able to brush up my Shakespeare, as the song goes, live comfortably, and travel extensively. London, Paris, Antibes, Monte Carlo in and out of season, Zurich, and Rome were my playgrounds. I rubbed shoulders, among other things, with the well-to-do, and became *au fait* with the ways of the world, which is to say the ways of the rich, the super rich, and the mega rich. *Darling Desire* was the child of my wanderlust. The rest, Mr. McNally, is history."

I tossed her a curve with, "And what of the child of your womb, Ms. Wright?"

"Gillian?" Sabrina said as if amazed that I would ask. "Gillian had the best of everything. I enrolled her in a fancy Swiss school from day one."

"You sent your daughter to the first grade in Switzerland?" I exclaimed.

"What's wrong with that? Little Swiss children go to the first grade in Switzerland."

"They live there, Ms. Wright."

"My daughter lived there, Mr. McNally. You don't think she got on a little yellow jet every morning toting a lunch pail."

The woman was insufferable, but I have to add, infectious. Sabrina Wright was a package. By that I mean there were no loose ends— no ifs, buts, or maybes. Like Faust, she would sell her soul to the devil in return for a bestseller and then buy it back with ten percent of the gross. "How often did you see your daughter?" I asked.

Puffing on her onyx holder, she said, "We met frequently at airports when our connecting flights criss-crossed. We dined in the VIP lounge. I always paid." She gave it a beat and then burst into a raspy guffaw. Chauncey, giving the impression that he was in on the joke, joined in. Moments later everyone in the bar was sporting a grin. Yes, Sabrina Wright was infectious.

"Why did you suddenly decide to tell her the truth?"

"It wasn't sudden. I had been thinking about it. And then one night– oh, you know– a couple of white chicks sitting around talking. I was trying to talk her into giving up Zachary Ward. He writes under the name Zack Ward."

"Writes?"

"In a manner of speaking. He's a reporter for a dreadful tabloid of the 'I Was Impregnated by a Martian at the Church Rummage Sale' variety. They met at a writers' workshop where he was the guest lecturer, which gives you some idea of the workshop's caliber."

I wanted to remind her of the precarious position of those who reside in glass houses but refrained. I know it's popular, especially in bombastic Palm Beach, to put down anything popular with the common folks, be it literature, music, or a hit film, and label it bourgeois. I refuse to go along with this line, not only because I am a member in good standing of the bourgeoisie, but because all art is valid, and appealing to the masses doesn't make it less so.

If Gillian was enrolled in a writers' workshop, that meant she aspired to emulate her famous mother. Was Sabrina unhappy over her daughter's career choice? Testing the waters, I said, "I assume Gillian aspires to be an author. *As is the mother, so is her daughter,* the Old Testament tells us."

Quick as a cobra on the offensive, she snapped, "In this case, Mr. McNally, it would be more a case of a bastard emulating a bitch."

The lady had wit, however acerbic, and I was beginning to enjoy her company, but then I have always been an easy mark for well-turned ankles and calves. With anyone else, the black-tipped cigarette might have been construed as overplaying her hand, but Sabrina Wright overplayed every move, making the Mata Hari weed almost unnecessary.

Reluctantly I extinguished my English Oval in an ashtray and encouraged Sabrina to go on with her story. "You told Gillian you were her natural mother and she fled. Is that more or less what happened?"

It was Sabrina's turn to douse her smoke and she did so by first removing it from the holder before tamping it in the ashtray. Chauncey, ever helpful, removed it and provided us with a clean one. Would he save Sabrina's black-tipped butt and press it into his memory book?

Sabrina told Gillian the truth because she thought her case against Zack Ward would be more compelling coming from a flesh-and-blood mother than from a surrogate parent. "I wanted her to know how sincerely I had her best interests at heart," Sabrina explained.

"What have you got against Ward, other than his profession?"

"I believe," Sabrina said, "that his only interest in Gillian is to pump her for information about me for his rag. Gillian is a rather plain girl and Zack is very attractive, if you get my drift. She has had beaus but never one as comely as Zack, or as ardent. When I made my confession, she was, of course, surprised but pleased. We had a good cry and celebrated the occasion with champagne."

Sabrina didn't say that getting rid of Ward was in her best interests, too. She did say that it was several days later when Gillian began to pester her mother to disclose the name of her father. "I know she told Zack her news, and he immediately saw in it the scandal about me he was longing to write about. Of course the story would be worth twice as much in dollars and notoriety if it named the father. You see, I told Gillian that her father was a man of great wealth and pedigree. Given the combination of my name and her father's, the story would not only make Zack's career, but his fortune. A week later Gillian and Zack left New York for Palm Beach."

"Why Palm Beach?"

With a gesture that said she had gone this far so why not go all the way, she answered, "Because I told her she was conceived here and that her father still lived here. At the time, I was in Fort Lauderdale on spring break. Gillian's father was slumming."

"Zack notwithstanding, why, after all this time, are you reluctant to tell Gillian who her father is?"

"Because I struck a bargain, Mr. McNally, and I intend to comply with the rules. I was given a great deal of money by my paramour, as I told you. Enough to raise my daughter in style and live a life that granted me the time and the experience to write and become the darling of publishers as well as investment bankers." Sticking out her chin, she added, "And I will go to any length to honor his anonymity. Any length," she repeated.

"What are the odds of Gillian and Zack finding what they came looking for?"

"A million to one, but even those odds are too close for comfort. That's why I sent Robert to see what they were up to and to wheedle Jill into returning home."

I had forgotten all about the missing Robert. "Is he Robert Wright?"

"No, he's Robert Silvester, but he is my Mr. Right. Robert is my editor and was fresh out of college when they assigned him to my first book. You know how it is with a first book. When we weren't lunching together, we were on the phone. To cut expenses, he moved in. When *Darling Desire* was published to great acclaim, we celebrated by eloping to Las Vegas."

As she filled me in on her marital exploits, I began doing a little arithmetic. She was eighteen when she had Gillian, who was nearing thirty. That would mean Sabrina Wright was nearing fifty. Sofia had told me that Sabrina's first novel came out about a dozen years ago– when Robert Silvester was fresh out of college. Unless he was a dolt, which I doubted, that would make him closer in age to Gillian than to his wife. Interesting.

"Robert made a reservation at the Chesterfield," she went on, "and checked in four days ago. He called me the night he arrived. The following evening he called to say he had found them and was dining with them that evening. He said he would call when he got back to the hotel, but he never did."

"Did he say where he found them?"

"I'm afraid not. There was really no reason to ask."

"Did you try calling him?"

"Yes. When I was connected to his room, it just rang and rang. I left a message for him to call me when he got in, but he never called. I hoped he was still with Gillian, trying to talk some sense into her. When he didn't call the next day, I again called the Chesterfield. They told me Mr. Silvester had checked out that morning. I couldn't imagine what had happened but hoped he might be on his way back to New York, although that didn't seem possible. I mean, he would have called me before leaving. When I didn't hear from him that day, I flew down here the next day, yesterday. So now I'm at the Chesterfield."

"Have you questioned them about your husband?"

"Not directly. I'm sure they don't know Robert is my husband. I just asked them if Mr. Silvester was still registered. I told them he was a friend and that I knew he was going to be in Palm Beach this week. They said he had been there but had left. I asked if he had left a forwarding address and they told me he had not. I didn't want to seem too interested.

"I'm sitting on a time bomb, Mr. McNally. My daughter is here with that awful Zack, looking for her father, and now my husband, who was here looking for my daughter, has disappeared into thin air. If any of this gets out, it will create a cause célèbre that will be heard around the world."

And sell a lot of books. I hated to start the clock ticking on that time bomb, but I thought the lady should know that Lolly Spindrift had not only announced her arrival but had also alluded to Robert's disappearance. This had her reaching for another cigarette without benefit of holder. She was so quick on the draw she had it lit before Chauncey could strike a match. "I don't see how . . . "

"I do. Lolly must have a shill at the Chesterfield who happened to be at the desk when you arrived and heard you inquire about Mr. Silvester. Maybe no one at the hotel knows Robert is your husband, but I'm sure Lolly does, dot, dot, dot."

"The man that got away," she moaned. "Do you realize that if Gillian's father sees that item he will think I'm in Palm Beach in search of him?"

She had a point. Not knowing Sabrina's husband was missing, Gillian's sire would surely think he was the man that got away– especially since he was. Sabrina's concern also confirmed that Gillian's father was alive and well and living in Palm Beach.

She put her hand on mine. It was ice-cold. The lady was truly frightened. "Will you help me, Mr. McNally?"

SABRINA TOOK ONE look at my fire-engine-red Miata and opted to take a cab back to her hotel. Smart move. While she was not exactly traveling incognito, neither was she here on a book-signing tour, and my car, unlike my professional methods, is more Palm Beach kitsch than discreet, but it does keep me amused. In this world of card-carrying terrorists, West Nile virus-carrying mosquitos, and E. coli-carrying cows, I zip happily along in my Miata like there's no tomorrow, because there's a good chance there won't be one.

I told Sabrina to sit tight and I would be in touch. I didn't know when, or what, I would have to offer when I did, but that is, after all, the standard line when parting with a distressed client. It gives them hope and me a chance to ruminate over the facts and a bite of lunch. I decided to take the case, that is, try to locate Robert Silvester, for two reasons.

The first one was because I liked the lady. She had what show folks call pizzazz. It's a word, like pornography, that's hard to define but you know it when you see it. Having been handed a golden parachute and tossed out of the family Cessna, she refused to sink, meekly, into the abyss. Against all odds, she had defied gravity and soared. Instead of disappearing, she had literally lit up the sky with her talent and a zillion book covers with her startled gaze. What's not to like?

Reason *numero* two? Greed– or did you think I was about to OD on altruism? My father takes great pride in the abundance of moneyed names, both old and new moola, on McNally & Son's client roster. Were I to be responsible for adding Sabrina Wright to that list, it would go a long way in mitigating my trespasses at Yale, lo those twenty years ago, as I have long forgiven those who trespassed against me. Now, like the message inscribed on a sundial, I number only the sunny hours.

I crossed from West Palm into the land of conspicuous consumption via the Flagler Memorial Bridge and then along Royal Poinciana Way, passing golfers on The Breakers Ocean Golf Course, all consuming conspicuously, before heading up Ocean Boulevard, alias the A1A.

I believed everything Sabrina Wright told me was true. What wasn't said was what she didn't want me to know, such as who had introduced her to Discreet Inquiries. If it was a former client, that person could or could not still be living in Palm Beach. Was it this former client who also recommended that we rendezvous at a pub where we were least likely to be seen by those who matter in the Town of Palm Beach, or had Sabrina programmed a list of such joints into her computer for when the need arose, be it for the writing business or monkey business?

The idea that her Palm Beach confidant might be Gillian's father also crossed my mind. If Sabrina had broken her part of the bargain and contacted him, perhaps to warn him of Gillian's arrival, he may have given her my name should the need arise. She had said that she would go to any length to honor his anonymity. To what length would he go to make sure she did?

Next we had Robert Silvester, the subject of my nascent investigation. My first impression was that he might have joined forces with Gillian to escape Sabrina, but that was before I knew why, and with whom, the girl had fled. Mr. Right was acting on his wife's behalf, but, and I forgot to ask, did he know Sabrina's secret? He must, or she would not have sent him in search of Gillian, who would tell him when he caught up with her.

Then why did Robert come to Palm Beach alone? Why didn't Sabrina accompany him? Why did he check out of the Chesterfield after he found Gillian, and where had he gone to?

Was Gillian a plain Jane forever in the shadow of her charismatic mother? Did her attractive suitor talk her into going in search of her roots, or had it occurred to her that being acknowledged by a father whose blood was blue and bank account green would legitimatize her in more ways than one?

And let's not forget Zack Ward, a tabloid reporter hot on the trail. To what length would he go to expose Gillian's father?

Finally, we had Lolly Spindrift, who had inadvertently opened this can of worms. He would make every sacrifice, including canceling his subscription to *Playgirl,* in return for the real scoop on Sabrina Wright's presence in Palm Beach.

In retrospect, there was more to the case than Sabrina's plot outline, and the cast of characters alone promised a page-turner. As the old drinking song had it, *This is number one/the fun has just begun* . . .

I turned off the A1A and onto the graveled driveway of my favorite restaurant– the Chez McNally on Ocean Boulevard.

THREE

FOR THOSE WHO wonder why a charismatic bachelor in possession of a functioning medulla oblongata– one who is approaching his fourth decade– chooses to live at home, the answer is Dollars & Sense. I occupy my own snug garret in our faux Tudor palace, tucked beneath a charming but leaky copper roof. The drip, drip, drip of the raindrops makes my three-room suite– sitting room, bedroom, and bath– *très* bohemian, an ambiance difficult to come upon in South Florida where postmodern is all the rage.

The lord and lady of the manor are currently on a long-overdue holiday, cruising the Caribbean on a luxury liner from which Father can ship-to-shore the office every day and inquire of his private secretary, the formidable Mrs.

Trelawney, as to the day's receipts and, no doubt, Archy's whereabouts.

Mother, Madelaine by name, suffers from a touch of hypertension and has grown a tad forgetful in her golden years, but remains a gentlewoman of immense charm. A gardener who raises only begonias, she has as many varieties of that tropical plant as are recognized by certified horticulturists, and then some. Her newest, an Iron Cross, was about to come into its own just as she and the Gov were due to ship out of Ft. Lauderdale. Mother consented to go only after we had secured a member of her garden club to look after the new arrival and its numerous relations.

Looking after Archy were Ursi Olson, our cook-housekeeper, and her husband, Jamie, our houseman. Ursi's cooking is one of the perks of living at home, another being the Atlantic Ocean just across the A1A from our abode where I can indulge my passion for swimming two miles every day, weather and time permitting. Our climate and my job permit far more often than they deny. While Ursi would not know a *cordon bleu* from a 4-H Club, she could make anything edible delectable, which accounts for the continuing shrinkage of my waistbands.

Hobo, our canine of blended heritage, peeked out of his gabled cottage as I emerged from my car. Satisfied that I was not a thief, bill collector, or religious zealot in search of converts, he returned to his afternoon siesta. I always get the feeling that I should apologize to our quadruped sentry for interfering with his power nap.

"Archy," Ursi exclaimed as I entered the kitchen, "I wasn't expecting you."

"I wasn't expecting me either," I told her, "but I had a noon appointment that cut into my lunch hour and thought you might whip up a snack to fill the void."

"Well," she pondered, "I could do something with what's left of last night's roast pork."

Jamie, who is as verbose as a stone, was seated at the table reading his newspaper. Tearing his eyes away from the latest Palm Beach brouhaha– the rabbi of our local temple punched a board member in the face after a heated argument and the recipient did not turn the other cheek– greeted my arrival with a grunt or a groan or, perhaps, a burp.

Taking my place at the table, I asked Ursi if she knew Sabrina Wright. As she poured olive oil into a skillet, Ursi cooed, "Oh, Archy, I love her. I'm on the list at the library for her latest book."

Ursi also loves the afternoon soaps, the evening sit-coms, and films in DeLuxe Color and stereophonic sound. I haven't seen a satisfying flick since Louise Fazenda rolled down her stockings for Mack Sennett. "How long is the list?" I wondered aloud.

Now slicing an onion, followed by a green pepper, Ursi told me the library ordered no less than five copies of Sabrina Wright's novels upon publication, but even with this extraordinary number in stock, one had to wait weeks before getting their hands, and eyes, on Sabrina's latest assault on desire. "I met her today," I announced as if stating that I had run into an old friend.

Ursi paused in her efforts to resuscitate last night's roast and let out an "Ah." Jamie's head twitched, but from experience I knew that he had not missed a word of the conversation. In my years of discreetly inquiring around the Town of Palm Beach I have learned that the best way to find out what is afoot upstairs is to nose around down-stairs. The domestics along Ocean Boulevard keep in con-stant touch, and a word from me to Ursi and Jamie would travel around our little island faster than a speeding bullet trying to outrace the man of steel.

Having no leads, I took my first chance in the case and sowed a few seeds into the fertile ears of our accommodating couple to see what, if anything, they would reap. I let it be known that Sabrina Wright was in Palm Beach in search of her daughter who had run off with a man Sabrina found odious. This was as much as I could say without betraying Sabrina's confidence, and it was more a sin of omission than a lie. Like all natives, it did not occur to Ursi to ask why the couple had come to Palm Beach, but she would have commented on their choice of destination had they gone elsewhere. As onion and pepper, along with slices of leftover baked potato, were tossed into the skillet and enveloped by the fragrant olive oil, it occurred to me that once Ursi and Jamie passed on this version of Sabrina's reason for being here, Lolly's man that got away would acquire a third persona— Gillian's beau.

Jamie, without so much as a nod, understood that I would be grateful for anything he could come up with regarding the whereabouts of Sabrina's daughter and her current flame. I have often slipped Jamie a few large greenbacks in appreciation of services rendered, a fact that would drive my sire up a wall and get me expelled, yet again, from a safe harbor. But in my business the riskiest thing one can do is not tempt the fates.

The aroma ascending from Ursi's skillet had me salivating as she lovingly sautéed the vegetables before adding the sliced roast pork and a touch of sherry. She left it on the flame long enough to warm the pork through and crisp the edges, then quickly deglazed the pan. As she transferred the contents to a warm plate, drizzling the lot with the savory pan juices, she complained, "You would think Sabrina Wright would know better. All her heroines fall in love with the wrong man, only they turn out to be the right man in the end."

"That's because in her novels Sabrina is calling the shots. In real life, Ursi, she can't do that."

My ragout was placed before me, along with several thick slices of Ursi's own sourdough bread and a bottle of ice-cold Brooklyn lager. Nirvana.

"Then she should let her daughter follow her heart," Ursi offered with my lunch.

It was clear that Ursi Olson had read too many Sabrina Wright novels.

WHEN I RETURNED to the office, the first thing I did was call Lolly Spindrift to see if he knew anything more about Sabrina Wright's visit to our Eden than his blind item intimated. I was not too sanguine, as gossip columnists in general, and Lolly Spindrift in particular, tell all they know or think they know, keeping secret only their own libidinous behavior. Lolly's column is called "Hither and Yon," which in other words means Palm Beach and anyplace elsewhere he can beg, borrow, steal, or invent a scoop about the rich and famous.

"Lol? Archy McNally here."

"You cad," he attacked. "You never call to whisper sweet nothings into my eager ear even after I gave you three mentions this month."

"Getting a mention in this town in July, Lol, is as newsworthy as telling your readers the pope attended mass last Sunday."

"But unlike the pope, dear heart, your dalliances bring a blush to my cheek and a longing to my savage breast;

however, I never tell, although I have a file with your name on it that would make the contents of Pandora's box look benign."

"Let's keep it under lock and key, Lol."

"It depends, Archy."

"On what?"

"How nice you are to Lolly."

Deflecting having to take him to dinner at some expensive bistro, I announced, "There's a new bartender at Bar Anticipation who's right up your alley."

"And how would you know?"

"A wild guess, Lol."

"Well, guess again. I've sworn off bartenders. The last one . . ."

It was a half hour before I was able to stifle his account of unrequited love. After making the necessary sympathetic sounds, I posed, "A favor, Lol?"

"I knew you wanted to pick my brains, Archy. What about pumping me over dinner this evening?"

The guy's conversation was peppered with all kinds of innuendo that, believe me, was intentional. Lolly Spindrift is small of stature and favors white double-breasted suits, ascots, Panama hats, and expensive restaurants. His petite size belies a ravenous appetite and the word "abstemious" is not in his lexicon. At a buffet dinner party given by a PB matron of great wealth and little charm, I watched him consume healthy portions of all twenty delicacies on the smorgasbord table, belch daintily, and in lieu of a doggy bag, take home the chef.

"The Pelican Club?" I offered.

The Pelican Club is a private dining and drinking establishment housed in a somewhat dilapidated two-story shingled house near the airport and is the favorite watering hole of the young, the bad, and the beautiful of Palm Beach and vicinity. Founded by a group of like-minded men, yrs. truly among them, who find the traditional clubs a bit too fussy and stuffy and, let's face it, unobtainable to the likes of us, the Pelican does not discriminate in any way, even to those who find us déclassé. For proof I give you the astounding number of traditional club regulars who find the Pelican an intriguing diversion.

"Get real, Archy. I wouldn't be caught dead in that joint."

If Lolly's roving eye roved in the wrong direction at the Pelican, he might get caught just that way on his initial visit.

"I hear the *foie gras* at Testa's will leave you panting," he informed me.

So will the bill, I thought. "Look, Lol, I can't make it tonight," I lied, "but I'll advance you a rain check if you advance me a little info."

"Can I trust you, Archy?"

"Of course not. That's what makes me so irresistible."

"That's what my bartender said and he was right. Okay, Archibald, what do you want to know about whom and why?"

"Sabrina Wright. What else do you know about her visit besides what your spy at the Chesterfield told you?"

"My spy?" Lolly exploded. "You jest, young man. I don't have any spies. Not that I wouldn't if I could afford them. I have to scratch for every item and can show you the broken fingernails to prove it."

"Then how did you know she checked into the Chesterfield and asked if her husband was stopping there?"

"So she *is* looking for her husband. What joy. Can I quote you?"

Me and my big mouth. I had just told Lolly more than I was going to learn from him. It was too late to retrieve my words so I had to eat them, which did not sit well with Ursi's stir-fry. "Quote me and kiss your *foie gras* good-bye. How did you get the item?"

"From an anonymous caller," Lolly answered. "He told me Sabrina Wright had just arrived in town and was staying at the Chesterfield. He said she was here looking for a certain man. I called the hotel and they confirmed that she was registered, but when I asked to be connected to her room I was informed that she was not taking calls. Like Garbo, she *vanted* to be alone.

"I could tell my avid readers that Sabrina was in town, but I wouldn't touch the bit about a certain man, which was pure hearsay and too specific. There are libel laws, so I dreamed up the man that got away, which could mean any man she had even so much as shook hands with."

"You didn't recognize the caller?" I asked.

"Not at all, and I don't think he was disguising his voice."

"But you're sure it was a man?"

"Archy, when it comes to recognizing men, I have no equal."

"Thanks, Lol, I . . . "

"Not so fast, Mr. Hit-'n'-Run. What is going on here? First I get an anonymous tip on Sabrina Wright, and then I get a follow-up call from Archy McNally of Discreet Inquiries. You don't have to be a whiz kid to know that there's something rotten in Palm Beach. Tell Lolly what you know or I will be very, very cruel to Archy."

"You're bluffing," I said with more bravado than conviction.

"Really? Item: The girl dancing cheek-to-cheek with

Archy McNally on the moonlit deck of Phil Meecham's yacht, the oh-so-social *Sans Souci,* didn't look like Connie Garcia, but then I wasn't wearing my glasses, so I could be wrong."

"That's blackmail," I accused.

"You bet your sweet tuchas it is, baby. Cross me and the item runs tomorrow."

Consuela Garcia is my light-o'-love and has been for longer than I care to remember. She is a Marielito who toils as social secretary to Lady Cynthia Horowitz, one of Palm Beach's more obnoxious chatelaines. Connie is a lovely señorita with a figure that brings to mind the dancer Chita Rivera of *West Side Story* fame. The musical play, to be sure, not the film, as Chita was not given the film role she had created on Broadway. But then Hollywood has not made an astute casting decision since replacing Myrna Loy with Anna May Wong as the daughter of Fu Manchu.

Connie and I have an open relationship, which I fear does not translate well into *Español*. I think it means I can dance cheek-to-cheek with a curvaceous blonde at one of Phil Meecham's naughty mixes, and Connie thinks it means she can neuter me for doing so. Clearly, my need to head off Lolly's item was of paramount importance to that which I hold near and dear.

Thinking fast, which is something I do very well when Connie reaches for a carving knife, I blabbed, "Look, Lol, I'll level with you." Here I told him the same story I had told Ursi and Jamie.

Recalling the laws of libel, Lolly demanded, "How do you know this?"

"Ms. Wright has hired me to find the culprit and her daughter." McNally's luck held out when Lolly, like Ursi, did not ask why the couple had fled to Palm Beach.

"My, my, Archy, aren't you rubbing shoulders, and what a delicious tidbit," was Lolly's expected reaction. I could see him licking his lips and filling his Mont Blanc with acid. "Do you think he was my anonymous caller?"

"I'm sure he was," I answered.

"Why did he expose himself to me, so to speak, dear heart?"

"He didn't. You wouldn't know who he was if I hadn't told you. I think he did it to goad Sabrina."

"This gets better by the moment. Ta, ta, Archy, see you in church."

I had to again head Lolly off at the pass and took my second chance of the case, a wild one, to accomplish this goal. "Lol, can I ask you not to print a word of this just yet?"

"You could, lover, but your plea will fall on deaf ears."

"What if I told you I could set up an exclusive interview for you with Sabrina Wright?" There is nothing, besides bartenders and food, that Lolly Spindrift likes better than the word exclusive followed by a celebrated name. I could almost hear his brain calculating the pros and cons of my offer. "To publish or not to publish, that is the question," I intruded upon his deliberations. "One quickie blurb or an exclusive with Sabrina that might very well be picked up by the wire services and attributed to Lolly Spindrift."

After a prolonged silence, he sighed, "She will speak to me? Promise?"

"Scout's honor."

"I'm not feeling too kindly toward the Scouts these days, Archy."

"Sorry, Lol. How 'bout my word as a gentleman?"

"Good grief, that's worse. You have forty-eight hours to deliver, dear heart."

"You're on, Lol. And the bartender works the day shift."

"Why, you little devil," Lolly giggled.

I hung up, praying I could talk Sabrina into talking to Lolly Spindrift. My trump card was that anonymous caller who had to be Zack Ward trying to flush out Gillian's father. Ward was a loose cannon, and I could see why Sabrina wanted him stopped before he learned all and told all. But how did he know she had come to Palm Beach and was asking for her husband when she registered at the Chesterfield?

Sabrina would see the necessity of keeping Lolly from writing anything further until we had time to figure out what to tell him that would both defuse the man-that-got-away item and keep Lolly from learning the true reason for Gillian's coming here.

What to tell Lolly I would leave to Sabrina's creative genius. Remember, I had only consented to look for her husband. Never had a case taken so many diverse paths so quickly with so little hope for a quick solution. On that ominous note, enter Binky Watrous pushing his mail cart, a wagon that is indistinguishable from those that clog the aisles of supermarkets from coast to coast. Binky's, mercifully, does not contain a screaming two-year-old reaching for everything he has seen advertised on the telly.

"Hi, Archy."

"Good afternoon, Binky, my boy."

Depositing a small packet of envelopes encased in a rubber band on my desk, Binky gave me a depressing forecast of my afternoon epistles. "The usual fast-food menus, requests for charitable donations, and a flyer from an X-rated video distributor in Miami."

"Your job, Binky, is to deliver the mail, not read it," I reminded him.

Binky suffers from EDS. Employment Deficiency Syndrome. Since leaving school he has held more jobs than Mother has begonias, all terminating disastrously for both employer and employee. While clerking in a liquor store in Delray Beach, Binky was held up at gunpoint. Ordered to empty the cash register, Binky told the intruder that the register was controlled by the digital scanner that reads the price labels, therefore the thief would have to make a purchase if he wanted to get his hands on the loot.

Remembering the dinner party he was giving that very evening, the miscreant asked Binky to recommend a pretentious *vin blanc* to complement his poached salmon. Summoning all he had learned while training to be a liquor store clerk, Binky talked the man into a pricey white Graves. Pleased, the bandit took home a case, along with the contents of the cash register. This is just one painful example of the entries on Binky's CV. The full picture is available from the U.S. Department of Unemployment under the Freedom of Information Act of 1966.

I had been instrumental in securing Binky the position of mail person at McNally & Son, and the appointment seemed to be working rather well to date– touch wood, cross fingers, toes, eyes, and remember to light a candle to St. Jude, the hope of the hopeless. Binky is a personable young man, some ten years my junior, who looks remarkably like that famous movie star, Bambi. Older women, like Mrs. Trelawney and Sofia Richmond, find his liquid-brown eyes to die for. Binky's contemporaries of the fair sex, alas, do not.

Ignoring my grievance, Binky asked me if I was free after work. "What do you have in mind, Binky?"

"Apartment hunting" is what he came up with.

Since securing employment with us and optimistic

about the future, Binky is eager to move into his own pad with cohabitation very much the driving force of his quest. He recently spent his last dime having his collection of Victoria's Secret catalogues bound in vellum. This is not a healthy sign. Binky lives with the Duchess, the sobriquet of his maiden aunt, who has supported him since the death of his parents when Binky was just a tad and who is as eager to be rid of her ward as he is to find a soul mate.

Removing a tiny scrap of newspaper from his jacket pocket, Binky proceeded to read aloud: " 'For rent with option to buy . . . ' "

"You can't afford to buy," I cut in.

"I will some day," Binky assured me. "By virtue of my unique talents, I am destined to be an entrepreneur, not an employee."

The only talent I have ever recognized in Binky Watrous is one for fatuity. "And how do you envision moving from the mailroom to the boardroom?" I foolishly asked.

"I intend to modernize the mailroom, Archy."

Never knowing when to withdraw while ahead, I rushed in where wiser men would dare not tread. "How, may I ask?"

"Pneumatic tubing," he proclaimed with great pride.

Had I the room, I would have fainted.

"From my desk I will be able to shoot the mail all over the building in record-breaking time," he went on, like a pitchman in a carny show.

In spite of our glass-and-chrome facade, McNally & Son is a Victorian enterprise within, thanks to its founder and CEO. Prescott McNally has been playing the part of the squire for so long that he actually believes he is one. A rectitudinous attorney, he reads only Dickens and sports an unruly guardsman's mustache, hoping to emulate the

English actor Sir C. Aubrey Smith. However, in my humble opinion, he comes off as Groucho Marx, especially when enjoying an ear of corn.

"The only thing pneumatic tubing will help break around here, Binky, is your neck," I assured him.

Not heeding the warning, as is his wont, Binky continued to read the advert: " 'For rent with option to buy. Mobile home . . . ' "

"You're going to live in a trailer park?" I cried.

"What's wrong with that? The Duchess thinks it's perfect for me."

The Duchess would put her stamp of approval on an opium den in Macao if she thought it would get Binky out of the house. I was, for reasons that will soon be clear, getting a bit anxious over Binky's find.

" 'Kitchen,' " he continued, " 'dining area, parlor, bedroom, and bath, partially furnished. Contact Hermioni Rutherford at the Palm Court.' "

Like I always say, expect the worst and you're seldom disappointed. Sgt. Al Rogoff of the PBPD, my friend and sometimes partner in crime busting, resides at the Palm. Was I to be spared nothing this dastardly day?

FOUR

CULOTTES. I HAD not seen a pair in ages and often prayed that I never would again but, like all my petitions for divine intervention, this, too, had gone unheeded. If more tears are indeed shed over answered prayers, my eyes are as arid as the Gobi in August.

Along with the navy-blue culottes came a white middy that lacked only a whistle on a string. Inside this remarkable outfit was Hermioni Rutherford, hope of the homeless. Red hair, the shade of which did not appear on Mother Nature's palette, and tortoiseshell glasses completed the picture of a Palm Beach realtor of the lower echelons. In a town where eighty-seven percent of the inhabitants are millionaires and where a good number of them run up a four-digit utility bill each month to keep the beach house cool, Hermioni's clientele content themselves with an electric fan oscillating over a bucket of ice cubes.

Binky pulled into the allotted carport of the mobile home once removed from the stationary trailer Al Rogoff called home. As we emerged, Hermioni charged me with all the grace of a smiling linebacker. "Mr. Watrous," she stated.

"I am Mr. McNally," I replied. "This is Mr. Watrous."

Eyeing Binky, she asked, "Are you two considering this as a couple?"

That went a long way in confirming my initial opinion of Hermioni Rutherford. "Mr. Watrous is contemplating making the Palm Court his bachelor digs"— weighty pause— "if what is being offered meets his needs."

"I see." Turning to Binky, she continued her interrogation. "May I know your occupation, Mr. Watrous?"

Before Binky began his litany of jobs held and lost, I answered, "Mr. Watrous is in pneumatic tubing."

"Who are you?" Hermioni questioned. "His spokesperson?" Did I detect a note of hostility in her query? Well, if I was ruffling her feathers, the feeling, I am sure, was mutual. However, she seemed pleased with showing the trailer to one in pneumatic tubing. Binky also looked happy with this job title. "Are you thinking of buying or renting, Mr. Watrous?"

"Renting," Binky told her, "but you never know."

I kept a watchful eye on Al's trailer as Hermioni and Binky got acquainted. I had purposely left my Miata in the garage at the McNally Building and had come in Binky's car, hoping to get in and out of the Palm Court without being seen by Sgt. Rogoff should he happen to be off duty and at home. If Binky did take up residence here, I did not want it to appear as if I had encouraged the move. Binky, I fear, is not one of Al's favorite people.

Into my line of vision came a rather attractive young lady just leaving the trailer that separated Al Rogoff's from the one up for grabs. She acknowledged our presence with a discreet nod before getting into a black Mercedes 190, modest but tasteful, and driving off. Binky had seen her, too, and I hoped her appearance would not cause him to sign a lease before investigating the premises.

"Shall we go in?" Hermioni suggested.

Three steps led to a concrete front porch that could hold one chair and little else. This was girdled by a wrought-iron fence painted a hideous green. Hermioni pointed to the trailer's number painted over the front door in gold-flecked fluorescent white. "Eleven-seventy, just like the Bath and Tennis Club," she announced. Here all resemblance to that posh establishment ended.

A mobile home, or trailer, is in essence a railroad car divided into diner, parlor, and sleeper. The kitchen of number 1170 contained a card table, one place mat, and one chair. A look in the cabinets and drawers revealed one cup and saucer, one dinner plate, one soup plate, one bread-and-butter plate, one water glass, one fork, one knife, one soupspoon, one teaspoon, an eggbeater, and a timer.

The parlor was furnished with one club chair, one end table, one lamp, and one television stand minus the telly. The bedroom held one twin-size bed and beneath its counterpane, one fitted sheet, one top sheet, one blanket, and one pillow with pillow slip. There was also one chest of drawers and one wardrobe in the sleeper.

"It was a divorce," Hermioni explained, "and everything was divided equally."

Binky looked a tad crestfallen, so I encouraged him with the promise, "Never fear, Binky. We will go to the

Wal-Mart and furnish you with everything from stemware to bedding to Jockey shorts, and come January we will scour the white sales. The rest of your life is before you, young man."

"Who are you?" Hermioni wanted to know. "His decorator?"

Looking out the parlor window, Binky asked, "What do you think of the view, Archy?"

Trailer courts are usually laid out in a grid with a disposal area unsuccessfully hidden behind a stockade fence at the far end of the vertical avenues. Each cement-block-mounted home has a carport and a patch of lawn the size of a handkerchief. Binky's parlor windows provided a marvelous view across the avenue of trailer number 1171.

"There is nothing wrong with this vista that good curtains can't enhance," I assured him.

Hermioni had very little to say as we paced the boxcar, mostly because there was very little to say. What you saw is what you got. "We will need references, of course," she cautioned, "from local residents as well as proof of employment and two months security on signing a lease. Do I understand that this will be a single-occupancy lease?"

"For the time being," Binky answered. For Binky, hope springs eternal.

"The Palm Court is a respectable community," Hermioni told us lest we didn't know, "catering to retirees and professionals. While we don't exclude young families with children, neither do we encourage them."

"What do you think, Archy?" Binky asked.

"What I think, Binky, doesn't matter. What do you think?"

Hermioni and I stood our ground as Binky make a quick tour of the trailer, pausing only to scan the place mat on the card table depicting a map of Palm Beach Island. His brown eyes glassy, his limp blond hair fringing his now perspiring forehead, Binky looked more like a frightened child than a prospective tenant, and Hermioni, I was sure, fought the urge to take Binky into her arms and cradle him against her ample bosom.

"I'll take it," Binky finally blurted to the place mat.

"Oh, good," Hermioni cried like a proud mother. "I will give you my card and you can come to the office to complete a formal application and leave a deposit whenever it's convenient."

Having earned her commission, she was more than ready to abandon us in pursuit of her next ten-percenter. Looking at me, she said, "I will leave you two alone as I'm sure you'll want to go over everything without me looking over your shoulders." Hermioni was now playing Goody Two-shoes with as much sincerity as a baby-kissing politician. "Just close the door when you leave and the spring lock will fall into place– not that there's anything much to take. Hee, hee."

No sooner had she gone out the door than she popped back in again and called out, "Did I tell you that I also represent a cleaning service that will do for you once a week or more often if requested? Our domestic engineers are all bonded, of course."

"Mr. Watrous can do for himself, thank you," I called back.

"Who are you?" Hermioni demanded. "His father?"

Exit Hermioni Rutherford, and not a moment too soon.

After a brief silence that had Binky looking as if he wanted to change his mind, I said, "Congratulations, Bink. You are a man with a pad to call his own. Be it ever so humble and all that jazz."

"Did you see the girl next door, Archy?" Here, any trace of second thoughts vanished.

"I saw a woman leave the trailer next door, Binky, but that does not mean she is your neighbor. Many people enter and leave the White House, but not all of them are the president." Giving that a moment's thought, I added, "But coming from Palm Beach County, one never knows, does one?"

Undaunted, as is Binky's wont when it comes to speculating about the opposite sex, he went on, "She was some looker, eh?"

"Where you should be looking," I admonished, "is into your wallet. Have you got the loot for the two-months' security?"

"The Duchess said she would help me," was Binky's not-surprising answer. Having invested over twenty years in Binky, a few more bucks, with the promise of the end in sight, wouldn't break the bank.

"Well, Binky, if you can tear yourself away from your castle, I think it's time to call it quits."

"I'll drive you back to the McNally Building, Archy, and thanks for your help."

"Help? I did nothing but hang around," I assured him.

"He who waits also serves," Binky informed me. This keen observation can be found framed and hanging on the walls of courthouses where prospective jurors wait, endlessly, to be called to judge their peers. Juror was one of Binky's periodic gigs.

Murphy's Law— anything that can go wrong, will— prevailed as we stepped out of Binky's incipient love nest and almost collided with Al Rogoff, chomping on a stogie and toting a plastic garbage bag. Al is a big guy. Beefy, in the vernacular, and seeing him in his leisure togs is like coming upon Smokey the Bear decked out in Bermuda shorts and tank top. Astonishing, I believe, is the most fitting adjective, and Al was just as astonished to see Binky Watrous and Archy McNally on the street where he lives.

Removing the stogie from his mouth, Al gaped. After ogling Binky as if he were breaking parole simply by being at the Palm Court, Al turned his attention to me and exclaimed, "Don't tell me Bianca hired you."

"Bianca? No, we came to see Hermioni Rutherford. Who's Bianca and why should she hire me?" I asked.

"Bianca Courtney," Al answered, the stogie back in his mouth. "She's the dame who lives there." He gestured with the garbage bag toward the trailer from which we had seen the young lady surface earlier.

Al Rogoff has several colorful epithets to denote the female gender, none of which will earn him points with the more politically correct denizens of our democracy. However, before you label Al Rogoff crass, let me state that he is a closet balletomane and an aficionado of classical music and the performing arts more associated with the erudite than with a police sergeant who resides in a trailer court and subsists on a diet of hamburgers, beer, and chocolate pudding.

Al enjoys playing the uncouth slob in public, allowing only a select few, myself included, to get to know his Dr. Jekyll alter ego. Furthermore, I'm reasonably certain that I'm his only friend who knows his middle name is Irving.

"Why would Bianca Courtney hire me?" I asked.

"She's got some crazy idea that a murder has been committed and the perp is getting away with it."

"Is she in danger?" Binky asked Al. Binky has a recurring Walter Mitty fantasy of turning into a masked crusader at the behest of a damsel in distress.

"Only of making a pest of herself," Al told him.

"What's the story, Al?" I asked.

"You looking for work, Archy?"

"No. Just an interested citizen."

Al again removed the stogie from his mouth, shrugged, and explained, "Bianca worked for a rich broad who married a guy twenty years her junior and drowned a few months after the marriage. Bianca thinks the guy did her in."

"What do the police think?"

"Granted, the circumstances looked a little queer, but we checked it out and ruled it an accident. When she moved in next door and learned I was a cop, she started hounding me to reopen the case."

"On what grounds?" I questioned.

"Female intuition," Al barked. "There's no reason to re-open the case because there never was a case to begin with."

"What makes you so sure?"

"Motive," Al stated. "The guy had no reason to murder his bride unless you think having twenty years on him was just cause."

I was beginning to enjoy this. There is nothing like a little bit of intrigue to stir the creative juices. I wondered if I could interest Sabrina Wright in this plot with a few variations, to be sure. The young He would become a young She and the old She would become an old He. But I had the feeling the new transgender heroine would not end up with her heart's desire, namely, the spoils of marriage to the old and the wealthy. And I was right.

"He doesn't benefit from her will?" I guessed.

"You got it. She made a will leaving everything, which is plenty, to the children's wing of St. Mary's Hospital and didn't change it after her marriage. He gets to keep the Jag she gave him for a wedding present."

"So what's Bianca's gripe?"

"Revenge, that's what. The marriage cost her a cushy job. Companion to the rich dame. Nice digs, three squares a day, and a regular paycheck every week. She rented the trailer when her lady boss got herself a new companion of the opposite sex."

As interested as I was in Bianca Courtney's plight, I was more interested in escaping the Palm before Al began to wonder what we were doing there if not to speak with his neighbor. If I wanted to hear more I could always invite Al to lunch at the Pelican and get him to talk while he devoured a hamburger, fries, and Bass Ale, at my expense.

"Well, I . . . " Binky began before I nudged him toward the car and away from Al Rogoff.

"Good seeing you, Al." I cut Binky off. "Call me and we'll get together for lunch."

Poor Binky was bursting to tell his news, but with a gentle pressure on his arm, I kept increasing the distance between him and Al Rogoff.

"See you," Al said, hoisting his garbage bag and heading for the disposal area.

Just as we got the car doors opened, I heard Al shout, "Hermioni Rutherford? She's with the real estate outfit that runs this place."

I waved at Al and tried to get into the car, but it was too late. He retraced his steps, garbage and all, demanding to know why we were talking to Hermioni Rutherford.

The moment of truth had arrived and there was no place to hide. "Binky has taken a lease on this trailer," I said. "Number eleven-seventy, just like the Bath and Tennis."

"Oh no," Al moaned.

"Love thy neighbor as thyself," I reminded Al before he vented his wrath.

"Yes," Binky agreed, thinking no doubt of Bianca Courtney.

With Binky safely in the car, I walked up to Al and whispered, "There are worse things in life than having Binky Watrous for a neighbor."

"Name two," Al challenged, waving the shopworn stogie in my face.

Looking at my watch, I said I didn't have time at the moment but would think of a few, perhaps even three, before hell froze over. Moving purposefully past me and coming up to the car window, Al looked in and advised Binky, "We have a rule around here, buddy. Don't come knocking when the trailer is rocking."

Exit Al Rogoff, and not a moment too soon.

As he drove out of the Palm Court, Binky wondered aloud, "Don't come knocking when the trailer is rocking? What do you suppose that means, Archy?"

"For someone so eager to cohabitate, Binky, you have a lot to learn."

"I'm not a virgin, Archy."

Give unto me a break.

THE MCNALLY CLAN meets every evening at seven for cocktails in Father's den where he mixes our martinis in a perfect silver shaker filled with perfect little ice cubes, pouring the result into perfect Baccarat crystal glasses and garnished with perfect green olives. The only thing not perfect is the brew itself, thanks to the *seigneur*'s heavy hand with the vermouth. In this, as in all things, Father is consistent when he measures out the ingredients including, so help me, the exact number of ice cubes.

Topics of conversation at this family gathering are limited to who did what that day. If I'm on a case, I will give Father a progress report. He, in turn, will nod his approval or vocalize his disapproval after which he will keep us abreast of the antics of his more prestigious clients or drop a few of the names he rubbed shoulders with at last season's Glitz at the Ritz Ball.

Mother, if she's had a letter from my sister, Dora, in Arizona, will report on the family there with emphasis on the grandchildren, Rebecca, Rowena, and my godson, little Darcy. Or, after hearing a guest speaker at the C.A.S. (Current Affairs Society), she will tell us, in detail, what the lecturer had to impart. Mother joined the group out of concern for the ozone layer without quite knowing what ozone is.

I recall one guest speaker, a Ms. Glynis Ives, self-proclaimed authority on the British royal family, reporting that when King George VI and his queen, Elizabeth, visited the United States in 1939, they brought with them gallons of British water to be used for brewing their tea and had insisted on hot-water bottles for their beds– in Washington, D.C., in the springtime.

What this has to do with current affairs I do not know, nor would I dream of asking. But I record such information in my journal under the heading "Incidental Intelligence."

As you can see, we lead a privileged lifestyle due not to my father's flourishing law practice but to the man who greased the way to Father's success– his sire, Freddy McNally. Freddy was a bulb-nosed, pratfalling burlesque comic on the Minsky circuit who worked with such headliners as the exotic dancer Trixie Forganza and Her Little

Bag of Tricks. Grandpa Freddy invested not in the stock market but, on his many visits to Florida in the Roaring Twenties, put his money into Gold Coast real estate at a dime an acre. When Wall Street laid that egg, Freddy's act soared.

While Father is not ungrateful for Freddy's foresight, he is not exactly joyous over Freddy's chosen profession. The lord of the manor would prefer to have it believed that the McNally dynasty began with him and, based on my expectations, will no doubt end with him.

With two-thirds of the family not at home, our household was a microcosm of Palm Beach in the summer months when the population drops to nine thousand, from a winter high reputed to be close to thirty thousand. Since the pater and mater had gone to sea, I had been taking my evening libation at the Pelican where the bar is presided over by Mr. Simon Pettibone, the club's general manager, factotum, and, on numerous occasions, father confessor.

Simon Pettibone is a dignified African-American who, along with his wife and children, keep the Pelican in tip-top shape and solvent, and accounts for the length of our membership waiting list. At this early hour I was Mr. Pettibone's only customer. Priscilla Pettibone, Simon's beautiful and sassy daughter, was busy setting tables in the bar and dining room and the Pettibone son, Leroy, who wears the *toque blanche*, was in the kitchen whipping up delights. This left Mrs. Pettibone, our den mother, who I assumed was upstairs in their apartment over the shop getting dolled up to greet the evening diners. Simon was watching the television screen showing a running tape of the day's stock quotations.

"Are we up or down?" I asked Mr. Pettibone.

"Sideways, Archy," he answered. Simon Pettibone was

also something of a Wall Street guru, whose tips were sought by club members who enjoyed a roll of the dice at that legal gambling casino in lower Manhattan. Anticipating my order, he began to prepare a frozen daiquiri.

"I had a drink with a woman today, Mr. Pettibone, who ordered a Pink Lady."

Mr. Pettibone paused in his work, closed his eyes, and recited: "Two ounces gin, one teaspoon grenadine, one teaspoon cream, one egg white, shake with ice and pour. Cherry, optional."

This was a game Simon Pettibone and I played ever since I had come upon a vintage mixology handbook and discovered such alluring alcohol bracers as a Sazerac, a Sweet Potootie, a Seventh Heaven, an Arise My Love, and, my favorite, a Soul Kiss. One evening at the club I ordered the latter and was rendered flummoxed when Simon Pettibone, without so much as a blink of the eye, mixed bourbon, dry vermouth, Dubonnet, and orange juice in exacting proportions and presented me with my order.

Not only did Simon Pettibone know the ingredients of all the drinks in a book that was a relic of Prohibition, he also added a few that were not in my mixology guide. To wit: an Oliver Twist– a martini with both olive and lemon. I never asked Mr. Pettibone from whence came this profundity of the mixologist's art.

Placing my daiquiri before me, he said, "I have a poser for you."

"I'm at your service, Mr. P."

"Do you know the name Henry Peavey?"

It had been a long, hard day, so I thought about this short and easy. Not having Sofia Richmond to fill in the blanks, I came up with nothing. "I'm sorry, Mr. Pettibone, I can't say it means a thing to me. Should it?"

"I don't know myself, Archy. Mrs. Pettibone got a letter from her cousin's son, Lyle Washington, who lives in Sacramento. Lyle is the son of Hattie and Sam Washington. Henry Peavey was Hattie's father. Jasmine, Mrs. Pettibone, is a cousin of Sam Washington, not Hattie, and both of them are gone now.

"It seems Lyle was cleaning out the attic in the house left to him by his parents when he came upon his grandfather Peavey's diary. His letter said it could be worth a fortune."

"Why?" I responded.

"Beats me, Archy. I said Jasmine is related on the Washington side of the family, and she's never been very close to them as they've always lived in California. She knows even less about the Peaveys. Lyle wrote to Jasmine because, as he said in the letter, he understood we saw a lot of notables here in Palm Beach, and he thought we might be helpful to him."

"And that's all he said?"

"That's all, Archy. It looks to me as if Lyle just took it for granted that we, or at least Jasmine, knew the Peaveys and the significance of finding Henry's diary."

"Did Mrs. Pettibone call Lyle?" I asked.

"She did, and got no answer. Lyle is divorced and lives alone. She called Lyle's daughter, who was just as mystified as we were. All she knew was that she got a call from her father who told her he was going south and for her to keep an eye on the house."

"South?" I echoed. "Do the Peaveys have relatives in the South?"

Mr. Pettibone shook his head. "We don't know and neither does Lyle's daughter."

"I think, Mr. Pettibone, all you can do now is wait for another communication from Lyle."

"I agree, Archy. But you have to admit it's a tantalizing puzzler."

I would admit. I would also admit that after dealing with the trials and tribulations of Sabrina Wright, Binky Watrous, Hermioni Rutherford, Al Rogoff, and, by proxy, Bianca Courtney, I deserved an English Oval. Therefore, I lit one.

"I thought you gave those up," Priscilla said in passing.

"This is only my second today," I told her.

"They say there's never a second without a third," Priscilla called over her shoulder.

I would admit that, too.

FIVE

IT WAS ONE month after the summer solstice, which gave me just enough daylight to get in my swim before joining the Olsons for potluck. In honor of this mauve decade, I selected a pair of mauve trunks adorned with or-ris braiding and a matching mesh belt. I pulled a hooded white terry robe over my shoulders and ambled across the A1A, barefoot. Amazing how traffic grinds to a halt when my wraithlike figure appears in the waning twilight. Will I meet my maker on one such balmy evening when a giddy teenager in a Porsche attempts to drive through me?

There are many who flee southern Florida in the sum-mer for cooler climes and we natives are prone to say unto them, "Ta-ta and don't hurry back." There is nothing like having an ocean all to yourself after a hard day in the salt mines. My shadow grew long as I walked across the tepid sand and the Atlantic was beginning to cool under a white moon, almost full, just peeking over the horizon. I swam my laps beneath a red sky, a mile north, before retracing my wet path back to my starting point. If it ain't Eden, it's a reasonable facsimile thereof.

When the family is all in residence, we usually breakfast in the kitchen with Ursi cooking and serving, after which she often joins us for a cuppa before Father and I leave for the office and Mother rushes to her beckoning begonias. Jamie Olson is sometimes present, lacing his black coffee with Aquavit while waiting to see if Mother wants to go shopping at Publix, which I believe is the only supermarket in the world that offers valet parking, or hit the local nurseries in search of an orphaned begonia in need of TLC. For these excursions Jamie drives Mother's wood-paneled Ford wagon.

Evenings, we dress for dinner in the formal dining room where Father officiates and pontificates over the fine quality of his wine cellar, which, I must say, is superb. Being alone, I joined Ursi and Jamie in our commodious kitchen for the evening meal, and when the sire is away the offspring will play at selecting a wine of reputable vintage to enjoy with the fruits of Ursi's labors.

Tonight, it was fricandeau, or loin of veal to the common folks. This she larded and braised and presented with roasted potatoes and onions, asparagus in lemon butter sauce, and, for color, glazed baby carrots. For openers there was a spinach salad *avec* bacon and mushrooms, tossed with Ursi's own warm bacon vinaigrette. If this is not the average American's bill of fare on a warm summer evening, please remember that Palm Beach is not the average American seaside resort.

My contribution was a 1982 cabernet sauvignon. For

appearances' sake we toasted our benefactor, wishing him calm seas and a safe return. Silently, I offered an invocation to Poseidon, adjuring him to treat my kin with more respect than he had shown poor Odysseus. I acknowledge the old gods because I am a firm believer in never burning my bridges and, who knows, if culottes can make a comeback, why not the original Olympians?

As expected, Ursi had spread the word of my involvement with the famous authoress Sabrina Wright. "They all knew that she was in town," Ursi said, "thanks to Mr. Spindrift, but it was me who told them why she was here. You could say I had an exclusive."

"Any reaction?" I asked.

"Well, they all agreed that Ms. Wright should stick to her books and let her daughter elope with the man she loves."

That was predictable and did nothing to further my cause in locating Robert Silvester and, should he still be with them, Gillian Wright and Zack Ward. Sudden thought: Had he ever been with them? Did Robert Silvester in fact find Gillian and Zack? He told his wife he had, but it's what my father would call hearsay. Then the guy disappears and therein lies the crux of the matter. Where had he gone, and why?

But Ursi had done my bidding. Lolly had told them Sabrina was in town and Ursi had connected me with the writer. Both Lolly and Ursi had the ear of those that mattered— granted on different strata, but due to necessity the twain doth meet on Ocean Boulevard. Now, interested parties would know whom to contact if they had anything to share.

Jamie's mandible, except when chewing, was as rigid as always, but then Jamie only spoke when he had something to say. I had dropped an ant in the pants of the Palm Beach noblesse and now had to wait on their sagacity, which, thankfully, did not hinge upon our national security.

Dessert was raspberry sorbet with Ursi's own decadently fudgy brownies, plus a few actual berries for their antioxidant powers. Stoically refusing seconds, I withdrew to my leaky penthouse and settled in for the evening. Not having dressed for dinner– summer flannels, lavender polo shirt of Sea Island cotton, white tasseled loafers, and no socks of course– I went directly to my desk, got out my journal, and began recording my interview with Sabrina Wright and the case of "The Man That Got Away." I thought a more apt title might be "The Men That Got Away," not realizing at the time just how prophetic my own musings would be.

The men, of course, would include Gillian's natural father, who had fled some thirty years ago; Zack Ward, who followed suit a week ago; and then Robert Silvester, just a few days ago. Originally, Gillian's father and Silvester must have believed he was the subject of Lolly's blind item. I omit Zack Ward because I'm sure he tipped off Lolly. Now that the Olsons had gotten my message out, Gillian's father knew, or would soon know, that Sabrina was here in search of Gillian and her lover. Would he believe it? If he did, would he find it inconvenient to have both his old flame and the result of their indiscretion on our tight little island? Too, he must be wondering why Gillian had sought asylum in Palm Beach. The guy's feathered nest was suddenly rife with thorns.

I had no idea how I was going to go about finding Robert Silvester. Both he and Zack Ward were strangers in our midst and therefore would not be privy to the gossip Ursi and Jamie had spread around Ocean Boulevard, so they could not link me with Sabrina. And even if they did, it was unlikely they would contact me. The deer does not attract the attention of the hunter.

So why did Zack tip off Lolly? Role reversal. Sabrina's prey was playing the hunter. This case had all the trappings of a bedroom farce, which comes with the territory when you get in the middle of domestic fisticuffs.

I undressed, washed, and donned a blue-and-white striped silk robe. I poured myself a small marc and, refusing to break the rule– never a second without a third– I lit an English Oval.

At this juncture, as in the spring, a young man's fancy turns to thoughts of love. It is said that the average man thinks of sex once every thirty-seven seconds. I have no doubt that Binky Watrous was canvassed on that one. If you think I was mulling over the idea of calling Connie Garcia, you are wrong. In fact, I was thinking of Bianca Courtney and her crusade for justice. More to the point, I was thinking of Bianca Courtney and her position between a boy and a bear– Binky Watrous and Al Rogoff.

What Bianca needed was a sheik in a blue-and-white striped silk robe to sweep her onto his Arabian charger and gallop off into the sunset. I have these heroic fantasies– every thirty-seven seconds. Was guilt a by-product of this fantasy? Absolutely not. I am true to Connie in my fashion; hence I remain single, which makes me more a puritan than a libertine.

Being a firm believer in the sanctity of marriage, I will not take the fatal step until I am prepared to draw a blank every thirty-seven seconds and become monogamous in thought, word, and deed, till death do us part. Being as far from that goal as the distance between our planet and infinity, I remain footloose and fancy-free. A cop-out? Sure.

But it proves that one can rationalize anything, crawl into bed, stroke your cheek good night, and savor the restful sleep of the just.

"MR. MCNALLY? THIS is Robert Silvester. I believe you're looking for me."

Was I just lucky, or was I the plaything of an author in search of a plot? To appreciate the full impact of this morning call on my febrile brain, let me begin with enumerating on the roods I bore before the mountain came calling on Mohammed.

For breakfast Ursi presented me with eggs Benedict. For those who only know from scrambled to fried to hard boiled, this delight is a toasted English muffin, upon which is placed a succulent slice of frizzled Canadian bacon, over which we have a poached egg. The resulting composition is then doused with a delicate Hollandaise sauce. Once one of my favorite egg dishes, it now brings back memories I would rather forget. Other loving couples have *their* song. Connie and I have eggs Benedict.

One afternoon in the not-too-distant past, I was lunching at Testa's with a charming young lady, unaware that Connie was also taking her midday meal there. Seeing us, Connie came directly to our table, toting her brunch plate. I thought she intended to join us– uninvited, I might add. In the manner of civilized people, I rose to introduce her to my companion. What Connie did was open the waistband of my lime-green linen trousers and slip in two perfectly prepared eggs Benedict.

So much for breakfast and remembrance of things past but not forgotten. I drove my Miata into the garage beneath the McNally building, exchanged a few words with

Herb, our security guard, and took the elevator to the executive suite. Dear Mrs. Trelawney accepted my expense report with neither meticulous analysis nor sarcastic comment. *En garde,* I thought, reaching for an imaginary épée. She signed it with a flourish and handed it back to me. Poised for battle, I waited for her first parry. My father's private secretary has two passions in life: serving the master and giving me a hard time, not necessarily in that order.

I was loath to turn my back on her and leave. Mrs. Trelawney wears a gray wig and, for all I know, packs heat. "Thank you," I ventured, sadly. A day without sparring with Mrs. Trelawney is like a day without sunshine.

"I have you down for a microwave," she stated.

"I beg your pardon, Mrs. Trelawney."

"A microwave oven," she expanded. If she thought this clarified her meaning, she was wrong.

"I seem to have come in in the middle of the movie, Mrs. Trelawney. Could you go back to the opening scene?"

Looking over her glasses she said, "You didn't come in in the middle of the movie, Archy. You came in in the middle of the workday."

This was more like the Mrs. Trelawney I had come to love. My spirits rose as I geared for combat. "Does your spy in the garage below report the time of everyone's arrival, or just mine?"

"Just you, Archy." She spoke without a trace of shame.

"You missed your calling, Mrs. Trelawney. One of those alphabet organizations is where you would have risen to the top of the class. FBI, CIA, KGB, G-E-S-T-A-P-O."

She nodded knowingly, as if agreeing with me. Mrs. Trelawney has the irritating habit of defusing a barb with a smile. "And you should have been a hairdresser," she shot back. "Love your suit."

She referred, no doubt, to my three-buttoned, pale pink linen ensemble of which I was particularly fond. Growing more conservative with the passing years, I no longer wore it with my lavender suede loafers but now opted for a pair of shiny black brogues with cooling perforations at the tips. I thought I looked smashing, but Mrs. Trelawney was the kind of gal who would gladly kick the crutch from Tiny Tim's grip and tell him to walk like a man.

Round one. I declared it a tie and made to depart. "See you in court, Mrs. Trelawney."

"Just make sure you bring the microwave with you."

I froze. "Okay, I give up. Am I supposed to say, What microwave?' "

"Binky's microwave."

"Binky?" I echoed. "Do you mean . . ."

"I mean, we're giving Binky a housewarming and I have you down for a microwave oven. Is that clear?"

Nothing could be clearer. I glanced at my watch. Mickey's small hand was on the ten and his big hand was on the three. I was aghast. Minutes after ten in the morning and everyone knew that Binky had rented living space last night and a housewarming was already being planned? "Did he distribute change-of-address notices this morning?" I complained.

"He told Evelyn Sharif in Records that he found a place last night, with your help. Evelyn told Sofia Richmond in the library, and Sofia passed it on to me. The housewarming was my idea," she concluded, as if she had just invented the wheel.

From Sharif to Richmond to Trelawney, a perfect 6-4-3 double play: Binky had a gaggle of middle-aged women vying to make him comfy, like doting mothers gussying up a dorm room for their little freshman. It was those Bambi eyes that evoked the mother instinct in older women and indifference in their daughters.

There are two things I detest in this vale of tears, and they are eggs Benedict over heather-gray briefs and office parties. Being the scion of the firm's ruler, I am forced to contribute financially to the latter but reserve my right to be a no-show at the gala. There is something almost morbid about seeing those you toil with in their cups. Bottoms are pinched, tops are ogled, and, on occasion, romance by misadventure follows. This differs from death by misadventure in that both parties can get up and walk away from the scene of the crime.

"Why should I give Binky Watrous a microwave oven?" I wanted to know. We did not have such an appliance in our home, thank you. Mother would never force a begonia and Ursi would never force a baked potato. Like Julian, the last Roman emperor to defend the old gods against the Christian hordes, so we McNallys fought valiantly to keep the digital world from encroaching upon our doorstep.

No fax, no e-mail, no voice mail, no PC, no WP, no CD, and no DVD. However, you might find the odd pair of B.V.D.'s in father's chiffonier.

"Remember, you're Binky's best friend," she announced.

"Says who?"

"Says Binky," she argued.

Binky has diarrhea of the mouth and constipation of ideas. Not wanting to singe Mrs. Trelawney's ears and, by propinquity, her darnel tresses, I toned it down to, "Binky speaks with a profusion of words and a paucity of facts."

"You're still down for a microwave oven." With this she ticked my name off her list of donors. "Your father is giving china. Service for four. A starter set, don't you know."

"Father? You spoke to the boss?"

"This morning at half-past nine, as usual. I told him I would give you his regards as soon as you came in."

"You are a national treasure, Mrs. Trelawney, and will take your rightful place in history alongside Pearl Harbor, the *Lusitania*, and 'The Fall of the House of Usher.' " I was losing my cool.

"Flattery will get you wherever you want to go."

"Right now I want to go to my office and cry."

"Fine. Then go for the microwave."

"Just how much does one cost?" I asked.

"About a hundred, but it depends on the size. And go with a known manufacturer; you don't want to go cheap on this. Remember, he's your best friend."

"I don't have a hundred to spare," I pleaded like one being audited by the IRS.

"You will when you cash in that swindle sheet. Have a nice day, love."

THE PHONE WAS ringing when I entered my office.

"Mr. McNally? This is Robert Silvester. I believe you're looking for me."

I wanted to say I was looking for a microwave oven but refrained from doing so. After a significant pause I decided to play it with moxie and answered, "As a matter of fact, Mr. Silvester, I was just about to call you."

"Really? And do you know where I am?"

"I do now. I have caller ID."

Robert Silvester laughed. "I don't believe you, but you

have a whimsical sense of humor, and if you're going to be dealing with Sabrina, you'll need that in great abundance."

"You know I've seen your wife?"

"I do now." Again the laugh. It was a pleasant sound, not at all mocking. "It was I who gave Sabrina your name."

I got the feeling I was being jerked around– with humor– and I didn't like it. "You told your wife to hire me to look for you? How clever."

"So, I am the man that got away."

"Let's say you're in the running, Mr. Silvester."

"How did Ms. Spindrift know Sabrina had come down here looking for me?" Silvester asked.

"Mr. Spindrift. Lolly is a he."

"How quaint."

"I'll tell him." Not wishing to get into a discussion about men named Carroll and Adrian, I asked, "Why did Zack Ward tip off Lolly that Sabrina was in town looking for some guy?"

"He didn't," came Silvester's immediate reply.

"Then who did?"

"For all I know it may have been Sabrina herself."

Lolly had told me the caller was a man, but I wasn't about to tell him that. Instead I told him what I thought of the inference. "I'm not amused, Mr. Silvester."

"Please, call me Rob."

"I'm still not amused, Rob."

"If you give me a chance, I'll tell you what I know," he said.

"I'm listening."

"Not on the phone, it would take too long. Besides, I'd like to meet you in person. Do you lunch?"

"Only when I'm hungry."

"Would Harry's Place at The Breakers suit?"

"To a T."

"Good. Let's say twelve-thirty or one."

SIX

THE BREAKERS WAS originally created as Henry Flagler's Palm Beach Inn. Originally build of wood, it twice burned to the ground before the current phoenix rose from the ashes. It's said that the second conflagration was started by a PB matron giving herself a home perm with a curling iron.

I don't know which came first, Cornelius Vanderbilt's weekend cottage in Newport, also called The Breakers, or Flagler's inn. I do know Cornelius never ran a B & B at his place, but then Cornelius never had a drawbridge named after him. Henry's Palm Beach cottage, Whitehall, is now the home of the Henry Morrison Flagler Museum. Its size and opulence makes Versailles look like a pretentious bed-sitter with formal gardens.

Besides the Ponce de León ballroom where revelers

usually gather in support of some charity rather than seeking eternal youth– that they leave to skilled laser wielders– The Breakers also houses several fine restaurants. Harry's Place bills itself as a genuine English pub and is the closest thing to fast-food dining a place like The Breakers would admit to. I told the maitre d' I was joining Mr. Silvester, and as he showed me to the table, my host rose to greet me.

"Mr. McNally," he said, extending his hand as he eyed my apparel. "I was certain it was you."

There are times when my reputation precedes me. Had I known I was to meet with Robert Silvester today, I would have worn the summer uniform– chinos, dark blue blazer, and loafers by the Italian shoemaker currently in fashion. (If you get caught in a pair of Mr. Gucci's flats, you're giving your age away.) The winter uniform finds the toffs in gray flannels, dark blue blazer, and loafers by etc. As it happened, I was happy to have come as myself, as Robert Silvester had come as Everyman.

Not surprisingly, the guy was a good fifteen years younger than his wife with the kind of clean-cut good looks popular with Hollywood teenage idols of the forties and fifties. Think of a blond Farley Granger, e.g. Silvester's hair was an attractive reddish brown, worn parted on the left and showing a hint of gray at the temples. I got the feeling that, contrary to the norm, the gray came from a bottle, perhaps in an attempt to look more like his wife's husband than her son. A dozen years ago, on his honeymoon, he would have had to show proof before he could order a bottle of champagne to toast his bride. Still, his bright blue eyes and genial smile rendered him more cute than classically handsome.

"What will you have?" he asked as I sat. "This," pointing at the drink in front of him, "is a pint of Guinness stout. When in Rome . . ."

I wasn't in Rome, so I ordered a frozen daiquiri before playing my first, and only, card. "You know your wife hired me to find you, so I'm obligated to report this meeting to her and tell her you're staying at The Breakers."

He smiled his Hollywood smile, exposing his Hollywood pearly whites. "You stopped at the desk before coming in here and asked them if I was registered."

I flashed him my jumbo charmer 150-watt smile and assured him that I had. "Zachary Ward and Gillian Wright are also registered, with all of you in separate rooms. How sad for the lovers."

My drink arrived and the waiter hovered. "Give us a few minutes," Silvester told him. Alone once more, he said to me, "You're very good at your job, Mr. McNally. I see I made a wise choice. And I will probably call Sabrina and tell her we're here before you do." He lifted his stein. "Your health, Mr. McNally."

I drank to that and decided not to tell him he could call me Archy. "So much for my case. Do I still get fed?"

"But of course. Does a ploughman's lunch interest you?"

"Not in the least, but the shepherd's pie is the best you'll get this side of the Atlantic."

He signaled the waiter and ordered the shepherd's pie for two. "I'm sure Sabrina filled you in on what we're all doing here."

"She did. But she was rather coy on how she got my name."

Silvester nodded knowingly. "Typical Sabrina. Never give anything away on page one that you might need later on. It's the writer's instinct. The less you tell, the more the reader must turn pages to find out what he wants to know. With Sabrina, life imitates art." He drank his Guinness and managed it without leaving a trace on his upper lip. "When Jill left New York, Sabrina guessed she had come here. You do know why?"

"I do."

"Sabrina wanted to follow immediately and drag Jill home. I talked her into letting me come down alone, find Jill, and see if I could talk her into coming home. I have been acting as arbitrator between Jill and her mother since Sabrina and I were married." He seemed to think this over, then said, "Perhaps referee would be a more apt job description."

As he spoke I filled in the blanks. Fresh out of some Ivy League college with a baccalaureate in English lit, Silvester went to work for a big publishing house with a dream of trees that grow in Brooklyn and valleys full of dolls. He moved rapidly from assistant to associate editor to editor. One day the dream landed on his desk in the form of four hundred laser-printed pages. Robert Silvester had a winner and he showed his appreciation by falling in love with the fictional heroine of *Darling Desire*.

When he met the author he experienced a classic case of transference. Sabrina Wright had been places and done things Robert Silvester had only read about in the novels he usually returned with the customary "Not for us" rejection letter. If Silvester was bewitched by the fictional *Darling Desire,* he was dazzled by her flesh-and-blood counterpart. This one was not only "for us," it was "for him."

Sabrina's interest in the bartender at Bar Anticipation told me she had a thing for younger men. Robert Silvester was prime, and as an added attraction, as if any were necessary, he was the guy who could shape her novel into a bestseller and guide her career. Not wanting to share her editor, she had married him. Both must have thought they were getting the best of all possible worlds, and if fame, fortune, and sex were the criteria, they had.

During the early days, Gillian was in Switzerland, learning how to speak French atrociously and ski beautifully. When she finished being finished, she returned to a famous mother and a stepfather who resembled the ski instructor in Lausanne, who had introduced her to the arts of sex and the slalom.

"Sabrina is headstrong and adamant when it comes to getting her way," Silvester was saying. "She's always dictated to Jill rather than reasoned with her and poor Jill was ready to make the break. Sabrina's disclosure gave the girl just the excuse she was looking for to act on her own. There is nothing like a worthy cause to justify our actions. Jill's quest is her own Holy Grail.

"I thought if I could keep mother and daughter apart until I had a chance to talk to Jill, it would save a confrontation between the two that would settle nothing. My error was to call Sabrina and tell her I had located Jill and Zack. She insisted on coming down immediately."

"She didn't tell me that," I thought aloud.

Silvester's shrug said that was a given. "Knowing Sabrina was practically on her way here the minute I said I had located Jill, I checked out of the Chesterfield and into here with Jill and Zack, without telling Sabrina. My purpose was to keep the warring parties from hand-to-hand combat until I had some time alone with Jill. I'd reconciled the two before and hoped I could do it again."

"And have you?" I asked.

Silvester shook his head. "No. Jill is more determined than ever to find her father."

Our lunch arrived and Silvester eyed his mound of mashed potatoes suspiciously. "I should have had the tossed green salad."

Having no such scruples, I asked the waiter to bring me a beer to go with the meal. "Dig in," I told Silvester. "It'll put lead in your pencil."

"My pencil, Mr. McNally, is not wanting." As if to prove it, he went at his shepherd's pie with gusto.

"Tell me, do you know who Gillian's father is?"

Without skipping a beat, he responded, "Cross my heart and hope to die, I don't. Sabrina will take the secret to her grave."

"And when did you learn that Sabrina was Gillian's natural mother?"

Not looking me in the eye, he stated, "At the same time Jill got the news."

I wanted to know if he had shared in the champagne toast, but the guy was embarrassed enough at the disclosure and I saw no reason to add insult to injury. I wondered what other secrets Sabrina Wright kept from those she loved and, no doubt, so did they. As far as I was concerned, the case, which I hadn't wanted from the beginning, was closed. I would bill Ms. Wright for twenty-four hours, plus expenses, and leave her and her kin to sort out their differences while running up a tab at The Breakers your average Joe might mistake for a telephone number. But I did want a few answers before I left the clan to their fate.

"Will you tell me how you got my name?" was number one on my list.

Silvester waved his hand as if shooing a pesky fly. "Of course." He gave me a name that sounded vaguely familiar and went on to say, "We were at college together. He's from these parts and in our junior year he got himself into a bit of a jam during the Christmas break. A little booze, a little pot, a fast car, and an underage girl in the passenger seat is the way it went, I think. His father hired you to patch things up and he returned to school singing your praises. I never forgot your name or the fact that you owned a collection of silk berets in a variety of pastel shades."

I recalled my silk-beret period with a nostalgia I'm sure Picasso must have felt for his blue period. This link brought to mind my former client and his son. Good people, and it was the boy's first offense, which is why I agreed to help him. "What did he do after college?"

"Wall Street," Silvester answered. "I called him to see if you were still in business down here. He contacted his father and that's how I got your number. I told Sabrina I was going to enlist your help, but as it turned out that wasn't necessary. Having given her your name, I was sure she would contact you when she got here."

Next query. "She asked me to meet her in a bar of dubious reputation. Any idea how she knew the place?"

Like a weary martyr, he sighed audibly. "My guess is she got one of the Chesterfield's employees to give her a rundown of the area's more notorious watering holes and then chose the one most renowned as a meeting place. Even under stress, Sabrina Wright must amaze, amuse, and mystify her gentlemen callers. I take it she treated you to all three, Mr. McNally."

She had, and with great style. After years of poking around in other people's dirty laundry, I can say with considerable confidence that the answers to most of life's mysteries are simplistic and obvious, from the pyramids to Sabrina Wright, as Robert Silvester had just confirmed.

It's the commonplace that's more likely to contain surprises behind its familiar facade.

My first thought regarding Lolly's anonymous caller was that he or she was a clerk at the Chesterfield who knew Sabrina Wright had registered at the hotel and had heard her ask for Robert Silvester. The informer made a grab for his, or her, fifteen minutes and settled happily for anonymous fame when Lolly printed the item. Simple and obvious. Yet I couldn't help but ask, "Why did you suggest Sabrina herself might have made that call to Lolly Spindrift?"

Silvester grimaced. "A caprice, nothing more. I've been dealing with Sabrina's impulsive behavior for so long that nothing she does surprises me, but, as I'm sure you know, she did not make that call."

"And neither did Zack Ward?"

"No, Mr. McNally, I'm sure Sabrina painted a picture of Zack replete with twirling mustaches and black cape but he's not like that at all. He is a brash young man but not a devious one. True, he works for a rag, and he is ambitious, but one has to start someplace. Even Raymond Chandler wrote for the pulps."

I didn't tell him that I rather liked the original pulps with their lurid cover art and even had a few stashed away in a box of memorabilia I intend to leave to my godson, Darcy. The one touting *The Blue Dahlia* on its cover must be worth a fortune.

In keeping with Silvester's white paper on Zack Ward, I stated rather than asked, "And he doesn't court Gillian because of her famous mother."

Silvester shook his head. "Did Sabrina tell you Jill met Zack in a writers' workshop?" When I acknowledged this with a nod, he asked, "Did she tell you that Jill was enrolled in that workshop under an alias?"

He didn't wait for a response because we both knew she hadn't. As I had noted when I met her, Sabrina Wright is a package. Now I knew she never allowed anyone, including her husband, to get under the wrapping.

Silvester explained, "Jill joined the workshop more as a diversion than with any serious intent to pen a novel. She also dabbled in acting classes, art classes, and Yoga, all with a 'no comment' from her mother. It's not easy being the daughter of a successful woman and less easy when the woman is Sabrina Wright.

"Jill had learned early on that when people discovered her relationship to Sabrina they treated her with either indifference or scorn. In her early days as an actress, a noted producer offered her a big part in his next play if her mother would finance it. After that, she ventured out into the real world under an assumed name. As far as I know, she and Zack saw each other for a few weeks before he knew who she really was."

"Then why," I quizzed, "is Sabrina certain Zack Ward is more interested in a Sabrina Wright exposé than in her daughter?"

He wrestled with that one before capitulating, but not without reluctance. "Zack is young and rather attractive. He didn't make a fuss over Sabrina, if you know what I mean. To compensate, she had to find a plausible excuse to make herself, and not Jill, the reason for Zack's presence in our lives. Enough said?"

The thought had crossed my mind but I had given motherhood and prudence the benefit of the doubt— and come up skunked, yet again. In my formative years I had dated both Polly and Anna. Together, they had made a lasting impression. If the writer and her editor were in a give-and-take relationship, poor Rob was coming away empty-handed.

Even if what he was telling me was true, it didn't mean that Zack Ward wasn't the instigator behind Gillian's search for her father, and I said as much to Silvester.

"I honestly don't know if he did or didn't talk Jill into coming down here," Silvester said. "But if it was Jill's brainstorm, Zack is with her all the way. The two are in love, Mr. McNally. Make no mistake about that."

I wasn't about to make any mistakes because I was no longer involved in the rather sordid affair, but as Silvester's lunch guest, I felt I had to feign interest. Okay, I'm not kvetching. Who's above getting the inside scoop on the antics of the rich and famous? Not Archy.

However, I couldn't help but give ol' Rob a little nudge in the ribs. "And if Gillian did happen to find her papa, Zack would pull the plug on his laptop?"

Silvester signaled our waiter for the check. "I'll tell you what, Mr. NcNally. Why don't you ask Zack that question?"

I STOOD IN the sitting room of Robert Silvester's suite at The Breakers, staring at Gillian Wright and Zachary Ward. A line from the intro of an old song echoed in my brain: *Here I stand with deep regret, an innocent victim of etiquette.* That I was, and you could drop the "innocent" without doing bodily harm to the rhyme's message.

When Silvester invited me up to meet the couple, I refused with the lame excuse of having an appointment with my tonsor. He insisted it wouldn't take long and said so while signing the check. Not wishing to bite the hand that feeds, I acquiesced. "But just for a minute," I said, running a hand through my hair.

Leaving the restaurant, he admitted, "I told them I was

lunching with you here, and they're anxious to meet you."

I didn't need a crystal ball to know that Gillian Wright wanted to dub me her knight-errant in charge of her crusade to unearth Daddy Warbucks. Sorry, kid, but I misplaced my DNA testing kit. Why me? Because they were the new kids on the block and believed I was the only game in town. Having crossed another bridge I didn't want to leave in flames, I agreed to the meeting for the chance to politely refuse my investiture in person. Silvester called from the desk and told them we were coming up.

"It's a pleasure to meet you, Mr. McNally," Sabrina's daughter welcomed me.

Gillian Wright could be called plain only in contrast to her showy mom. On her own, the young lady was rather pleasing to the eye, and this eye is a connoisseur of the species. She had her mother's dark eyes and a mop of curly light-brown hair. As a child she must have been a true blonde. She sported a healthy tan and wore a pair of indi-chic bell-bottom slacks and a man's dress shirt with the tails hanging out. Rather than emulate or compete with her high-fashion mother, Gillian chose to dress down in a more subtle, yet edgy, style in an attempt to appear as if she had better things to occupy her mind than the current length of madam's hemline. Unfortunately, it didn't work.

I'm a very social animal in the Palm Beach area and as such, come in contact with the local citizenry on tennis courts, golf courses, and across crowded rooms. I could not look at Gillian Wright without trying to ascertain if she bore a resemblance to one of the prominent men in my circle. My chances of coming up with a match were hampered by the fact that in Palm Beach we are blessed with more prominent men than grace the hallowed halls of the Racquet and Tennis Club on New York's Park Avenue.

Gillian's wry smile told me she probably knew what I was thinking.

"It was very clever of you to find Rob." This from Zack Ward who, with his black-rimmed glasses and a head of expensively layered brown hair, brought to mind a young college instructor bucking for tenure.

"I didn't find him," I quickly corrected. "He called me and gave directions."

"But," Zack Ward amended, "if Rob hadn't called you, how would you have gone about looking for him? I ask as an investigative reporter."

"I don't give away trade secrets. I answer as an investigative snoop."

This garnered a nervous laugh all around and saved me the embarrassment of telling the pushy young man that I hadn't a clue as to how I was going to locate Robert Silvester.

"Won't you sit down?" Gillian invited.

"Sorry, but as I told Mr. Silvester, I have an engagement and would come up just long enough to meet you and Mr. Ward. It's been a pleasure, however brief."

This left Gillian no choice but to pounce. "Mr. Mc-Nally, you know why I'm here and I would like to hire you to help me find my father."

I think the statement took every bit of courage she possessed, which wasn't much to begin with. If Sabrina was a brazen peacock, her daughter had all the verve and color of a dormouse. It was heartening to see Zack Ward take her hand as she made her plea.

"Ms. Wright," I said, "you could advertise or make a statement to the press. That would flush him out."

"Oh!" she exclaimed as if I had suggested removing a wart with a stick of dynamite. "I would never do that. Did you see the piece in the paper the other day announcing Mother's arrival? I was mortified. How did the reporter know she was here?"

"I think a clerk at your mother's hotel is the guilty party," I answered.

"I don't want the press involved in this in any way, Mr. McNally. It would prove humiliating to both me and my father."

"Not to mention Sabrina," Silvester wisely stated.

"Sabrina has nothing to do with this," Ward said with a belligerent edge to his delivery.

"I beg your pardon, Zack," Silvester addressed the bespectacled young man, "but Sabrina has everything to do with this. She made a bargain and she intends to keep it. Why can't you respect her position?"

This verbal salvo had obviously passed among the trio ad nauseam since Silvester had caught up with the pair. I felt like what I was, an outsider trapped in the inside of a family feud. "May I say something?" I cut in before the furniture began to take wing.

"Please, Mr. McNally," Gillian Wright said in earnest. "I would value your opinion."

"You do me a great honor, but I don't know the solution to your problem. What I do know is that if your father wanted to establish contact with you, he would have done so a long time ago and is still very capable of doing so if he wishes. Your mother is a famous woman. He wouldn't have to hire Archy McNally to find you."

"We thought of that . . . " Ward began, but Gillian cut him off.

"Let me tell it, Zack," she insisted. "It takes two to make a bargain, Mr. McNally, and two to uphold it. Maybe my father is as reluctant to go back on his word as my mother is and for the same reason. Each thinking the other wants to stick to the agreement.

"He may even think my mother never told me the truth, as she hadn't until a few weeks ago, and felt he had no right to do so if she desired not to. Or, if she had, that I have no desire to know him. You see how many variables there are in this situation? I don't think we can assume anything. All I want is to meet with my father privately, without causing harm to any concerned, and if he refuses to acknowledge me, I will accept that and walk away without sorrow or malice. That I swear to you."

I wanted to applaud but felt it would undermine her sincerity. "You don't have to swear anything to me, Ms. Wright. I'm not an interested party." Thank God, I thought to myself.

"Then you won't help?" she said, clearly struggling to hold back tears.

"You have to appreciate my position," I lectured. "Your mother is my client, and she is vehemently opposed to what you're doing. Even if I were so inclined, I can't take your case. It would be a conflict of interest on par with a divorce lawyer representing both husband and wife."

"You told me earlier the case was through," Silvester noted. I wondered whose side he was on.

"It is," I said. "With regards to all of you, I'm afraid." Softening my tone I went on, "Take my advice, Ms. Wright, or Jill, if I may: Run off with your beau and give, 'happily ever after' a try. It's worked for others."

"I'm not going to give up looking for my father, Mr. McNally."

"That may prove a very foolish decision, young lady, and a very dangerous one." And with that, I took my leave.

SEVEN

HERB FLAGGED ME from his kiosk as I pulled into our underground garage. When I reached his post, he was standing by the door displaying a shiny chrome object with the lid open that might have been a relic from the Spanish Inquisition.

"How do you like it?" he asked.

"I would hate to get my foot caught in it," I assured him. "What are you trapping?"

"Trapping?" he cried. "I'm not trapping anything. It's a waffle iron."

I'm a pancake man myself, but not wishing to offend, I said, "Whatever turns you on, Herb."

"It's not for me, Archy. I bought it for Binky's house-warming."

Words failed me. This was clearly getting out of hand.

If everyone in the McNally Building bought Binky a gift, he could open a Circuit City. "Did Mrs. Trelawney suggest the waffle iron?"

"She did," he answered.

"Rather pushy, don't you think?"

"You have to admit, Archy, it's better than having to decide for yourself. I would have bought him a bottle of hooch."

"Well, you should have. Binky won't know what to do with that contraption."

"It comes with an instruction book," Herb said as if he represented·the waffle-iron industry.

"Binky Watrous can't read," I declared disparagingly.

"Then how does he deliver the mail?"

"Pneumatic tubing, that's how."

Herb scratched his head and grunted, "Sometimes, Archy, I don't get your drift."

"Sometimes, Herb, neither do I."

In my office I found a message telling me that Connie had called. I also found a consumer guide magazine, sandwiched between the afternoon mail, opened to the page rating microwave ovens. I dropped it in my wastebasket.

Before calling Connie, I asked our switchboard to connect me with the Chesterfield. The desk clerk told me that Ms. Wright was no longer in residence. True to his word, Silvester must have called his wife as soon as I left The Breakers, and Sabrina had lost no time in joining her family. By now mother and daughter would be locking horns, with Silvester and Ward acting as intermediaries when they weren't tossing a few stink bombs of their own into the melee. And people wonder why I refuse to get spliced.

In retrospect, I had no regrets terminating the case and my association with Sabrina Wright. Her lure was sirenic and best enjoyed from a safe distance. Get too close and you're caught in the undertow. She was a survivor, for which I admired her, but in rough seas survivors toss cargo and crew overboard to lighten the load. That's how they survive.

Silvester had given me the answers to the questions that had been bothering me: How Sabrina had gotten my name and the reason for the covert meeting at a pub in West Palm. Having met Gillian and Zack, I was convinced that they had not made the call to Lolly Spindrift and stuck to the premise that the leak had come from the hotel. True, the evidence was circumstantial, but men have been known to hang on less convincing evidence.

Silvester had also filled me in on why he had arrived in Palm Beach without his wife and why he had tried to keep Sabrina at bay while he talked to his stepdaughter. The pieces all seemed to fit, but as I cogitated over the events of the last two days, I wasn't satisfied with the picture that emerged. There was something missing. Was it something I had forgotten to ask? If so, whatever it was kept eluding me. I knew it would surface when least expected, but as the case was no longer on my docket, there was no urgency.

Final thoughts on "The Man That Got Away": What was Gillian's father thinking at this moment, and what wouldn't I give to know his name? Also, what wouldn't I give *not* to have to tell Lolly Spindrift his interview with Sabrina Wright was kaput?

When I got Connie on the line, she said she had called to see if I was still among the living. It's Connie's way of asking for a date. I invited her to join me for a cocktail at the Pelican after work. That's my way of accepting.

"I was there this afternoon, hoping to see you and buy you lunch," she said.

This was just the thing I had cautioned against when the Pelican board members decided to make the club coed. At Yale the rash move manifested itself in the fact that one now had to wear trunks in the swimming pool. If Connie had been planning to stand me lunch, what could I do but say, "Let's make it a night and have dinner."

"Why, Archy, what a nice idea," she said and rang off.

When my phone rang moments later, I thought it might be Connie calling to say she just remembered she was meeting a girlfriend that evening and could she have a rain check? I would pout, beg her to cancel, and issue a rain check good for a year and a day from the date noted above. Imagine my surprise when our switchboard person announced that Mr. Thomas Appleton was on the line, waiting to speak to me.

"Are you sure he doesn't want my father, Milly?"

"No, Archy. He asked for Mr. Archy McNally."

"Put him on," I said, not without a flutter of apprehension.

The Appleton family were to Palm Beach what the Cabots were to Boston and the Astors were to New York. Thomas was the current patriarch with a son in politics everyone said showed promise. With the Appleton money behind any future campaign, young Troy– I believe that was his name– would no doubt fulfill his destiny. I had seen both father and son around town on a number of occasions and had even watched Troy Appleton on his polo pony in a 22-goal challenge at the Palm Beach Polo and Country Club.

If Thomas Appleton wanted this McNally, he wanted Discreet Inquiries. If he wanted Discreet Inquiries, there was trouble in paradise. The only question was who had taken a chunk out of the apple, *père* or *fils*?

"Archy McNally here."

"Mr. McNally, I hope I'm not intruding."

"Not at all, sir. How may I help you?"

"I would like to have a word with you at a time and place we can mutually agree upon."

This meant that he did not want to come to the McNally Building or meet at one of his clubs and certainly not at mine. It was not an unusual request from one of his ilk. Experience taught me that he had already selected our *mutually* agreed upon turf, so I lobbed the ball gently back into his court.

"I leave the time and place to you, sir."

"How thoughtful, Mr. McNally. Are you familiar with the Palm Beach Institute of Contemporary Art?"

"I've heard of it, certainly, and have been meaning to visit but haven't got around to doing so."

"Then your time has come," Appleton said, "and you're in for a treat. I'm a patron and often take people around, so our meeting won't cause raised eyebrows should we chance to be seen. You understand, of course."

"I do, sir."

"Lake Avenue in Lake Worth," he told me. "They open their doors at noon; shall we be among the early birds?"

"We shall, sir."

"Have a look around and then meet me in the New Media Lounge on the second floor. Until tomorrow, Mr. McNally."

As you sow, so shall you reap. With the likes of Ursi and Jamie scattering the seed, there was no doubt that I had just gleaned Gillian Wright's natural father. Now three of us were privy to the thirty-year-old secret. I had told Gillian that learning her father's identity could be dangerous. A harbinger for Archy? Who said Palm Beach was dull in July?

Before leaving the office, I removed the consumer guide from my wastebasket, slapped a yellow self-stick note paper on its cover upon which I wrote, "NOT MINE– PLEASE REDIRECT," and dropped it in my outbox. That'll learn him.

I ARRIVED AT the Pelican in a buoyant mood only to be cast down to the depths by the sight of an eight-inch-square butcher block with a serrated knife clinging to its side by magnetic force.

"If that's a housewarming gift for Binky Watrous, I will shave my head and walk barefoot to the shrines of Guadalupe," I vowed to Priscilla Pettibone, who was displaying the impressive chunk of wood.

"In that suit?" she questioned.

"What's wrong with this suit, young lady?"

"Nothing, if you're trying to pass for a neon sign," she sassed. "And it is for Binky. It's a chopping block. Very handy for cutting up lemons and limes for drinks and veggies for dinner."

"Binky will add chopped fingertips to the minestrone. And just how did you come to learn of the charity event to turn Binky's kitchen into a chef's nightmare?"

"From Connie," Priscilla said. "She was in this afternoon, looking for you. Connie has lousy taste in men, in case you haven't noticed." Turning, she sashayed off in her silver mini and matching top with the assurance that every male eye in the place followed her every move. One day a shrewd fashion photographer will walk into the Pelican and walk out with our Priscilla.

As Mr. Pettibone served my daiquiri, I wondered how Connie had gotten word of the Binky fiasco. As if my

thought had conjured her up, Connie came into the bar
area looking splendid in slim-fitting black pants, spectator
heels, and a charmingly buoyant white halter. Her dark
hair cascaded to her bare shoulders. Priscilla now had the
attention of only half the men in the Pelican. I got a peck
on the cheek before Connie took the stool next to me.

"I'll have whatever he's having," she said to Mr. Pettibone.

I lost no time in venting my indignation at what was
fast turning into a United Way for Binky Watrous.
"Priscilla bought Binky a chopping block, Herb in security got him a waffle iron, I have been ordered to purchase
a microwave oven– *et tu, Brute*?"

"Oh, oh, the ladies are fawning over Binky and little
Archy is having a tempter tantrum."

"Don't be ridiculous," I said, reaching for my drink.

"Get a life, Archy," Connie advised, not for the first
time.

"No, my dear, it's a microwave I have to get, remember?" When Connie's drink arrived, I ordered a second.

"Mrs. Trelawney told me you were acting like a two-
year-old over this." She took a sip of her drink and proclaimed it "Delicious."

"You spoke to Mrs. Trelawney and she invited you to
join the magi bearing gifts."

"Yes. I called you this afternoon and when you didn't
answer I tried Mrs. Trelawney. She told me you had gone
to lunch, so I came here looking for you."

"As a matter of fact," I said, "I was lunching at The
Breakers."

"In that suit?" Connie exclaimed as if I had gone to
lunch in my birthday suit.

"What's wrong with this suit?" Actually I was getting

bored with both the question and my response. I took refuge in my second frozen daiquiri.

"I bet you were the only man at The Breakers in pink," Connie wagered.

"I was the only man at The Breakers who didn't look like every other man in the joint." Feeling the need, I pulled out my English Ovals and lit one. "And don't tell me you thought I had given these up," I warned.

"Okay, I won't. And, for your information, I'm thinking of getting Binky bedding, twin size, I'm told."

"Don't you think that's rather intimate, Connie?"

"I'm not going to share them with him. My God, Archy, you are acting like a spoiled brat, and you know what I think?"

"No. Nor do I care to."

That didn't stop her. "I think you're jealous," she accused.

I almost jumped off my stool. "Jealous. *Moi,* jealous of Binky Watrous? Are you out of your Iberian mind?"

Connie smiled the smile she had smiled when she shared her eggs Benedict with me at Testa's. This was not going well. I pulled on my English Oval for comfort, and as always, it did not disappoint. Was anything enjoyable also good for you? Sex? Yes, sex is indeed both enjoyable and healthy. Proof? I had read of a great sultan who kept a harem of one thousand wives. Every night he sent his faithful servant to select one to share his bed chamber. The faithful servant died at the age of fifty. The sultan lived to one hundred. Conclusion? It's the chase, not the act, that does a man in. Later, in the quiet of Connie's condo, we would discuss bedding.

"Let's face it, Archy. Binky is ten years your junior . . . "

"Nine," I said.

"Ten," she said. "He's setting up his own household as most of us do when we reach our majority. Before you know it, he'll be married and settled down."

Those two sentences were rampant with not-so-thinly disguised innuendo. Connie was treading on thin ice and she knew it. I was spared defending my puritanical ethics and my chance for a romantic interlude by the arrival of Mrs. Pettibone, bearing a dish of shrimp surrounding a paper cup of spicy red sauce.

"Compliments of the chef," Jasmine Pettibone said as Connie and I helped ourselves to what the Italians call *il sapore di mare,* or the fruit of the sea. The little crustaceans were carefully shelled, perfectly prepared, and absolutely succulent. Leroy's sauce lost nothing in the transfer from bottle to paper cup. Fresh shrimp is one of the rewards of living not too many miles from the Gulf of Mexico.

Addressing me, Mrs. Pettibone said, "Simon told you about Lyle, my cousin's boy, out in California."

I answered that he had and went on to say, "I have no idea what it's all about. Any further developments?"

"What's all this?" Connie said, momentarily distracted from Leroy's offering by the promise of gossip. Momentarily, and not a nanosecond more.

As I related to Connie as much as I knew, Simon Pettibone joined us from his side of the bar.

"Henry Peavey," Connie said, shaking her head. "Doesn't mean a thing to me. What about you, Archy?"

"As I told Mr. Pettibone, it means nothing to me either."

Huddled around the plate of shrimp, we might have been participants in a taste-test happening. It did occur to me that Mrs. Pettibone had intended to pass the goodies around to the other early diners just beginning to arrive at the club, but if Connie and Mrs. McNally's favorite son didn't keep their hands off the pickin's, she would have to abort her mission.

"There are more developments, Archy," Mr. Pettibone declared with a glance at his wife.

Jasmine Pettibone had been blessed with a particularly aristocratic bearing that had served her well. Now displaying what is politely called a full figure and with streaks of gray in her hair, it was still unmistakably clear from whence came Priscilla's lovely face and form.

"Lyle's daughter called this morning," Mrs. Pettibone told us. "She heard from her father."

"So," I said, "the mystery is solved."

"Hardly," Mrs. Pettibone said. "Lucy– she's Lyle's daughter– wasn't home when his call came. He left a message on her answering machine."

"Saying what?" Connie asked. Now she, too, seemed to be caught up in the mystery of Henry Peavey.

"Saying that he had arrived and was making contacts, and that it just occurred to him to tell Lucy not to answer any questions or make any statements to the press should they try to contact her," Mrs. Pettibone stated with a resolute nod of her head.

I said, "And that's it?" at the same time Connie said, "The press?"

Mr. Pettibone gave us both a nod. "And don't ask where he arrived at, because he didn't say."

"He originally told his daughter he was going south," I reminded the Pettibones.

"South of Sacramento goes all the way to the Argentine," Connie informed us. Consuela Garcia is practical to a fault.

"The plot certainly thickens," I told them. "Well, keep us posted. I'd like to know what Lyle has gotten up to."

"So would I," Mrs. Pettibone answered.

The club was starting to fill, but I noticed that our favorite corner table was still vacant. "What's Leroy tempting us with this evening?"

"A crown roast," Mrs. Pettibone announced as she moved away with the remainder of the shrimp.

Leroy's crown roast is a couple of rib sections of a loin of lamb arranged in a circle and roasted with strips of bacon wrapped around the lower section and also covering the ends of the rib bones, to prevent them from being scorched while cooking. Stuffing the cavity of the crown is optional, but I knew that Leroy's recipe called for an apple-and-raisin filling held together with cubed country bread and garnished with mace, sage, nutmeg, garlic cloves, and enough melted butter to soften a stone. When served, the tips of the rib bones are decorated with paper frills. Truly a feast for a king and therefore aptly named.

Picking up our drinks, I led Connie to our table, and once settled, I noticed the attractive diamond earrings and bracelet she wore. When I complimented her on her expensive taste, she laughed and said, "You like them? They're part of my collection of summer diamonds."

Now Palm Beach is the land of in-your-face ostentatiousness, but summer diamonds? "Pray tell, what are summer diamonds?" I asked.

Thrilled with the chance to show her smarts, Connie blurted, "Some-are diamonds and some-are not. Get it?"

"I'll pretend this conversation never took place if you promise never to call costume jewelry by any other name."

"The earrings are real, the bracelet is not, for your information," she said, not hiding her displeasure. "You get so uppity when you break bread at ritzy diners. Were you at The Breakers with Sabrina Wright?"

"So you've heard?"

"Who hasn't? Mrs. Marsden told Madam you were on the case," Connie said.

Mrs. Marsden is Lady Cynthia's housekeeper and a confidant of our Ursi's. Do you begin to see how Thomas Appleton got the message?

"As a matter of fact, Archy, Sabrina Wright was one of the reasons I wanted to see you today."

"Really? And I thought you were pining to see me. Don't tell me you want an autographed book."

"No. Madam wants to meet her," she said.

"So does half the world, I would imagine. What's Lady C's interest?"

Connie rolled her eyes toward the Pelican's ceiling, which was in need of a paint job. "It's got to do with her latest project."

Lady Cynthia Horowitz had two passions in life: young, handsome, male protégés (and she's a septuagenarian) and projects. She has championed the cause of nesting plovers, humpback whales, bald eagles, and hirsute violinists. Her last brainstorm was an ingenious scheme to install Art Nouveau pissoirs on Worth Avenue. Really!

Cartier, Tiffany, Hamilton, and Verdura, among other local merchants, were appalled at the idea, but I understand many older gentlemen who spend countless hours trailing after their wives on that boulevard of expensive and useless merchandise joined Lady C's committee in earnest.

Priscilla breezed by and asked us if we were having the special. We were, and I ordered a bottle of cabernet sauvignon to go with the meal. Then I said to Connie, "Okay, let's have it. What has your boss got the wind up over this week?"

"She's going to write her memoirs," Connie announced unhappily. "She thought she might get some helpful hints from Sabrina."

Her memoirs, was it? The lady had lived a long life, and had had at least as many husbands as fingers on her right hand, all rich and one titled. She was a living Sabrina Wright novel. Did she imagine a book-signing party at the Classic Bookshop on S. County Road where the couturier and graphic artist Michael Vollbracht recently appeared to push the reissue of his book *Nothing Sacred?* The dishy primer is famous for Vollbracht's sketch of the late Marjorie Merriweather Post holding up a box of Grape-Nuts.

No one knew more about sex, money, and manipulation than Lady Cynthia Horowitz, and I said as much. "There's nothing Sabrina can teach the Madam, Connie. She's been there, done that, and lived to tell about it. Besides, I'm off the case."

"So soon?" Connie seemed surprised.

"Yeah. I found her daughter and the guy she ran off with." It was a slight exaggeration, but who found whom was now a moot question, and when in doubt, take the credit, I always say.

"Madam doesn't believe the man that got away was Sabrina's daughter's lover," Connie said. "Nor do I."

Nor does Thomas Appleton, does he? I kept that to myself, however. With Connie, I often share and confide, but given the *dramatis personae* of this charade, I immediately decided to play my hand close to the vest. Besides, I still was not sure what Thomas Appleton wanted to see me about. Not contemporary art, that's for sure.

"And who does Madam think the guy is?" I asked.

"Sabrina's young and gorgeous lover," Connie gushed.

That figures.

EIGHT

THE NEXT MORNING I called upon Sofia Richmond once again to get some background information on the Palm Beach Institute of Contemporary Art. When I'm able, I like to do a little homework before meeting with a new client, if indeed Thomas Appleton would become a client. As he was a patron of the museum, it wouldn't hurt to bone up on its history so as to appear smarter than I am. Who knows, the guy might ask questions.

I didn't have to delve into the Appleton family closet, as its contents were more or less in the public domain. If it contained a skeleton, as I now suspected it did, its name was Sabrina Wright.

The PBICA, as it's familiarly referred to in print, owes its existence to the philanthropists Robert and Mary Montgomery. He is a noted attorney. The Montgomerys renovated the Lake Theater, a landmark art deco movie house that now houses the PBICA, after purchasing it from the Palm Beach Community College. The facility formerly held the contemporary art and design collection of J. Patrick Lannan. When the Lannan Foundation relocated the collection to Los Angeles, they donated the building to the college.

The PBICA purports to be a venue for major national and international art in all media and a meeting ground for the diverse populations who live in and visit the Palm Beach region. Who could find fault with that?

I got there minutes after it opened its doors to the public and wondered whom I could bill the three-buck admission charge to— Appleton or Sabrina? It was most likely to show up on my expense report as a miscellaneous disbursement, a category that often comprises fifty-five percent of my expenditures, much to Mrs. Trelawney's chagrin. I ambled around, fascinated with what I looked upon, before making my way to the second floor and the New Media Lounge.

Thomas Appleton was already there, seated before three television screens. He rose when I entered and came to meet me.

"Mr. McNally, thank you for being prompt." He offered his hand and we shook.

"I glanced at the exhibits before coming up and was most impressed," I said. "I intend to come back when I can give them more attention."

"Shall we sit?" When we did, Appleton pointed to the screens. "Each shows a video presentation by a current artist. As you can see, there is no audio." Pointing to the earphones on an ultramodern glass-top table, he instructed, "One must use these, which allows for a private viewing. The two computer stations you see are connected to the Internet. With them, visitors are able to surf Web art sites worldwide via a list provided by the museum. The Lounge is the concept of our new director, Michael Rush."

"The medium is the message," I quoted.

Thomas Appleton looked like Kriss Kringle, clean-shaven and out of uniform. Round face, ruddy complexion, and a shock of white hair combined to give the impression of a jolly gent more inclined to be an insurance salesman than a multimillionaire bon vivant, sportsman, and sidekick of presidents and kings. I had heard he was usually under par on the golf course, but judging from his waistline, I would imagine he was more a devotee of croquet than tennis. In Palm Beach, croquet is taken quite seriously, with teams competing from other states as well as the land of the game's origin.

Being early, the New Media Lounge was empty except for us, and knowing Appleton wanted to conduct our business as quickly and as privately as possible, I thought it prudent to get down to the particulars before he changed his mind or was spotted by someone he knew, in which case I would have to play the guy who came to service the earphones.

"It's all very interesting, Mr. Appleton, but not the reason for our meeting," was how I approached the delicate subject.

"Very true, Mr. McNally, and I respect your directness. Time, as they say, is money."

I could have said that not being officially in his employ, time was bleeding my wallet, but one didn't talk that way to an Appleton without being blackballed from places that didn't solicit my business. It was a no-win situation and one in which I felt very much at home.

"I understand that you represent the author Sabrina Wright," he finally stated.

"Represented, sir. My business with her has been concluded as of yesterday."

Was it my imagination or did those ruddy cheeks lose their glow? "Are you saying Sabrina, that is Ms. Wright, has found what she came here looking for?"

"I am, sir."

I knew what the guy was thinking, but did he know I knew? For a moment I thought about putting that heretofore jolly face at ease by telling him he was among friends, but I didn't know how much Appleton was ready to 'fess up to, and more to the point, I had not forgotten my prediction that knowing the identity of Gillian Wright's father could be dangerous. He had invited me here, therefore the onus was on him to say why he wanted to see me.

In the ensuing silence Thomas Appleton stared at the three television screens as if he were waiting for the commercial to end and the show to begin. He sighed, rolled his shoulders, and finally said, "The girl, Gillian, ran off with a man, came here, and Sabrina hired you to find them. Is that correct, Mr. McNally?"

It was the story I had spread around, but the fact that he was asking for confirmation suggested that he didn't believe it. No fool, Mr. Appleton.

With a show of surprise, I poured a little oil on the fire and stated, "You're familiar with Sabrina's daughter's name." What the hell, I liked the ambiance of the PBICA, but I had no intention of spending the entire day here.

"To be sure," he said. "It's no secret. I mean the woman and her daughter do get their names in the press."

If he insisted on shadowboxing, I would simply leave

the ring. "I'm sorry, sir, but client confidentiality is sacrosanct even after I've closed the books on a case. If your purpose, for whatever reason, is to learn why Ms. Wright hired me, I'm afraid I'll have to abort this meeting." I half rose to prove my resolve.

Appleton restrained me with a hand on my elbow. "Of course, Discreet Inquiries. Friends have told me the name factually delineates your work ethics. My compliments, Mr. McNally. But the truth of the matter is, I did ask you here for just that reason."

"Then I can see no further reason to continue this game of cat and mouse, Mr. Appleton. It's been a pleasure, I'm sure."

"Oh, not so fast," he again held out a restraining hand. "Can we make a deal, Mr. McNally?"

With a shrug I countered, "That depends, sir. What's in it for me?"

He smiled. "I like you, Mr. McNally. I like you very much. I even like your white cotton trousers and your red-and-white-striped hopsack jacket. I hope it starts a trend."

"If it does, Mr. Appleton, I will give the ensemble to Goodwill. I like to think of myself as one of a kind."

Now he laughed with gusto. "And judging from your ethics, Mr. McNally, you are just that."

Without a pause, I said, "But it's my ethics you want to compromise, Mr. Appleton."

"So it is. Will you hear me out?"

"Only a fool refuses to listen, sir. What are you putting on the table?"

"A thirty-year-old secret. Interested?"

"And what must I give in return, sir?"

"First, your word that you will never repeat what I tell you, and second, you will tell me if Sabrina Wright's visit

to Palm Beach has anything to do with that secret. Deal?"
He actually held out his hand, which I shook for the second time that day.

"Deal," I responded.

He took a deep breath and exhaled the words, "Gillian
Wright is my natural daughter." With that, he raised his
eyes upward as if he expected the ceiling of the New
Media Lounge to come down upon us in retribution for
either his productivity or his confession thereof. It
didn't.

"This is not Sabrina's first visit to our Island," he expanded on his confession. "She was here some thirty years
ago when we were both students. It was labeled spring
break and Fort Lauderdale was the hot spot for that holiday. As I recall it was a hundred and ten in the shade and
very drunk out. Sabrina and I had what some poet called a
brief encounter."

"Playwright, sir. Noel Coward," I corrected.

"Playwright or poet, the result was Gillian," he said.

To add a little romantic nostalgia to the tale, I asked,
"Was Sabrina very beautiful, sir?"

"Let's say she was available, Mr. McNally."

"Please, sir, call me Archy."

"And you call me Tom."

There is nothing like talk of sexual transgressions and
ethics bashing to evoke intimacy between men of good
breeding. Having melted the ice, we fell into the drink and
went with the floe.

"I'm afraid, Tom, the reason for Sabrina's visit has
much to do with your brief encounter."

He nodded as if resigned to his fate. "I thought so," he
said. "I am not an insensitive man, Archy, and I didn't
exactly leave Sabrina in the lurch. In fact, monetarily

speaking, she was far better off after our brief encounter, believe me."

Now that he had opened up to me I saw no reason to pretend I didn't already know his secret. Also, certain that Appleton would never talk to anyone about this conversation, I felt I wasn't compromising my former client's position by revealing facts of which Tom Appleton was already painfully aware. "She told me as much," I revealed, "and I'm not one to cast the first stone."

"She told you everything?" he asked.

"Everything but your name. She did not divulge that."

"So if I hadn't called you, you would never know . . ." His voice died away and he shook his head woefully. "What fools we mortals be," he lamented. Then, perhaps to rationalize his actions, he added, "I couldn't take that chance, I had to know what she's up to. I'm a widower, Archy, and I would now gladly acknowledge Gillian and to hell with what anyone might say, but such a move could prove disastrous for those innocent of any wrongdoing. You know my son is involved in state politics?"

"So I've heard, and with a bright future, they say."

Appleton started in his chair. "More than bright. There's talk of a run for the Senate, the U.S. Senate, that is, within the next four years. Any hint of a scandal would cause his backers to run scared."

"He has nothing to do with the brief encounter," I said.

"But he has everything to do with me, and in politics guilt by association is a fact, not a figure of speech."

"I assume your son is happily married," I ventured.

"He's married, Archy, that's for sure. She's photogenic, and that seems to make them both happy. She's given him the requisite number of children, boy and girl, employs no staff off the books, subscribes to no less than four charities, the recipients of which are Asian Americans, African Americans, Native Americans, and Hispanic Americans, and she wears her hair in the style of the late Jacqueline Kennedy Onassis. They're what the pols call a dream couple, and I don't intend to turn the dream into a nightmare." In the manner of a harassed executive being confronted with a hostile takeover, he leaned toward me and pleaded, "What the hell does Sabrina want, Archy?"

"Only to protect you," I assured him.

I believe that we humans come equipped with a sixth sense that, at this early stage of our evolution, we cannot access at will, but the uncanny thing does make itself known for no discernable reason at the oddest of moments. This was one of them. Call it intuition, inspiration, instinct, precognition, or plain old gut feeling, but when I spoke those words to Thomas Appleton, I knew as sure as I was sitting in the New Media Lounge of the PBICA that Sabrina's mission was to protect herself first, and Thomas Appleton only as long as it didn't jeopardize her position.

Why was she so unyielding in her determination to keep the name of Gillian's father a secret? Because of the deal she had struck with Appleton? I no longer believed that. In fact, my gut feeling said Sabrina Wright didn't give a damn for Thomas Appleton per se after all these years, yet she was willing to sacrifice her daughter's affection, such as it was, to protect him. This was not the stratagem of a survivor.

Appleton's eyes searched my face like a child wanting to believe in the tooth fairy when common sense, and the kid next door, told him it was all a crock. "Tom," I said, "Sabrina knows your name and address, correct?"

"Sure," he answered.

"Therefore she didn't hire me to find you. Correct?"

"I know all that, Archy, but who's the man that got away?" he questioned.

Never had so many been so concerned over five words from a gossip column that didn't mean a thing to anyone, including the columnist. I explained their meaning to Appleton as best I could and gave him what I believed to be their source.

Still skeptical, he said, "Sabrina came down here looking for her husband?"

Having reached the point of no return, I told Appleton exactly why Sabrina had come to Palm Beach, reiterating yet again, "She's here to protect you, Tom." Of course, what I had to say didn't alleviate his fears, it just shifted them from mother to daughter.

I hate to hear a grown man moan, but that is exactly what Thomas Appleton did when he heard my story. Or should that be Sabrina's story? "She told Gillian the truth?"

In our society what passes for the truth is usually the lie everyone agrees upon– hence Appleton's incredulity. He couldn't agree with her less. Sabrina had broken the commandment, and reprisal was swift and exacting. Gillian and Zack go after the Holy Grail, Silvester and Sabrina follow to make sure they don't find it, Lolly runs a blind item and Archy is toe-to-toe with an Appleton in the New Media Lounge of the PBICA. You go figure.

And another county is heard from. Good grief, Zack Ward. I almost forgot about him. If Appleton thought he had reached the nadir of this conversation, I had a bulletin for the old bean.

"Sabrina didn't disclose your identity to Gillian," I insisted. "In fact she's down here to make certain that Gillian does not learn who you are. I can tell you that Sabrina is determined that Gillian, or anyone else for that matter, will never know you are Gillian's father. Her sole concern is protecting your anonymity, Tom."

"Why?" he wondered.

Two minds with but a single thought. Appleton was having as much trouble as yrs. truly trying to figure out Sabrina's munificence. My job was to placate not incite the man, so I answered, "Because she entered into a pact with you . . . "

"For which she was well paid, believe me."

The rich can't resist reminding you of the fact. Be that as it may, I went on, "She's holding up her end, as agreed."

Still perplexed, he groused, "Whatever induced her to tell Gillian the truth? It was my understanding at the time that the infant would be put up for adoption and then Sabrina would adopt her. It was the most expedient thing to do at the time, and lord knows, it's worked for others. Why? And why now?"

I told him what Sabrina had told me. "She doesn't like Zack Ward, the guy Gillian is dating and getting serious about, and she thought the girl would be more receptive to the advice of her flesh-and-blood mother."

Appleton frowned, "Now she and her boyfriend are down here looking for her flesh-and-blood papa. It's bizarre."

"Not really," I protested. "If you learned your father was not your real father, wouldn't you be curious to know who was?"

"Archy, my father was one of the richest men in the world. If someone told me he wasn't really my father, I would tell that S.O.B. to bug off."

Hey, the guy had a point.

"And just who the hell is this Zack Ward anyway?" he nearly bellowed.

Were this a film I would yell, "Cut," and we would break for lunch. This would give me time to compose a response that would not cause Thomas Appleton's heart to pause for an unhealthy period of time. This not being the case, I had no choice but to keep the camera grinding and hope for the best. "I was meaning to tell you about Zack," I said. "I believe he's a reporter for a trashy tabloid."

Appleton's cheeks glowed to a point where I feared spontaneous combustion would turn his head into a burning bush. He opened his mouth, but gasps, not words, emerged. "Can I get you some water, Tom?"

Closing his eyes, he answered slowly and sincerely, "I don't suppose you have any cyanide on you."

"Afraid not, Tom. But let's be realistic. As we speak, Sabrina is talking those two into returning to New York, and she will never reveal your name to them or anyone else," I repeated for good measure. "And that should settle it."

"That should settle it?" He mimicked. "Archy, that's what Chamberlain said when he got back from Munich."

He had a point there, too.

As if thinking aloud, Appleton reasoned, "If Sabrina told Gillian the true story of her birth because Sabrina thought it would work to her advantage, what would stop her from revealing my name to the girl for the same reason?"

Point number three, and he took the set. "It's a fear you may have to live with, Tom," I said.

"I do not and I will not." He spoke like a man used to getting his way regardless of the consequences. "Where is Sabrina, Archy?"

"They're all bedded down at The Breakers," I told him.

"I'm going to call and meet with her."

"Do you think that's wise?"

"No, but I have to impress upon her that I will go to any length to protect myself and my family from any scandal."

There was that menacing phrase again, and I didn't like it. I didn't like it one stinking iota.

NINE

GIVEN THE AMOUNT of time and energy I was putting into a case that was closed and a family affair that was none of my business, "The Man That Got Away" could now be retitled "The Man Who Wouldn't Go Away." I didn't owe Sabrina Wright a thing but couldn't resist one last conversation with the lady to warn her of the imminent call from her former, if brief, lover. If nothing else, it would be interesting to see what her reaction would be to hearing from him after all these years– and to my being a third party to their little secret.

Did I also want to impress upon her my unique ability to ferret out the most obscure Palm Beach mysteries without really trying? Sure. I might even turn up in a Sabrina Wright novel as a PI named Danny Desire.

I made the call from my office, asking the desk at The

Breakers for Mr. Robert Silvester. It worked. I was immediately connected to his suite and doubly rewarded with
the now familiar sound of . Sabrina's deep-throated
"Hello."

"Archy McNally here," I announced.

"Mr. McNally, what a coincidence. We were just talking about you," Sabrina said.

"I take it you are not alone."

"No. Robert is with me. Why do you ask?"

"I want to pass on a bit of information that is intended
for your ears only."

There was a pause during which I thought I could hear
a sharp intake of breath, or was there static on the line? "Is
your daughter with you?"

Now there was no mistaking the anxiety in her voice
when she answered, "No. She and Zack are out hunting."

Was it open season on runaway fathers? And just how
did one go about tracking down a man you had never seen
and didn't even know existed until a few weeks ago? "I
hope they're not knocking on the doors of the local gentry.
The people in these parts don't take kindly to nosey
strangers. They're apt to shoot first and ask questions
later."

"I believe they went to the local library to scan the
newspapers dating back to nine months before Gillian's
birthday. Clever, don't you think?"

I thought it was rather dumb, and from the mocking in-
flection in Sabrina's delivery, so did she. The young people's endeavor did prove just how hopeless poor Gillian's
chances were of finding her father after a trail gone cold for
thirty years. Did she expect to turn up an item listing all the
couples who had engaged in sexual congress in southern
Florida nine months before her birth? "I take it you haven't

been able to talk her into abandoning the search and going home."

"You take it right, Mr. McNally, but I've made them an offer they might find hard to turn down," she boasted.

Did this family never tire of bartering their lives away? "May I know what it is?"

"Certainly," she answered with an enthusiasm that was far too coy to be genuine. "I will give Zack an exclusive interview for his rag if he and Gillian will give up this asinine charade. Believe me, Mr. McNally, it's against all my principles to be misquoted in a lousy tabloid, but if it gets Gillian off the scent, I'll do it."

Whoever would have thunk it? Sabrina, sacrificing her principles for the sake of a one-night stand. *Noblesse oblige* or *noblesse* desperate? This was bad news for Tom Appleton.

"What will you disclose in the interview?" I asked.

"As little as possible," she said. "I've had practice in saying nothing to the press in several thousand words. If he dares mention Gillian's father, I will deny everything."

Right now the odds seemed to be with Tom, but Sabrina clearly wanted to see the last of this charade, as she termed it, and the lady was at the end of her tether, which had never been very long.

I gave her my professional but uncalled-for opinion on her offer. "Judging from what Gillian told me, I doubt she will allow Zack to accept, tempting as it may be."

"Of course," Sabrina exclaimed like a doting mother, "you met the children. What do you think of them?"

"Like I said, I think they're two very determined people. You would do well, Ms. Wright, to go back to New York and leave them to their groping in the dark. Sooner or later they'll come home, sadder but wiser."

"And more angry than ever," she cried. "And estranged from me forever, I dare say. No, that would never do. We must resolve this thing here and now, Mr. McNally, and go back home together, as a family. A happy family. In short, Gillian must acquiesce to my better judgment and resign herself to playing out the hand she was dealt, as I was forced to do."

This woman was in possession of a pair of *cojones* that would put the Dallas Cowboys to shame. Like Frank Sinatra, Sabrina Wright did it *her way,* and pity the daughter who refused to acquiesce. And now here comes Archy, the bearer of news that might help or hinder her case– Appleton's case?– Gillian's case?– or none of the above? Not having a stake in the matter, I rolled the dice, knowing they were loaded.

"I said I had something to tell you, Ms. Wright."

"So you did. And just what is it that's meant for my ears alone? My bill?"

"That will come in the mail," I promised. "You are going to get a phone call, Ms. Wright. I pass this on as I believe I owe it to you as a former client. *He* is going to call. Very soon, I expect."

"He? I don't follow, Mr. McNally. Who is *he?"*

"He is Gillian's father."

If earlier I'd thought I had detected a sharp intake of breath when I mentioned the reason I was calling, I now heard the most horrific sound known to our species– silence. I waited a good minute before I asked, "Are you there, Ms. Wright?"

"I take it you're not joking," she said.

"No, ma'am. *He* is going to call you."

"How do you know this, may I ask?"

"You may," I said. "I know this because he told me so."

A pause. She was thinking, but unable to see her face, I had no idea what she was thinking. "Mr. McNally, I demand to know how all this transpired."

"It was that blind item in the paper. Remember? He thought you were down here looking for him. He contacted me, we met, and Bob's your uncle."

"We can do without the levity," she cautioned, employing the royal pronoun. "And just how the hell did he know you were involved on my behalf?"

She was seething and running scared. Like Chauncey's common face and noble tail, this, too, was a lethal combination. "I'm afraid I can't tell you that, Ms. Wright, without giving away the tricks of my trade."

"Damn your tricks, mister. You tell me what you know or I'll sue you from here to hell and back again."

I heard a voice in the background that I assumed to be Silvester's wanting to know what was happening. Without bothering to cover the phone's mouthpiece with her hand in the time-honored tradition, Sabrina told her husband to "shut up." A moment later she was back on my case. "Did you hear me?" she shouted.

"Let's not lose our heads, Ms. Wright. You hired me to do a job and in the course of my investigations, on your behalf, I was approached by this individual. Still acting on your behalf, I told him just why you were in Palm Beach. The truth, Ms. Wright. I told him the truth, or should I say, I told him what you told me?"

"What are you getting at?" She was practically ranting. A stratagem I would never have attributed to the fair Ms. Frigidaire. Was her hair in disarray? Doubtful. But I bet Silvester's was.

To be sure, her response spoke volumes. "I'm getting at nothing," I lied, "but before you have your attorney present me with papers, just remember who I will call to bear witness on my behalf."

That did it. The tornado fizzled into a languid breeze. "Mr. McNally, forgive me. You must understand what's happening here. Without warning I get a call telling me I am about to hear from someone I have not seen or heard from in thirty years. Someone with whom my emotional involvement led to dire consequences. Is it any wonder I lost my cool?"

"No, ma'am. But don't blame me. I thought I was being helpful."

"You are, Mr. McNally. You are." She had it all together once again, and like a good general, was now sensibly getting the lay of the land. "What does he want? Did he say?"

"He wants to make sure that you will never betray him."

"Didn't you tell him I was down here for that very purpose?"

I told her I had done just that. "But he's worried. He's most upset that you told Gillian her point of origin."

"So am I. I've made two mistakes in my lifetime," she philosophized. "One was opening my heart, the other was opening my mouth. I parlayed the first to my advantage, and I will not allow the second to negate what I worked to achieve. I thought Gillian would be more sensible about my plight and empathize with what I had done for her. Instead, she insists on going against my wishes and digging up the past. It is not acceptable, Mr. McNally."

It would never occur to Sabrina Wright that had she been a more empathetic mother, Gillian might not be obsessed with finding her father who she hoped might give her the love Sabrina had forgotten to include along with fancy Swiss finishing schools and a generous monthly allowance.

I, too, had made a mistake. Calling the lady to warn her

of the voice from the past with which she would have to deal in the immediate future. Instead of a thank-you, I got flak, which just goes to show you that the most perceptive seer of the twentieth century was the great Dorothy Parker, who preached: *The do-gooders of the world are the louses of the world*. Case closed.

"Mr. McNally," my nemesis said, "can you assure me that no one else on our planet knows who *he* is?"

"If they do, they didn't hear it from me, and they never will."

Not able to let go until she had tried one more time, she questioned, "And you will not tell me what compelled said person to call you?"

"No, ma'am. I will not."

"Then I think our business is concluded, Mr. McNally. I will deal with my friend." Getting in the last word, she bid me, "Good day. I wish I could say it has been a pleasure."

Bitch was the only word that came to mind as I dropped the phone. I wondered how much of our conversation she was going to repeat to Silvester. I would imagine he had heard enough to know what was afoot, and wasn't he as curious as Gillian to know the name of his wife's former lover? That name, by the by, never passed our lips the whole time we talked, a fact that was going to soon boomerang and hit Archy on the back of his unsuspecting noodle.

"I will deal with my friend," Sabrina had said. The irresistible force was going to go head-on with the immovable object. Who, or what, would give remained to be seen. I would have to go head-on with Lolly Spindrift when I reported that the exclusive I had promised him with Sabrina Wright was off. That would cost me a fortune in wining and dining to appease his rage.

Speaking of which, I was in need of a drink, and what I got was Binky Watrous and the afternoon mail.

"Well, if it isn't Hannah Homemaker, in person. What's new at the trailer court, young man?"

With a fervent gushing I found boring, if not offensive, Binky informed me in great detail. Binky does not understand that a simple "How are you?" is a greeting, not a question.

"I signed my lease and Mrs. Rutherford gave me a key and a coffee mug with my name on it. Compliments of the Palm Court."

Compliments of the management? Did everyone at the Palm Court have a coffee mug with their name on it? Al Rogoff had never mentioned owning such a piece of crockery, but then there was much the sergeant didn't admit to. "And when does the actual move take place?" I asked as if I cared.

"I already started, Archy. I brought my shaving gear over this morning and most of my clothes. I'm going to sleep over tonight."

Not without his Victoria's Secret collection, I bet. The shaving gear brought to mind the mustache Binky used to sport when he was in love with a girl who fancied men with hairy upper lips in the tradition of Gable and William Powell. Binky's was a pale blond affair that was all but invisible except when it got rained on. Then it resembled the tassels of a wilted ear of corn.

"And I introduced myself to some of my neighbors," he gushed on like a garden hose that had sprung a leak.

I foresaw a mass exodus from the Palm Court that might cause the waters of Lake Worth to part. "What neighbors?" I asked as if I cared, and I did.

"Bianca Courtney." This was accompanied by a grin

that brought to mind a cat who has just moved next door to a creamery. "Do you remember her, Archy?"

I pretended to ponder the question before answering, "Vaguely. A chubby thing with a poor complexion."

"No way, Archy. Bianca is a dish. She invited me in for a cup of coffee."

Wasn't that nice? Please understand that for obvious reasons Binky and I have never competed for the affections of a lady fair, and I wasn't about to start now. That said, the memory of a pretty lass getting into her Mercedes is something that sticks to your ribs, like a hearty breakfast of eggs and porridge. And, as Binky didn't stand a chance with this one, I saw no reason to withdraw in his favor.

"Did she have a mug with her name on it?" I wanted to know.

"No, Archy. We drank from proper china cups, with saucers. Bianca is a lady."

Saucers certainly attested to good breeding. Could she be the victim of impoverished gentry, hence the motor home digs and the job as companion to a rich old lady? In short, a latter-day Jane Eyre? If so, Binky Watrous was not her Mr. Rochester and the Palm Court was no Thornwood. Picking up the packet of envelopes Binky had deposited on my desk, I made a show of looking for one that was affixed with a first-class stamp. "And what did you and the lady discuss, Binky? The joys of living in a corridor?"

A bit sheepishly, or so I thought, he said, "As a matter of fact, Archy, your name came up over the coffee and croissants."

Croissants? Not Jane Eyre, but Julia Child. Bless her heart. Binky was about as subtle as the writing on a latrine wall. Al Rogoff had told us of Bianca's quandary and even chanced that we were at the Palm Court at her bidding. To impress his neighbor, Binky had told her that his best friend ran Discreet Inquiries, explained its function, and, no doubt, hinted that he was in some way associated with the agency.

What did I think of all this? I loved it. Someplace in the back of my wicked, scheming, conniving, and perverted mind, I was thinking of just such a ploy to insinuate myself into the confidence, and perhaps the arms, of Bianca Courtney. How, was the question, and lo, Binky was the answer. Unthinking to be sure, but then few of Binky's actions are accompanied by thought. Conclusion: If Bianca and I hit it off, it's all Binky's fault.

To be sure, I wasn't going to tell him this. Let 'em squirm, was my modus operandi. Wide-eyed, I questioned, "My name? In what connection, pray tell?"

He told, adding, "I mentioned that I often help in your inquiries."

Just as I suspected. "Really, Binky? Refresh my memory."

"Well," he said, "remember that party at Manalapan Beach when I drove the pretty girl's car to your house so you could follow with her in your car?"

"And Hobo bit you and you wanted to sue."

"I was crippled, Archy."

"You had a scratch on your ankle."

Leaning on his mail cart as if to accentuate his former injury, he tried again. "What about the time I got a job in the pet store so you could follow up a lead?"

"And the parrot bit you."

Grasping at straws, he uttered, "When your sister was here last Christmas, I took little Darcy to the beach."

"And little Darcy bit you. Let's face it, Binky, you bring

out the feral instincts in man and beast. It could be your cologne." I stopped him from extolling the merits of Old Spice by returning to the point of this dialogue: "Did you tell Bianca I would call upon her for details of this alleged crime?"

"Sort of. You see, Archy, as much as she wants to hire you, she can't afford you."

I nodded my understanding in the grave manner of a doctor telling a patient the operation needed to save his life was priced beyond his means and referring him to the doc's brother-in-law, who happened to be an undertaker. "There's no charge for the initial interview; after that we can see what we can do."

"Like *pro bono,*" Binky spouted.

A few months of hauling mail in a law office and the guy spoke as if he were delivering scrolls to the Roman senate. "When did you say I might call, Binky?"

"I didn't, Archy, but I'll ask her tonight. She's invited me to dinner, seeing as my kitchen isn't set up as yet."

"How neighborly. What's she making, did she say?"

"Chinese takeout," Binky blustered like it was the bill of fare at the Ritz.

"With three you get egg roll," I told him.

"We'll only be two, Archy."

Sometimes I wondered if under that head of droopy blond hair there wasn't a wise guy screaming to get out.

TEN

THAT EVENING, I got in my swim, showered, parted my freshly washed hair neatly on the left, and combed the remainder straight back in imitation of the young Ronald Reagan in his Warner Bros. heydays. Not bad. Troy Appleton's wife wasn't the only one who knew how to use someone else's coiffure to win friends and get out the vote.

Satisfied with what I saw in the mirror (I'm very easy with me), I dabbed a bit of my personal and very expensive scent onto the back of my neck, donned a pair of Newport red Bermuda shorts over a matching shade of cotton briefs, and pulled a blue sweatshirt, emblazoned with a foot-long white Y, over my head. I never wear the thing in father's presence as it evokes stares and sighs of woe that would have neighbors believe the McNallys were putting on a revival of *Oedipus* with a Greek chorus of one.

Actually, I wore it last winter when I took Connie to a performance of *Puns of Steel* by the Princeton Triangle Club at the Alexander W. Dreyfoos Jr. School of Arts in West Palm. Connie was embarrassed, but I got a round of applause from the Elis present.

Regardless of the effect the lettered shirt has on the pater, the outfit would never do for family dining were he at home. But when breaking bread with the help in the kitchen on a balmy summer night, it was perfect.

I mixed myself a proper Sterling vodka martini in the den before joining Ursi and Jamie. I must say, I am certainly making the most of the master's absence, which, alas, must soon come to an end. Nothing is forever and rightly so, for I do miss Mother.

"Roast chicken with lemon and herbs," Ursi recited the bill of fare as I entered. Jamie had his nose buried in the evening paper with a bottle of beer before him. "And don't you look sporty, Archy."

"Thank you, Ursi. I do have good legs, don't I?"

This got Jamie to look up, scan my legs, and go back to his paper. A no comment, I've always thought, is the most telling comment of all. "What do we get with the chicken, Ursi?"

"Rice pilaf and a romaine salad with buttermilk dressing," she answered. "Very light and easy and just the thing for a hot summer night, don't you think?"

I did think. But, for starters, Ursi couldn't resist passing around one of her specialties: Miniature pizzas, no more than two bites per munch, with a variety of toppings. Not very light fare, but then they were just to get the juices flowing. Jamie, who drinks his beer straight from the bottle, put aside his paper to concentrate on the tray of finger food his wife had placed on the table.

"Now tell us all about Sabrina Wright," Ursi said as she puttered around the stove. "Did you find her daughter?"

"Let's say her daughter gave herself up," I told them. "The family is now together at The Breakers."

"And the young man?" Ursi asked, opening the oven from which the aroma of lemon chicken escaped to tantalize my taste buds.

"He's with her," I said.

"In the same room?" As she spoke, Jamie reached for a tidbit of bread, cheese, tomato sauce, and anchovy, but froze to await my answer.

"No, Ursi. They are in separate but adjoining rooms."

"Is there a connecting door?" Jamie's voice so startled us we stared at him as if he were daft. Picking up his mini pizza, he popped it into his mouth.

"Don't be crude," his wife reproached him. "Besides, connecting doors can be locked."

"From either side," Jamie said, scanning the tray for his next assault on the minis.

It was so unusual to hear the Olsons engaged in spirited repartee that I had allowed Jamie to get one up on me on the crusty delights. I had had an anchovy, a pepperoni, and a broccoli. I spotted another anchovy and got there before Jamie. He shot me a look and fished up a plain cheese-and-sauce. That should teach him to keep his eyes upon the food and his mind off bedroom doors.

"So your case is closed," Ursi said.

"It is," I answered, knowing I was making a public statement in the privacy of my home just like the musings of the man in the Oval Office.

"Is Sabrina Wright going to allow them to wed?" Ursi asked, removing the chicken from the oven.

"She can't stop them," I said. "Her daughter is of age, and so is her beau."

Under different circumstances I would have gone into more details of the case with Ursi and Jamie, but that would mean hearing the below-stairs gossip regarding Sabrina's visit. Should the Appleton name wend its way into the conversation, I didn't want to risk having to avoid hearing it. Jamie Olson may be as vocal as a clam, but he is also as slippery as an eel. Therefore I was relieved when Ursi announced dinner. "Are you going to have wine, Archy?" she asked, bringing the platter of lemon chicken to the already set table. The chickens had been expertly quartered by Ursi herself, garnished with parsley, and presented with the rice pilaf.

"I think I'll stick with beer tonight," I said, unfolding my napkin and placing it on my lap.

In lieu of grace Ursi said a *"Bon appetit."*

We had the romaine salad with our meal– crisp and cool– and dipped into a Dutch apple crumb cake for dessert along with iced Caffe Verona, ground fresh at our local Starbucks. I went up to my *aerie* sated, got out my journal, and recorded my last conversation with Sabrina Wright, officially ending the case. Having done my duty, I poured myself a marc and lit an English Oval in celebration of not having had one all day. Here, as often happens when I'm alone in my allotted space long past sunset, I ruminated on man's inhumanity to man and to Archy McNally in particular.

Binky had gotten his own pad, and Connie was, once again, tossing out hints as shrouded as hand grenades that Archy do the same. What she really wanted was to begin the begat, as the Good Book encouraged. I was very comfortable where I was and not yet ready for the dubious benefits of love and marriage.

Last evening, as predicted, we did go back to her place, a high-rise condo on the east shore of Lake Worth, a one-bedroom affair with a great view from her tiny balcony. I have been there so often I know she keeps the Absolut in the freezer and that you have to jiggle the handle of the toilet to avoid a perpetual flush.

She played her Spanish tapes, which are Greek to me, and after many passionate kisses which, like a spider's web, leads to a fly's undoing, we retreated to the bedroom where a framed poster of the film *Casablanca* hangs over the bed. We undressed with all the nonchalance of an old married couple.

Sparks didn't fly, but neither did they fizzle. We knew each other's erogenous zones and played them like skilled pianists on the closing night of a long tour. Okay, I'm making it sound far worse than it was. The truth is, it's sometimes better than the first time– but not all the time. Would marriage and a family make a difference? If so, how? For better or for worse? And don't you just know why the marriage vow covers both possibilities and all the stops between?

When Dora, my sister, visits on the holidays, do I look upon her, my brother-in-law, Ted, and their three lovely children with a wistful eye? Do I grow a little sentimental when I enter the kitchen just as Ursi's soap is interrupted by a commercial for Disneyland? The answer to both is– certainly I do.

However, as the Bard spoke of music's charm, Archy speaks of our modern-day poets, namely the lyricists, who give voice to the plaintive airs. *Down in the depths on the ninetieth floor* or *high as a flag on the Fourth of July*, these wordsmiths never fail to come up with a phrase to sum up our sentiments in twenty-five words or less. Lionel Bart said it for me when, in his musical, *Oliver,* he has Nancy rationalizing the fact that Bill Sikes will never marry her. Nancy says of wedded bliss, *Though it sometimes touches me/For the likes of such as me/Mine's a fine, fine life.* Charlie D. couldn't have said it better.

ELEVEN

THE CAPER OF the Trojan Horse or, beware Archy bearing a microwave oven. I dressed in jeans, a pink Izod, and penny loafers. The boy next door? One look in the glass told me I had achieved that goal without shouting its intent.

After breaking my fast with fresh squeezed orange juice, cinnamon French toast with pure maple syrup, and a cup of java, Paris set out for the rape of Helen. Really, it's just a figure of speech.

When I turned the Miata onto Ocean Boulevard, I glanced in my rearview mirror and watched a black stretch limo materialize like a mirage out of the sultry air. I didn't see it approaching when I pulled onto the boulevard, so it must have been parked on the road's shoulder, waiting for a chance to join the traffic– or waiting for me? In Palm Beach, stretch limos are a common sight, and a fear of the mechanical dinosaurs has never been among my many phobias, but in my business it pays to keep alert.

I moved south, passing the Palm Beach Country Club, and swung onto N. County Road. The limo came with me. I stayed on N. County to The Breakers Ocean Golf Course, went west on Cocoanut Row, ignoring the Flagler Memorial Bridge. I kept south to the PB Elementary School and then took a sharp right over the Royal Palm Way Bridge. When I got to the mainland, the limo was no longer visible in my rearview mirror. My thrill for the day? With what I had in mind, I hoped not.

Owing to the Inland Waterway that runs smack through Lake Worth, Palm Beach island is connected to the mainland by three drawbridges. It has long been thought that should a big heist take place on the island, the police could order all the bridges up, trapping the culprits on the island. Not a bad place to linger with a sack full of legal tender, I should think.

At a trendy appliance store I purchased a microwave oven like I knew what I was doing. Instinct told me not to buy the top of the line because it would contain a lot of frills not necessary to nuking a frozen chicken pot pie. I avoided the bottom of the line because it probably would have trouble melting an ice cube. Like Americans on Election Day, I went with the one in the middle, veering slightly toward the top. My guess was that Binky would spend hours trying to bring in the evening news on the gadget's fifteen-inch screen.

I had it gift-wrapped and a kind salesperson helped me carry it to my car. The microwave and Archy filled the Miata's front seat from there to the Palm Court, where I parked in the space reserved for number 1170. One space over was filled with a black Mercedes. My, my, what a surprise.

Toting the bulky package without help was cumbersome but not impossible. I hauled it up the three steps to number 1168 and rang the bell. The Greeks had landed.

Bianca opened her door, looked at the man on her doorstep holding a gift-wrapped crate, and said, "I didn't order it."

"It's not for you," I told her.

"Then go away," she said.

"If I may explain . . ."

"Are you selling computers, door to door?"

"No, ma'am. It's a microwave oven."

"I have one," she said. "Good day."

Before the door closed in my face, I explained, "It's for your neighbor Binky Watrous. I'm Archy McNally."

Her pretty blue eyes opened wide, from her ruby lips came an "Oh," and the faintest hint of color surfaced on her white cheeks. If Helen's was the face that launched a thousand ships, Bianca's was the one that got Archy to buy Binky a microwave oven. Who's to say which face will survive the test of time? This woman was made for color snaps, picnics in summer, football games in fall, sleigh rides in winter, and chasing around the Maypole in apple-blossom time.

"Mr. McNally. I am so sorry. What can I do for you?"

"Inviting me in would help my cause." My knees were beginning to buckle, but if I put the damn thing down I feared I would never be able to lift it off the floor.

She opened the door and backed away. "Please, please come in. I am so sorry. I didn't recognize you, Mr. McNally."

I looked for a corner to unload my burden. Then, remembering where I was, I lowered it to the floor of Bianca's kitchen moments before I would be in need of a truss. Pretending I wasn't about to expire, I smiled at her while I got my second wind, which was long in coming. She smiled back, displaying a near perfect set of teeth. Was there nothing wrong with the woman?

"There was no reason you should have recognized me, Ms. Courtney," I said. "I believe we saw each other only fleetingly the other day, when Binky rented number 1170."

"Please, my name is Bianca. Won't you sit a moment? I was just going to make a pot of coffee. Will you join me?"

I sat, gratefully, in a good reproduction of a classic Windsor chair, which, along with one other, went with a table of matching pine. There were cafe curtains on the little kitchen window, and by stealing what I hoped was a subtle glance into the parlor, I got the impression of chintz and pastels and sugar and spice and everything nice. I felt like the big, bad wolf, but not strongly enough to call off my expedition. I was, after all, here to help.

"I haven't had my second cuppa this morning, so I don't mind if I do," I accepted.

"Good. Regular or decaf?"

"Regular. I need the jolt."

She laughed as she filled a Mr. Coffee with water. "So do I. You said the microwave was for Binky, Mr. McNally?"

"How can I call you Bianca if you insist on Mr. McNally? It makes me feel like an old man. Friends call me Archy and I hope you'll join the throng."

I watched her hesitantly measure the amount of coffee, which told me she was new at the task. Today, she wore Capri pants in a black toile pattern, a crisp white sleeveless blouse, and neat little flats. Her brown hair was combed back and held from her face with a simple clip above each ear. If I had to guess her age, I would say early twenties, give or take.

"Yes," I told her, "the microwave is for Binky, and perhaps I should explain. It's a housewarming gift . . . "

"How kind of you," she interrupted.

I gave her a modest shrug. "As a matter of fact, it was me who rallied the office into contributing to Binky's rather spartan digs."

"He told me you were best of friends," she said, setting out cups and saucers. There was even a sugar bowl and a creamer, which she filled with half-and-half.

I enjoyed watching her move about and estimated her waist at a waspish twenty-two inches. This reminded me to refuse any sweets should they be offered with the coffee. "I brought the microwave here thinking I might catch Binky before he left for the office, but I was too late. He told me about his friendly neighbor, so I thought I might impose upon you to store the gift, saving me the trouble of carting it to the office and back here again."

"You're not imposing at all, Archy." Our coffee ready, she played hostess.

"You had Binky in for dinner last night?" I helped myself to the half-and-half but refused the sugar. Cutting back on smoking had sparked my appetite, which had never been wanting to begin with.

"Chinese takeout," she said, avoiding the sugar and the half-and-half. "We both had the chicken and snow peas with extra fried rice. Wicked, but delicious." I knew I wasn't going to be offered anything with the coffee, and just as well.

Here, as happens with new acquaintances who have exhausted the few topics of conversation they have in common, the mindless chatter petered out. We smiled at each other like two actors in search of a script. I had gotten in the front door, and now had come the time to establish a beachhead. "Your neighbor on the other side, Sergeant Al Rogoff, is also a friend of mine," I said.

"So Binky told me," she answered, unimpressed. "He interviewed me when I went to the police with a particular problem, but he wasn't much help. Did Binky say anything to you about my former employer?"

"He did, and, to be truthful, so did Al. Would you like to tell me your version?"

It seemed she would like nothing better. Bianca was a native Floridian, from Coral Gables, where her mother taught at the local high school and her father was a CPA with an expertise in restaurants, which, in southern Florida, made for a flourishing practice. She had a younger brother who was in New York in search of an acting career. She told me he had met another young man from out west who was in the Big Apple on a similar calling and the two were now sharing digs in Chelsea. Wasn't that nice?

Was she ingenuous or was Archy too quick to assume? I would reserve judgment.

It was all very middle class and ho-hum until tragedy struck when her parents were killed in an auto crash two years ago. Mr. Courtney, it seemed, had spent a little faster than he had made. Even their home was mortgaged to the hilt. Bianca, who was finishing at the University of Miami in her hometown, was forced to leave and go to work. Enter Lilian Ashman.

Lilian was a distant, distant relative of Mrs. Courtney's, who had married a widower twenty years her senior. Mr. Ashman had dabbled in Manhattan real estate, buying up blocks of Third Avenue before the El came down. When it did, Mr. Ashman became a multimillionaire and, a few short months later, a corpse. The grieving widow came south to take in the sun and the waters. She was sixty, admitted to fifty, and dressed as if she were thirty.

"It was embarrassing," Bianca said. "Having married a man twenty years older, I think she was compensating by looking for one twenty years younger. But she was kind. When she heard of my situation, she offered me a job as companion, which was little more than accompanying her on shopping sprees and attending countless cocktail parties and charity balls."

And, I thought, attracting young men into her company. Bianca had obviously never read Tennessee Williams's *Garden District*.

"Then she met Tony. Antony, without an *h*, Gilbert. He claimed to be forty but I think he was nearer fifty," she said with more honesty than rancor.

"How did they meet?" I cut in.

Her cheeks took on that flush that began at her throat and worked its way up. "Through the Personals in a magazine. But it was a very literary magazine, Archy."

Why do people think that the more upscale the periodical, the more credible those who peruse their Personals? It's a myth on par with lightning not striking twice in the same place. It does, and more often than you think.

Lilian went public in her quest for a mate by stating in print that she was looking for a man who appreciated the classics as well as the comics– a prudent romantic who enjoyed long walks. She got Antony who was a devotee of Ralph Waldo Emerson and Charles Spenser Chaplin– a hiker who had been on a walking tour of Provence.

"But he was handsome," Bianca admitted, "with a body

to match. Lilian couldn't take her eyes off him when he pranced around the pool."

And, I guessed, neither could you, you little minx. Things were looking up.

Antony said he hailed from Texas, spoke with a drawl, and hinted at links with oil barons. Eyeing Lilian's house, cars, help, and lifestyle, he popped the question after a relationship of one month. The foolish woman accepted. Six months later she was dead. Drowned in her pool.

"I told you how vain she was," Bianca said, stressing the point. "She had a personal trainer and a room filled with exercise machines which were used, not for show. She had the figure of a woman thirty years younger and she was an expert swimmer. She did fifty laps every day, including Sunday, and dove like a professional. So how did she drown?"

"You tell me."

Distressed, Bianca said it was believed that when diving, Lilian had hit her head on the bottom of the pool's Gunite surface and was knocked unconscious. Only Tony was present. He was seated, having breakfast, and saw her dive. When she failed to surface immediately, he was not concerned, because she often swam the length of the pool and back again, underwater.

"Is that true?" I asked.

Reluctantly, Bianca nodded. "When Tony finally realized that something was wrong, he went in after her, but it was too late. He sounded the alarm and I called the police. In ten minutes the place was crawling with uniforms, ambulance crew, and even Lilian's doctor. Tony had to be given a sedative to calm him. After a cursory inquest the police declared it an accident.

"The next day, when things had more or less settled

down, I saw Tony going into the exercise room, carrying one of the small barbells. What had he been doing with it? Tony never exercised, and in the two years I lived with Lilian I never knew her to work out anyplace but in the makeshift gym. Don't you see?" she cried.

"You think he took the barbell from the gym, used it to clobber his wife, after which he tossed her in the pool, hid the weapon someplace, and returned it the next day?"

"Isn't that obvious?" she said.

"I'm afraid not, Bianca. Did you mention the barbell to Tony?"

"No. I was afraid. But I did tell the police. They didn't seem to think there was anything unusual or suspect in what I saw."

"Who inherits, Bianca?"

She didn't like that and made no attempt to hide her annoyance at the question. "That again. Okay. When Lilian relocated here, she didn't have a will and her lawyer told her it would be very imprudent to die intestate. To please him, she made a will leaving everything to her favorite charities, thinking that she could always change it when and if she had other ideas about where to leave her money."

"So Tony doesn't inherit?"

"Oh, I think he's entitled to something as her spouse, but not the bulk of the estate. I know he's got lawyers working on his behalf, and he's still living in the house."

She looked so adorable when she pouted that I hated to zing her, but she knew it was coming. "So what's Tony's motive, Bianca?"

"Maybe he didn't know about the will," she said with little conviction.

"Murder is a serious business, and Tony doesn't sound

like the type who would kill on speculation. Did Lilian Ashman ever promise to name you in a new will?"

"She did. And I know what you're thinking. That I'm angry at her dying before she could keep her word and I'm looking for a scapegoat to blame."

It certainly seemed that way, and I had to agree with the police, but that wouldn't score me any points with Bianca Courtney. Being between cases, I saw no reason why I couldn't snoop around with Bianca as my guide. If nothing else, I would try to prove to her that Lilian Ashman's death was an accident and set her mind, and Lilian, at rest. Diving boards are known to be the bane of private pools. And it's a fact that many pool suppliers advise against installing them.

Our coffee, practically untouched, had grown cold, and I feared so would my welcome unless I gave Bianca some hope for her cause. "Tell me," I said, "did Tony ever make a play for you?"

This surprised her, but she didn't shy from the question or pretend to be modest in her answer. "He did and I thought it was disgusting and I told him so. He laughed."

"You don't like Antony Gilbert very much, do you?"

"I hate him," she replied with feeling.

An objective observer she wasn't, which did little to help her case. "So if you called and asked if you could drop by to pick up something you forgot, he would not object?"

The hope in her eyes was worth my phony effort to help. "You mean . . ."

"I mean I would like to meet him. That's all, Bianca."

"I know you're a professional investigator, Archy, but I haven't much money."

"I don't expect to be paid because I don't think you

have much of a case. But I am willing to stick my nose in because I like you."

I was rewarded with that fabulous blush and a smile— but not a kiss. However, all things considered, I had made progress in my courting of Bianca Courtney. This left me feeling like Oscar's take on the English gentleman galloping after a fox— *the unspeakable in pursuit of the uneatable*.

"It's none of my business," I ventured, "but how is your cash flow?"

"Lilian gave me the car and I was able to save almost all my salary in the two years I was with her. I had no expenses other than some personal needs. She was most generous with me. When she shopped for herself, she never failed to buy me something. I can get by for now if I'm careful and I'm on the lookout for gainful employment."

I rose to leave and Bianca got up with me. I took out my wallet and gave her my card. "Why don't you call Tony and see what's convenient for him, and then coordinate with me."

"I can't tell you how much I appreciate this, Archy. I'm not out to get Tony, but I do think the police should have asked a few questions before writing it all off as an accident." She had reached the door, and when she opened it for me she stepped back and exclaimed, "Wow. Just look at that."

The stretch limo was parked out front, blocking my Miata.

TWELVE

I STEPPED OUT, telling Bianca to stay put and lock her door behind me. Like a sensible girl she did as she was told. I hopped indifferently down the three steps as if the sight of a stretch limo at my doorstep was the rule rather than the exception. The driver was leaning against the limo, arms folded. He wore a black suit with matching tie and cap. As I approached he straightened up. My eyes fell on the bulge under the breast pocket of his jacket. My guess was, it wasn't a fountain pen.

When I had arrived at the Palm Court that morning, I noticed that Al Rogoff's carport was empty and had been glad of the fact. Now I wasn't so glad.

"Mr. McNally," the driver politely addressed me. "Would you mind stepping into the car for a few minutes?"

"Do I have a choice?"

"Of course," he answered. "But I hope you'll oblige us. This isn't what it seems, believe me. Mr. Cranston would like a few words with you."

Cranston? Richard Cranston? Was it possible? This was too bizarre to be real, but unless Bianca had slipped me a mickey and I was now on my way to the Emerald City in a stretch limo, it was happening. Or was it all a ruse? Was I about to meet my maker in return for some toes I had stepped on while pursuing my chosen profession? If so, did it have to be in a trailer park with the purchase of a microwave oven as my last recorded act? What a lousy way to go, and it was all the fault of Binky Watrous and his damned housewarming.

Richard Cranston, if it was *the* Richard Cranston behind those tinted windows, was a member of a prominent banking family. This did not stop him from adding billions to the family business via Silicon Valley and the computer revolution. In the last presidential election he had backed the winner with financial support amounting to millions while attaching himself to the candidate's campaign entourage as a welcome advisor. Rumor had it that Cranston was now being rewarded with a cabinet post or an ambassadorship.

The affiliation between the two men went back to their college days when they pledged the same fraternity. It was said that both the First Backside and Cranston's bore the brand of the fraternity's Greek letters. Thanks to his buddy, Cranston was currently the most visible and discussed Washington pol in Palm Beach since Joe Kennedy and sons' salad days.

The driver opened the door and held it. I put off the inescapable for a moment before entering and then found myself face-to-face with the man himself in surroundings as posh as a movie star's location van. Bar, TV, several telephones, and a hamper from which the aroma of hot coffee rose in the air-conditioned air.

With more courage than I was feeling, I said, "I thought I lost you on the island."

"We dropped you by the bridge and allowed my man in his VW Bug to continue shagging you. Like your red Miata, we are a bit conspicuous."

Two cars on my trail? This was getting weirder by the moment. If I didn't know the guy from a myriad of newspaper photographs and countless TV shots of him and the First Man forever hurrying from a copter to a waiting limo, I would think he was a rich PB eccentric having fun.

When he offered me coffee, I refused with, "No, thanks, I just had a cup."

"With the charming lady, no doubt." Cranston had a reputation for being something of a Romeo. Tall, lanky, and square-jawed, he emanated a boyish charm some women find irresistible. If he played the field, he did so with practiced circumspection. His marriage was solid, with three lovely and eligible daughters to keep the paparazzi and the gossips in business. "What about a proper drink?" he tried again. "The sun's not over the yardarm, but I'll never tell."

With what I hoped was a show of displeasure, I said, "Mr. Cranston, may I know why you followed me here and what you want from me?"

He took a silver box from the bar, removed the lid, and offered me a cigarette. Without a qualm I accepted. It wasn't an English Oval– I was now leaving home without them– but any port in a storm, eh, what?

Giving me a light, he said, "I would have contacted you through your father, but he's away at the moment."

"He's traveling . . . "

"On the *Pearl of the Antilles* cruise ship with your mother," he cut me short. "I know that. The next best thing was to corner you in a place were I would least likely be recognized and you led me right to it. However, if your friend Sergeant Rogoff was at home, we would have aborted the mission, but not for long."

The guy was telling me how much he knew, which was a lot. As for the unconventional meeting, I said earlier that local patricians in need of my help did not like to advertise the fact, but this near hijacking was an all-time first.

"You seem to know a lot about me, sir, so I assume you know what I do for a living, such as it is." He liked that and smiled his appreciation. "I take it you want to hire me?"

"I want information from you and I'm willing to pay for it," he said. "Consider me a client and start billing me."

This made as much sense as Einstein looking for the answer to the cosmos in a crystal ball. "Why me when you seem to have unlimited resources at your disposal to tell you what you want to know?"

"Because, Mr. McNally, you have access to a resource I neither possess nor wish to approach."

"Namely, sir?"

"Namely, Sabrina Wright."

My flabber was too startled to be gasted. Was there no end to this woman's liaisons? When her plane touched down in Florida, the sound must have been heard around the world. Was she involved with the government on the highest level? Espionage? Now I wanted that drink but like much I wanted in life, I had let my chances pass me by. "You speak of the popular writer, Mr. Cranston?"

"You know damn well of whom I speak, Archy. Tell me what she's doing in Palm Beach with her family."

As with Thomas Appleton, we were suddenly on a first name basis. Appleton? Was there a connection? *Oy vey!* I thought it best to play dumb until I knew just what was coming down the pike. I puffed deeply on the weed and choked. Mr. Richard Cranston slapped my back– hard.

"How would I know what she's doing here, with or without her family?" I coughed.

"Archy, I'm a busy man and I've spent all morning getting you where I want you, so spare me the crap. The moment Sabrina arrived in Palm Beach, she contacted you. You met in a sleaze joint where she enjoyed a Pink Lady and you had a vodka and tonic. The next day you had lunch with her husband, after which Sabrina left the Chesterfield Hotel and moved into The Breakers with her hubby, daughter, and one Zachary Ward, a stringer for a tabloid. Have I got it right?"

He had it so right I felt violated. Was that insolent bartender in his employ? The waiter at Harry's Place? The butcher, the baker, the candlestick maker? I noticed that the driver was still outside the car and well out of hearing range. This powwow was top-priority hush-hush, and I didn't like it one lousy bit. People who know too much are expendable.

"What's she after, Archy? I don't believe that bull in Spindrift's column. If Sabrina wanted me, she knows where to find me. So what is she after?"

My déjà was now so vu my head was spinning. "Why would she want you, Dick?" If I called him mister or sir, I would be the schoolboy playing to his master. No way. You give these guys an inch and they walk off with your life.

He puffed away, adding to the smoke we had both been exhaling. The air conditioner was now blowing it back in our faces and irritating my eyes. Was this the complaint of a true ex-smoker or of a guy who wanted out of this stretch limo?

"More to the point, Archy, what did she want from you?"

Seeing an ashtray on the bar, I tapped the ash off my cigarette as I answered, "I asked you first, Dick."

I had touched a raw nerve for which I was verbally trounced. The guy turned into a raging bull and ranted, "Don't get wise with me, buddy. Don't ever get wise with me. You tell me what I want to know or . . . "

"Or what?" I trounced back. The bull had picked the wrong matador to snort at. "You rub shoulders with a few hotshots and you think you can stalk citizens, drag them into your fancy car, and threaten them to learn what you want to know. Well, think again, *buddy*. The charming lady is at her window with a video camera in one hand and a telephone in the other. On a signal from me, she'll dial the police. Would you like to explain this meeting to the press?"

The guy turned the color of the long ash at the end of his cigarette. "I don't believe you."

"All you have to do is try to stop me from getting out of this car and you'll know if I'm lying or not." I reached for the door.

When his arm shot out to restrain me, the ash fell onto his lap. There is nothing like a hidden camcorder to drive a politician bonkers. "My apologies," he muttered, shaking his head. The man was in a bad way. "Please, hear me out."

Keeping on the offensive, I informed him, "I haven't got all day, but I'll give you ten more minutes."

He spoke very quietly when he said, "I'm going to be

offered the post of ambassador to the Court of St. James's." So, he was truly following in Joseph Kennedy's footsteps. Good thing he didn't have any sons– or perhaps he harbored political expectations for his daughters. "Any hint of a scandal, especially of a sexual nature, could put my confirmation in doubt, or I would have to withdraw my name out of loyalty to certain parties."

I trashed my cigarette with Sabrina's words echoing in my head. *"I became* au fait *with the ways of the world, which is to say with the rich, the super rich, and the mega rich."* She even hinted at her many sexual conquests along the way. Was Richard Cranston one of them?

Almost in answer to my silent musings, Cranston was saying, "Sabrina and I had a brief tryst a while back."

Finally. "Your wife, of course, didn't know about it."

He looked at me as if I were retarded. "My wife? I didn't even know my wife at the time." He finally got rid of his cigarette before it singed his fingers. "Now that my name is newsworthy, is she trying to muscle in on the publicity? Is that why she's here?"

Dickey's ego was bigger than his car. "If you'll excuse my saying so, I believe Sabrina Wright is a far bigger name than Richard Cranston if you're talking on a global scale. In short, she doesn't need you to get her name in print. She's not only a household word, she's an icon."

Imagination having no greater stimulus than a guilty conscience, he implored, "Then why is she here?"

Believing I would put his mind at ease and give the Court of St. James's what it deserved, I said, "Sabrina's daughter, Gillian, was adopted. The girl is here looking for her father. Sabrina wants her to stop the search and return home. Why she hired me is too complicated to repeat and it has nothing to do with your affair with the lady. The end."

He bowed his head and shielded his eyes. "The end," he repeated. "The end of the line."

"Sabrina Wright is not interested in you. I would swear to that if I were the swearing kind, which I'm not."

The guy looked like he was going to be sick. "Did Sabrina tell you she is the girl's natural mother?"

So he knew that, too. "Yes. But she didn't tell me the name of Gillian's father. All Sabrina wants to do is pack up the group and herd them all home. She's not interested in you, Dick, or any of her old flames. Relax, and there's no charge."

"Sabrina might not be interested in me, but her daughter is."

"Gillian interested in you? Why?"

"Because I'm the man she's looking for, Archy. I'm Gillian's father."

Numb from the neck up, I listened to a story that was almost verbatim to Appleton's saga of his brief encounter with Sabrina Wright. That was one hell of a spring break, let me tell you. And wouldn't Gillian be surprised. Her daddies were coming out of the woodwork. There was so much going on in my mind, I didn't even notice when Cranston had finished telling his story. "I can count on your discretion, Archy. Remember, you are in my employ, and if you ever did repeat what I just told you, I would deny it, sue, and guess who would win? Or, I would tell the world why you were expelled from Yale."

That hit me like a knee to the family jewels. "You know?" I foolishly asked.

"I know, Archy. Believe me, I know."

My head was aching. Were Cranston and Appleton acquainted? Given their backgrounds and social positions, they must be. Did their friendship go back thirty years? Why not? Did they know they had both bedded the then young Sabrina Wright? Doubtful. Gentlemen don't kiss and tell and these guys were the genuine article. And who paid Sabrina to go away and never return? Both of them, naturally. Only the man who believed he had sired Gillian would pay the piper, and both of these men believed they had.

Last, and foremost, Appleton and Cranston were political animals tuned into the highest of echelons. It was crazy. And scary. I still felt that knowing the name of Gillian's father could be dangerous, and I knew not one, but two candidates for the title. What I wanted to do was crown Sabrina with a hatchet, but that could wait. Right now I had to talk my way out of the car while I could still do so of my own volition.

"Your secret is safe with me and with Sabrina." Here I went into the same spiel I had given Appleton. I would have liked to tell him just why Sabrina was so keen on keeping his, and Appleton's, secret a secret, but held back. No man likes to be told he's been duped, especially a man with the pride and brass of Richard Cranston.

"She's down here to stop her daughter from learning the truth. Sabrina Wright is your ally, Dick, not your enemy. She's a very clever woman and she will do what she must to keep the bargain she made with you thirty years ago. Put your trust in her. It won't be misplaced."

The poor man appeared to be aging before my eyes like a citizen of Shangri-la who had foolishly run down the mountain. His pallor accentuated the dark circles under his eyes, which were now puffed from worry and fatigue. Cranston was a man living with his head on the guillotine's block since the day he read that item in Lolly's column. That insipid blind item had two important men in Palm Beach on the brink of nervous collapse, proving yet again that the pen is more lethal than the sword.

"Trust her? You have to be kidding. She told the girl she was her natural mother, which was against our pact. If the girl is here looking for me, she must have told her where she was conceived. Trust? She's about as reliable as a campaign promise. I said I wanted to hire you, Archy, and I still do."

"What for?"

"You know Sabrina. Stick with her and her family. Especially the tabloid reporter. Keep me posted on their every move."

With a gesture at the driver loitering just outside the car, I reminded him that he had people far more capable than myself to keep the group at The Breakers under surveillance. "I work alone," I told him, "and I'm in the habit of breaking for lunch and dinner, not to mention a good night's sleep. You could furnish a relay team to cover them around the clock."

He shook his head and ran his hand through his fashionably cut hair. It tousled and then fell back into place, perfectly. I hate men with hair like that. "Don't you see? That would mean telling people I'm interested in Sabrina Wright. They won't know why I'm interested and that would be worse than if they did because they would then speculate on everything from bigamy to satanic worship. You already know the truth and you're one person too many, but I can't do anything about that except use it to my advantage."

A very rich man once told me that the wealthy are often accused of milking their employees dry. That is, having them perform chores other than the ones for which they were hired. He claimed that this penurious behavior has less to do with saving a buck than in limiting the number of people surrounding them. The more sparse the court, the less worry about tattling, tell-all books, and the threat of blackmail. Hence, I could understand Cranston's fear, but that didn't mean I had to like his blunt assertion regarding the vulnerability of my insider status.

I didn't want to refuse him out of hand as my father would never forgive me, so I made him an offer he couldn't refuse because he had no choice. "I'll keep my ear to the ground and I do have my sources. If I run into Sabrina or any of her group, I'll feel them out and pass on what I learn. That's the best I can offer you."

He nodded, reluctantly. "Do you think I should meet with her, Archy?"

Better make an appointment, was what I thought. "That's up to you, but I would let sleeping dogs lie. Gillian hasn't got a clue and Sabrina is not cooperating. Get some rest and this, too, shall pass."

"Thanks, Archy. I'm sorry I tried to pressure you." He offered me his hand. "Friends?"

I accepted the olive branch. "I'll keep you posted when and if I can," I promised.

Still clutching my hand, he said, "The Court of St. James's. It means everything to me, Archy, and nothing is going to stop me from presenting my credentials to Her Majesty. Nothing."

THIRTEEN

THE LIMO MADE for the disposal area at the end of the block before executing a three-point U-turn and heading out of the Palm Court. As it passed me, Bianca appeared at her door and called, "Who was it, Archy?"

"Only a couple interested in renting number eleven-seventy. They didn't know it had been taken."

"I don't believe you," she said.

Not wishing to get into a discussion on the subject, I shrugged my regrets and waved a good-bye as I got into the Miata. When I drove out of the Palm Court, the limo was nowhere to be seen. Gone, I thought, but not forgotten. I motored aimlessly until I spotted a coffee shop. I parked and went in. The place was between breakfast and lunch, therefore just about empty. I sat in a booth, ordered a coffee and toasted English, and tried to figure out my next move.

When I had called Sabrina to tell her she was going to hear from Gillian's father, the woman had no idea who that might be– Appleton or Cranston. But, like the pro she is, she had aced my volleys and sent me packing with a sharp "Good day." When she tried to learn why Gillian's father had contacted me, was she hoping the lead would tell her which of the men she was likely to hear from?

It was only later that I realized the name Thomas Appleton had never come up in our conversation. But with Silvester present and a switchboard operator with easy access to the line, I had to assume she was loathe to name names, and that made sense.

When Sabrina told Gillian she was her natural mother, I had to also assume that she, Sabrina, couldn't resist bragging about her pedigreed conquest and life, however fleeting, in posh Palm Beach. No doubt she had reminded Gillian that, although she may have been born on the wrong side of the blanket, the comforter was spun from threads of pure gold. And, thanks to mama's business savvy, Gillian had been given all the advantages due her heritage. Did Sabrina also name all the royal bastards who had risen above the happenstance of their birth? She was, after all, a writer of romances.

A few days later, Gillian demanded to know who her father was. Here, Sabrina must have regretted her boasting. She refused to answer Gillian, not only to honor her bargain but also because she didn't know the answer. When Gillian announced that she was going in search of him, Sabrina must have been beside herself with fear. It was a wonder she sat still long enough for Silvester to come down here and try to talk the girl and Zack into returning home.

The waitress brought me my elevenses and it was just what I needed. One cannot think properly on an empty stomach. What I was thinking was that Sabrina should have sat still a little longer before chasing after Silvester. Her meeting with me had precipitated a chain reaction that was taking on all the characteristics of a bedroom farce.

But given the agendas of the concerned parties, this comedy was apt to revert to tragedy before the final curtain. Appleton had the countenance of Santa, and Cranston the tolerance of Scrooge, but even Santa was known to deposit coal in a dissident's stocking and what wouldn't Ebenezer do if he learned he had been bamboozled out of a small fortune? Small? Appleton had hinted at how generous he had been. Double it and you're talking a king's ransom. But both men would gladly absorb a financial loss if only Sabrina and Co. would go away. And both were hell-bent on not being named father of the year. Sabrina, for now obvious reasons, was poised to do what she must to keep either man from learning the truth. The situation was a scandal waiting to happen.

My first reaction after leaving Cranston's mobile office was to call Sabrina and read her the riot act, but now a calmer head and a fuller stomach prevailed. Let the titans do battle while little Archy slipped quietly off into the sunset, body and soul intact. Only Sabrina and Archy knew that Sabrina had played Russian roulette with two loaded pistols, and not even she knew which had fired the blank. But she didn't know I knew and I had no intention of telling her I knew. With this crowd, ignorance was not only sublime, it was judicious.

Archy knew too much about these three, and Cranston knew too much about Archy. Our government wasn't the only one to operate on a system of checks and balances.

From this moment on I would be the man that got away and prayed they would never come looking for me. When Father returned, I would unload my burden; until then I would play the ostrich and bury my head in Bianca Courtney's sandbox. I paid my check, left a generous tip, and headed for the Palace.

THE PALM BEACH police headquarters is housed in an edifice that would not be out of place in the hills overlooking the Côte d'Azur. Thus it had been dubbed the Palace by Sgt. Rogoff, who labors within the castle walls. The twelve o'clock whistle was about to toot when I parked out front, hoping to catch Al on his way to lunch if he was on desk duty and not patrolling the streets.

Should he emerge with policewoman Tweeny Alvarez, I would try to make myself invisible, which is not easy when you're sitting in a red convertible in front of a police station. Tweeny Alvarez had a thing for Al which I believed was prompted by the fact that he was the only man on the force who could best Tweeny at arm wrestling. I couldn't tell you if the feeling was mutual because Al wears only his sergeant stripes on his sleeve.

Tweeny is no Tallchief or Callas, but then Al Rogoff is no Nureyev or Domingo, so it was a standoff in the looks and talent department. However, I didn't know Tweeny well enough to say who her idols might be. Given Al's physique and manner, I would take an educated guess that Tweeny's favorite Hollywood dreamboat was either Kong or Godzilla.

Al came out, blinked in the bright sunlight of a Palm Beach summer day, and approached the Miata as if he were about to ticket me for illegal parking. Actually, it's the way Al approaches everything that gets in his path. "You waiting to be arrested?" he greeted.

"No, sir. It's take-a-flatfoot-to-lunch day, compliments of the Pelican Club, and your name leaped out of the hopper."

"That's what I thought," he groaned, getting into the car. Al Rogoff getting into my Miata brought to mind the fat lady at the circus squeezing into a girdle. "Tell me something, Archy; doesn't the Grill at the Ambassador Hotel ever have a take-a-cop-to-lunch day?"

"Heavens, no. Besides, you'd be out of place there," I told him, putting the car into gear and moving off. The Palace and the Ambassador triggered the image of Richard Cranston presenting his credentials to Her Majesty.

"I feel unwanted at the Pelican," Al complained. "I walk in wearing my uniform and half the guys in the room start looking for the nearest exit. Is the joint a front for a booking parlor?"

"It's not the uniform, Al, it's your demeanor. You come on like Eliot Ness entering a speakeasy. Relax. Give the boys a big smile and a friendly wave and see what happens."

Al folded his arms across his chest and looked at me obliquely. "Screw you, Archy."

Now the man was sounding more like himself, and I took heart. "Tweeny off today?" I ventured cautiously.

"She's at the range, qualifying," Al said.

"Is she a good shot?"

"Tweeny? From fifty yards she can knock a flea off a dog's ear without singeing his fur."

"Tell me, Al, is there anything Tweeny Alvarez can't do?"

"Yeah. The dame can't sit through *The Ring of the Nibelung* in one take. She gets antsy halfway through *Götterdämmerung.*" Al shook his head in disgust.

Poor Tweeny. She probably had been set for a romantic evening with Sinatra singing Mancini and she got Siegfried warbling Wagner. This romance did not bode well.

The Pride of the Pelican, Ms. Priscilla, welcomed us with an armful of menus and, "Well, well, the fuzz and the shamus. Are you in hot pursuit or can you stay for lunch?"

"We'll take the corner table, young lady, and I'll thank you to keep a civil tongue in your head."

"Oh, cool it, bub, don't get your Jockeys in a knot. Two malts, as usual?"

"You can." Sitting, I said to Al, "That girl is a piece of work."

"You can say that again. I saw the young Lena Horne on the tube the other night and she had it all, but you know what? Pris is prettier than Lena."

"And more sassy." I picked up one of the menus Priscilla had dropped on our table. "What are you having, Al?"

"I won't know how much of your money to spend until I know why you got me here."

I tried to raise one eyebrow as does my august papa— and failed. "Whatever do you mean?"

"Archy, we've been friends for years and you've never invited me to lunch without having me sing for my supper. So what is it you want to know?"

"You really know how to hurt a guy, Al."

"I hope so." Al slapped his forehead with the palm of his huge hand. "Hell's bells, I forgot to smile and wave. Should I go out and come in again?"

Priscilla arrived with our froth-topped beers in chilled pilsner glasses, perfectly drawn by Mr. Pettibone. With a nod, Al knocked back half the glass, leaving a white mustache on his upper lip, which he carefully shaved off with his tongue. But remember, he can sit through *The Ring* tetralogy and hum along. How do you figure a guy like this?

"Hamburgers and fries?" Priscilla guessed.

"I don't think so," I said.

"Why not?" Al questioned with indignation.

"Since I all but gave up the weed, I've been putting on weight and I have to watch my waistline. Besides, we should be cutting down on red meat. We're not getting any younger," I lectured with feeling.

Priscilla let out a chuckle. "Take it from me, gentlemen, the bloom is off the rose."

"That's not funny," I told her.

"It wasn't meant to be." Remembering her job, she recited the afternoon's special. "Grilled salmon. Very healthy, especially with a tossed green salad."

I looked across the table at Al who was shaking his head. Man does not live long on hamburgers and fries washed down with a few pilsner glasses full of suds. In the interest of keeping Al alive long enough to tell me what I wanted to know, I ordered for both of us. "Two grilled salmons, Priscilla, and the tossed green."

"Okay," Al relented unwillingly, "but bring me an order of fries on the side."

As Priscilla was withdrawing, I called, "Make that two orders of fries."

"What about your waistline?" she challenged.

"I'm not going to eat them. I just want to look at them and remember when I could."

Al watched Priscilla's departing form, which was done

up in a Pucci– a print wrap dress in light blue, black, and mocha– and sighed. Watching Priscilla in retreat after taking an order had become the fastest growing noncontact sport at the Pelican, an honor formerly held by our annual Running of the Lambs in the parking lot.

We were a bit early for a lazy Palm Beach summer lunch and were the only ones occupying a table in the bar area. There were a few men seated on stools watching market quotes on the TV and picking Mr. Pettibone's brain for tips. The dining room was nearly empty when we entered, but a steady flow of singles and doubles trickled in as we awaited our food.

While his mind was otherwise occupied, I inquired with a bored air, "What can you tell me about Bianca Courtney, Al?"

"She and Binky had Chinese takeout last night. Chicken and snow peas with extra fried rice. They ain't eating healthy like us."

"Are you a Peeping Tom, Al?"

"No. Kevin Woo delivered my order before going next door. Sweet-and-sour pork with two spring rolls."

"Kevin Woo? From what part of China does he hail, Belfast?"

Al finished his beer and looked about for Priscilla. "He's third-generation Floridian. His father is Tyrone Woo. He owns the Pagoda."

I was getting more information than I cared to know. "So Kevin Woo delivers the orders and rats on his customers. Did you ever think of moving into a fishbowl?"

"It's not like that," Al said. "We're a friendly group and we watch out for each other. We ain't no different from your gang. You got Lolly Spindrift– we got Mrs. Brewster."

Here, Priscilla breezed by and deposited a plate of crudités on our table. "It comes with the salmon," she informed us.

Staring at the raw vegetables, Al ordered two more beers and a platter of onion rings. "And a few dill spears while you're at it."

"And some of Leroy's fried mozzarella sticks," I added.

"Should I have Leroy fry the crudités?" Priscilla asked before wandering off.

"Where were we?" I said to Al when she was gone.

"On a diet, remember?"

"No, after that." Snapping my fingers as if a bulb had just lit up in my head, I exclaimed, "Yes, Bianca Courtney. What else can you tell me besides what she and Binky had for dinner last night?"

"Let's see. She had a visit this morning from a man driving a red car. Then a stretch limo pulls up outside her door and sits there until the guy leaves Bianca's pad. He gets in the limo for maybe twenty minutes, and it just sits there like there's a meeting going on. When the guy gets out of the limo it drives off, and then the guy gets back in the red car and follows it."

This left me not only flummoxed, but speechless. Our brews arrived and I drank to play for time. Mrs. Brewster had witnessed Cranston's cloak-and-dagger ploy and reported it to the neighborhood cop. Did the snoop get the limo's license number?

"I got a call at the station house this morning from Mrs. B," Al said, like I didn't know. "Nice dame, but old and nervous. She calls me if a UPS truck backfires. So who was in the limo?"

Nervous old ladies did not take down plate numbers. They wouldn't turn their backs long enough to get pencil and paper. "It was a client, Al. That's all I can say."

"How come a client met you at the Palm Court?"

Not even I could answer that with a story that was remotely believable, so I made no attempt to do so. "You said we've known each other for a long time, Al, right?" He nodded with a shrug. "Have I ever done anything to abuse that friendship?" He shook his head but spared me the shrug. "Then I have to ask you to trust me with this one. I can't tell you a damn thing about the limo, Al, but I promise I will as soon as I'm able."

"Has it got anything to do with Bianca Courtney and her deceased employer?"

"Absolutely not," I said with joy at being able to tell the truth, the whole truth, and nothing but the truth. Our onion rings, pickles, and mozzarella sticks arrived and we helped ourselves. I felt I had sweated off enough pounds over Mrs. Brewster's see-and-tell avocation to make up for the few ounces I was imbibing.

"Has it got anything to do with Sabrina Wright?"

My joy was short-lived. I grabbed a mozzarella stick to ward off the evil eye and to appease the gnawing in the pit of my belly. Lunch with Al Rogoff could be hazardous to your health. The best way to avoid answering a question was to ask one. "How do you know Sabrina Wright is in town, and why would I be involved with her?"

Al was working on a pickle spear. He really loved those things. "We read Spindrift, too, and we like to keep an eye on the visiting firemen, especially the big shots. And there was a rumor going around that she hired Archy McNally to find some guy who ran off on her."

There was that blind item again. Gadzooks, it had done everything but start World War Three. Bite your tongue, Archy, she's not out of Palm Beach yet. "Do you read Sabrina Wright, Al?"

"Hell, no. But Tweeny does."

Somehow I could not imagine Tweeny Alvarez reading anything but the Most Wanted list. Changing the subject without drawing attention to the fact, I said, "I imagine Bianca Courtney reads her, too."

"So tell me what you were doing at Bianca's?" Al asked.

I'm so clever it hurts.

"I was delivering a microwave oven," I said, munching my third mozzarella stick. Well, they're better than popping tranquillizers.

"Do I have to trust you with that one, too?"

I told Al everything, beginning with Binky's housewarming and ending with my conversation with Bianca. "I went as a favor to Binky, you understand. The girl, as you know, is young and foolish."

"The broad, as you and me know, is young and pretty," Al said, delivering a death blow to the English language. But don't ever mistake him for a fool. Many a felon has and lived to regret it for anywhere from ten years to life. "She told you about the barbell. It's a laugh, Archy. She wanted us to dust it for prints. The guy lives in the house, for chrissakes, and if his paws weren't on everything in the joint I would be suspicious."

"But did you ask him why he was seen returning it to the exercise room the day after the accident?"

"Yeah. And he didn't appreciate it. He knew Bianca was the snitch. The barbell was in the garage holding down a stack of newspapers waiting to be picked up for recycling. The housekeeper confirmed this."

Funny what people leave out of their stories when they're trying to prove a point. Now I was committed to visit Antony without an *h*. Maybe I could talk Bianca out of the visit and into a midnight swim. "One more question, Al. What did the forensic people say about the head wound?"

"The old dame must have hit her head on the floor of the pool when she dove off the board."

"Must have," I pounced. "But could the wound have been caused by something else?"

Al dismissed this with a wave of his hand, which actually created a breeze. "But she was alive and well when she dove in the pool and dead when we carried her out. Conclusion, she hit her head in the pool."

"And who saw her dive into the pool, alive and well?"

"Her husband, that's who."

"Anyone else?" I goaded.

"Archy, the guy gets next to nothing from her death. You know that and so does Bianca. He was better off when his wife was alive. Okay, he had to dip his wick a few times a week, but in return he got treated like a prince. Now he goes back to pushing rich old ladies around dance floors."

I must say Al's description of the marriage bed had a certain flair. Priscilla arrived with our grilled salmon, tossed greens and fries on the side. I took this moment to ask her if the family had heard anything from their cousin in California.

"Not a word," Priscilla said, "and Mom's been on the phone with cousin Lucy daily, but she hasn't heard a thing from her father since his last call."

Covering his fries with ketchup from a plastic squeeze bottle, Al asked, "What's this all about?"

I related the tale of Jasmine's cousin and the diary of Henry Peavey. "You know the name, Al?"

"Doesn't mean a thing to me." He removed a pad from

his shirt pocket, and reaching further down, he came up with the stub of a pencil. He jotted the name on his pad. "I'll run it through the local and national police registers and see what comes up."

"Thanks," Priscilla said. "I'll tell Mom."

I heard one of the men at the bar say, "It's Troy Appleton." Several people left their tables to get closer to the TV screen.

Curious, I called out, "What's happening?"

"The local station is showing Troy Appleton speaking on the steps of the capital in Tallahassee," Mr. Pettibone announced. "They say he's going to make a run for the U.S. Senate."

If he doesn't run for cover first.

I knew the Appleton family secret and Richard Cranston claimed to know my secret. Did all the people watching the popular pol have a little secret of their own that only one other person was privy to? Then, did all the people who knew their little secret have one of their own that was shared by one other person? If so, no one was left out– and no one was safe.

"How about another beer, Archy?" Al said.

"Why not, Sergeant? Gather ye rosebuds while ye may, even if the bloom is off the bud."

FOURTEEN

HERB GAVE ME a thumbs-up as I rolled past his glass closet and into my parking space. The signal meant that Mrs. Trelawney was asking for me. I knew he would be on the horn to inform her of my arrival before I was out of the car. Since my meetings with Appleton and Cranston, and especially with Cranston, I had become super sensitive to those who meddle in the affairs of others– yrs. truly included.

Electronic surveillance, hidden cameras in banks and offices and rest rooms, cell phones that are practically shortwave radios, and let's not forget the old lady who lives across the street and the kid who delivers our takeout dinners. Al Rogoff took down a name and said he would run it through a national register to see what came up. Who hasn't wondered what would come up were his name run through Big Brother's ledger?

The Internet leaves paper trails that are capable of delineating the life and times of everyone who was plugged in. Our biographies were being written as we lived them. Appleton arranges a meeting in a museum and Cranston in the backseat of his car. The museum was open to the public and at least three other people, Bianca, Mrs. Brewster, and the limo driver, had observed and recorded Cranston's not-so-clever ploy.

"Rat on me and I'll rat on you," Cranston had intimated when we parted. Well, Dickey boy, no man is an island, because we're all connected by that information highway which is swarming with pot holes, culs-de-sac, and sewer rats. And, as Al Rogoff might say, "Archy ain't got no credentials to present to the dame in Buckingham Palace."

The case I had agreed to take on for Sabrina Wright had lasted less than forty-eight hours, defied a solution, included a cast of thousands, and left me clinically paranoid. I needed to relax and unwind. I needed that midnight swim with Bianca Courtney. I would even consider a few fifty-minute hours with our resident shrink, Dr. Gussie Pearlberg, if I did not agree with Sam Goldwyn's malapropism: *A man who goes to a psychiatrist ought to have his head examined*.

When Binky stuck his head in my doorway a few moments after I had traversed it, I began to regret having gotten him a position at McNally & Son. Like a potent narcotic, Binky should be taken in small doses between long intervals. Now I had him in my back pocket where I did not need more bulge.

"Thanks for the microwave oven, Archy," Binky said.

News of my visit to Bianca had traveled faster than a

microwave oven could reduce a hot dog to ashes. "Did Bianca Courtney call you?" I questioned.

"No. I went home for lunch and stopped in to see her. She helped me carry it to my kitchen and she's going to show me how to work it."

I paused briefly, mulling his phrasing, before intoning, "I believe it comes with instructions," not mentioning my doubts about Bianca's own knowledge. "And you don't want to come on too strong with your new neighbor, Binky. It's really not necessary to knock on her door every time you pass it. Familiarity breeds contempt, as some closeted extrovert once said, and you should play hard-to-get."

Reflecting on this sage advice, Binky remarked, "I'm so hard-to-get, I've never been gotten."

This was true but not in the sense that either Binky or I had intended. Moving right along, I advised the boy to tend to his own garden. "You've just moved in. You've got a thousand things that need doing, and courting your neighbor is not one of them."

My words went unheeded as, unable to contain his excitement, he said, "Bianca told me that you're taking her case. Thanks, Archy. You know I'm available for legwork and reconnaissance, as usual."

Binky watches too much television and is beginning to talk like a script composed by ten scribes locked in a room with an unlimited supply of legal pads, pencils, and Jim Beam. The only thing I wanted to reconnoiter on Bianca's behalf was unmentionable, for which I did not need Binky's help– as usual.

"I'm sorry to say, Binky, that she doesn't have much of a case. I talked to Al Rogoff this afternoon and it seems the police are satisfied that Bianca's former employer met with an accident. After hearing the facts, I would have to agree."

Quick to tell me how well he had integrated into the ebb and flow of life at the Palm Court, Binky disclosed, "Al had Chinese takeout last night, too. Sweet-and-sour pork and spring rolls."

I was losing patience, a common consequence of a one-on-one with Binky. "What Al had for dinner last night does not change or help Bianca's case. Her only clue, the barbell, was being used as a paperweight in the garage and not for bopping the lady of the house senseless. This has been confirmed by the housekeeper."

"Why couldn't he have taken the barbell from the garage, used it to knock her out, then returned it to the garage?"

My exasperation took the form of a sigh that came from deep within. But we are told to suffer the children, so I explained, "Because he had no reason to do her in, Binky. He doesn't inherit anything but what might be due him as her legal spouse. In fact he may soon be looking for a rental in the Palm Court."

"I hope not, Archy. Bianca hates him."

"And I'm afraid she's allowed her feelings to warp her common sense. I did say I would go with her to meet this Antony Gilbert, and now I'm sorry I did." Fearing Binky would burst into tears at this, I quickly stated that I would honor my promise, "However futile the effort."

All smiles, Binky expressed his gratitude. "I'm glad, Archy. Bianca really appreciates my help in putting her in touch with you. Anything you do will make her feel better, and if you have to let her down, I hope you can do it easy, you know what I mean?"

Indeed I did know. I intended to let her down over a

cozy supper for two across a candlelit table overlooking a moonlit ocean. How to transport her in my red Miata from the Palm Court to a restaurant, unseen by her ever-watchful neighbors, would tax the expertise of a general moving an army across a terrain rigged with land mines. I had been known to rent a Ford or a Chevy for trailing on stakeouts and might have to resort to that maneuver in the courtship of Bianca Courtney. Then, poor Binky once again aided and abetted me in my determination to succumb to lust and debauchery.

"Are you having dinner with us tonight, Archy?" Binky asked.

"Us? Who's us?" Was I to be included in another Chinese take-out orgy?

"Connie and me. She's taking me to the Pelican tonight to celebrate my move to the Palm. I think she bought me something, Archy, because she wanted to know what my color scheme was in my bath."

"Really? And what is your color scheme?"

"The tile and walls and basin are white, so I told her white was my scheme."

And my scheme was unfurled before me like bunting at a political convention. With Binky and Connie at the Pelican, I could pick up Bianca without being seen by Binky and not have to worry about running into Connie. Things were looking up. It was a dastardly plan, but all's fair in love and war and wooing in a trailer park. And if Connie ever learned she was playing decoy for my philandering, she would make a spado out of me in *dos minutos*. The danger was an aphrodisiac to my senses. Lucky Bianca.

"I'm sorry, Binky, but I can't join you. I have a previous engagement. Give Connie my love."

"I'll tell her, Archy." Before leaving, he said with a contrived show of modesty, "I have to report to Mrs. Trelawney at four. What do you suppose that's all about?"

That was all about Binky's housewarming. The participating staff would get there fifteen minutes before four, with their loot, and shout surprise when the new leaseholder entered, all agog. What schmaltz. I had to remember to tell Binky to make a list of who gave him what so when recompense time rolled around in the form of Lucy's wedding, Moe's retirement, and little Jason's bris, he could respond in kind. "You know very well what it's all about, young man. You will walk into Mrs. Trelawney's office bereft of household furnishings and emerge better stocked than Sears. You'll not get it all into your car in one trip."

"I rented a U-Haul," he boasted.

"Don't you think that was a little presumptuous?"

"You always told me to come prepared, Archy, remember?"

Unfortunately, I do remember. That rash counsel led to Binky purchasing a gross of condoms, which he keeps in the trunk of his car. If he ever gets stopped and searched, I'd like to be present when he explains the cache. "Enjoy your moment in the sun," I told him.

"You won't be there?"

"No. I don't attend office galas; that's why I brought my gift to your door."

"To Bianca's door," he corrected.

"Yes. To Bianca's door."

Binky left momentarily, and returned with, "Who was in the stretch limo, Archy?"

Poor Dickey Cranston. The only person who didn't know about his car being at the Palm was Her Majesty unless, of course, she had ordered Chinese takeout from the Pagoda. "None of your business, Binky."

"That's what I thought. See you, Archy."

The phone rang. It was Connie inviting me to dinner at the Pelican. I told her, as I had just told Binky, that I had a previous engagement. "A business engagement," I stressed.

"What kind of business?" The ever-trustful Connie stressed right back.

"The kind of business that pays the rent, that's what kind."

"You don't pay rent, Archy."

"It was a figure of speech."

"Really? Well, make sure that's the only figure you'll be doing business with tonight."

Connie has a way of belying our "arrangement" that gets me right where I live. I told her I was seeing an old friend of my father's who was eighty-six, in a wheelchair, and thought senile was a river.

"Sounds like fun," Connie said.

"Not as much fun as dinner with you and Binky. What did you get the boy?"

"Two bath towels, two hand towels, and two facecloths. All in royal blue."

"But his scheme is white."

"The room is white," Connie said. "It must be like living inside a giant eggshell. It cries out for contrast." A moment later she was jabbering, "And have you heard about his new girl? She lives next door. Binky is acting like a schoolboy."

"I've never known Binky to act like anything but. And he's had crushes before this. In fact he's seldom without one."

"But never one right next door, Archy. With Binky it's usually out of sight, out of mind, but with this one he'll very seldom be out of sight. He's going to tell me all about her tonight."

Not if I killed him first and hid his body in the U-Haul. Binky would tell Connie how he had so gallantly brought Archy and Bianca Courtney together in the interest of justice. He would bare the saga of the microwave drop-off, the date to visit her former place of employment, etc., etc., and et al. By the time he finished, Connie would be shredding the royal-blue bath towels with her painted talons. God help me. But why should he? I'm a cad.

"Connie," I began, not knowing what would come next.

"Gotta go, Archy. Madam is buzzing. Can you get her a meeting with Sabrina Wright? She keeps asking."

"Sabrina Wright and I are incommunicado . . . " Click. The line went dead, but not for long. Before I could formulate Binky's demise, it rang again.

"Archy McNally here."

"You black-hearted swine. You two-timing sod. What happened to my interview with Sabrina Wright? I told my editor it was in the bag and he reserved space. I now have a lot of space to fill and nothing to fill it with except, hopefully, your obit."

"Lolly, give me a chance . . . "

"I did give you a chance. I revealed my source in return for a favor and got the shaft."

"You said your source was an anonymous caller."

"So I revealed my anonymous source, what difference does it make? What the hell is going on, Archy? Tell me, and no McNally finagling or I'll do you-know-what for you-know-who to read."

I was being threatened with blackmail from every corner. Now I had to placate Lolly, silence Binky and place him in the U-Haul, call Bianca to do you-know-what, and prevent you-know-whom from reading about it. What's a Discreet Inquirer to do? There just weren't enough hours in the day.

"Sabrina's not speaking to me, Lol. She ended our brief relationship before I could set you up with her. That's the truth."

"Sabrina Wright is yesterday's news," Lolly's tirade continued. "She's at The Breakers, still playing Garbo, but her daughter is all over town acting like a publicity-crazed starlet."

I was already seated, so I couldn't collapse into a chair. "What are you talking about?" Did I sound convincing? It made no difference. Lolly was so excited he wouldn't notice if I were, nor would he care.

"The girl, her name is Gillian, visits the library daily, and delves into the archives of our local periodicals. She's interested in any social items that date back decades."

"How do you know this, Lol?"

"Because she calls my editor and questions him about these items. Archy, the guy wasn't born when the stories ran. Colleagues tell me she also calls other rags, from here to Miami, asking the same thing."

This was the worst possible scenario come to fruition. Those star-crossed lovers didn't know what they were doing. Palm Beach is not only a small town, it's a burg that thrives on gossip, be it true, false, or so what? They say a secret whispered over lunch at Cafe L'Europe would be the topic of conversation at every dinner table along Ocean Boulevard that night.

Sabrina must be ready to kill both her daughter and Zack Ward. How long would it be before Appleton got wind of this, if he hadn't already? With Cranston's network of informants, he probably was told what the pair were about after their first phone call to the press. What had Cranston said? When people don't know the truth, they speculate. With Gillian looking for exposure rather than anonymity, they wouldn't have to speculate long before hitting on the truth. The boys, I'm sure, were ready to kill Sabrina.

In fact the whole stinking mess had the M word written all over it. But who would take the fall, Gillian, Zack, Sabrina– or Archy?

"Did you know the girl's boyfriend was a newshound for a trashy tabloid? I thought you said they came down here to elope. Looks like they're investigating something that happened before they were born." Lolly didn't know how close those words came to telling him what he wanted to know.

"It's what Sabrina told me," I contended. "And she did mention the girl's beau was in the writing business. But listen, Lol, I'll call Sabrina and see if she'll clue me in to what's going on and then I'll report what I learn to you over dinner at Acquario."

That gave him pause. "When?"

"As soon as I get through to Sabrina. For all we know, Gillian's boyfriend is down here on a busman's holiday, doing research on an old Palm Beach scandal for his paper."

"I don't see why she won't talk to you. Eric told me you two were quite chummy the other day."

And another county is heard from. Just what I needed. "Who's Eric?"

"The bartender you practically thrust upon me. You have great taste, Archy."

"You mean you . . . "

"I stopped in for a drink, as you urged me to, and invited him to a little social do on Phil Meecham's yacht. Trish Barnard was all over him, the floozy."

"Trish Barnard? I though she went for preppie blonds and I thought you had sworn off bartenders."

"It's summer, Archy, and the pickings are lean," Lolly described July in Palm Beach. "But it was all providential. Meeting Eric that is. Phil was looking for a bartender to work his parties and do odd jobs on the boat and Eric auditioned."

"How odd, Lol?"

"Don't ask."

"Okay, I won't. See you around the hangar, Lol."

"In case we miss each other, I'll call to remind you. You did say Acquario?"

FIFTEEN

IF "THE MAN that got away" were a musical composition, we would now be at what I believe is called the crescendo of the piece, with brass, strings, and percussion all at fever pitch. At the crash of the cymbals there would follow an eerie silence before the first soft notes of the next movement would commence. What the new movement would sound like depended upon the composer, for I was beginning to suspect that all that had transpired since Sabrina's arrival on our shores was being cleverly orchestrated by a person or persons unknown.

After meeting with Sabrina, I had referred to her quandary as a plot outline. Wasn't it uncanny that every dire consequence that outline begged was about to happen? It was as if someone were manipulating events based on Sabrina's synopsis, beginning with Opus One, that anonymous call to Lolly Spindrift– the snowball that was on its way to becoming an avalanche.

Who would benefit if the spit hit the fan? Everyone except the fathers-in-waiting. Gillian would get a name both prominent and wealthy. Zack would get a story that could catapult him to fame and riches. Sabrina would get publicity, which she didn't need, but to those who have it shall be added. Who knew the moment Sabrina had arrived in Palm Beach? Only the staff at the Chesterfield– and Sabrina.

Was she truly writing the *pièce de résistance* of her stalwart career and hanging around to see how the last chapter would play out? But Zack Ward was also a writer and didn't Gillian dabble in the art? Like Phineas Taylor Barnum's famous three-rings, there was so much going on at once, one didn't know where to look first. It was like watching a disaster movie from a velour recliner while munching a Milky Way.

MY APPEARANCE IN Mrs. Trelawney's office was met with rancor, not applause. "Where have you been, Archy? It's after three."

"Out buying a microwave oven, as ordered."

"And where is it?"

"With its owner. I delivered it to Binky's quarters."

This did not sit well with the squire's private secretary. "You were supposed to bring it here. The troops are gathering at four."

"I know, Binky told me." With that disclosure she scowled, which suited her mood. "Don't worry, he'll act surprised, he's been practicing all day. And you know I don't attend office functions."

"I thought, with your father away, you would make an

exception and take his place. Especially since Binky is your best friend."

"Hobo is my best friend, Mrs. Trelawney, and the only reason my father shows up is because they all take place right here and he has to pass through to get to the executive loo."

"Nonsense," she chided. "When Evelyn Sharif had her baby, your father gave her a year's supply of Pampers. Wasn't that thoughtful?"

I thought it was disgusting but kept it to myself and tried to look contrite as I placed my expense report on her desk.

"Didn't I just sign one of these?" she protested.

"It's been an exceptional week," I explained.

"I hope the microwave oven is not included under 'miscellaneous.' Gifts are not reimbursable."

"It is not listed under 'miscellaneous,' as you can see from the amount." It was listed under "supplies." "And expenses, as you very well know, are my only means of support, thank you."

"You could try something more honest, like robbing banks."

"If that is all, Mrs. Trelawney, I will bid you *adieu* until we meet again in May."

"May?"

"Yes. May it never happen."

"You missed your calling, Archy. You should have gone on stage like your grandfather." Without pausing to gloat, she took an envelope from the top of her desk and removed its contents. "I've been trying to get you all day. This is addressed to Mr. and Mrs. Prescott McNally and Archibald McNally." Adjusting her glasses she proceeded: " 'I hope you can join me for cocktails at Casa Gran tomorrow evening at seven. Very informal. R.S.V.P.

regrets only. Hope to see you then. Sincerely, Harry Schuyler.' "

"You're jesting," was all I could think to say.

"I am not. It came this morning, by hand if you please. Your father did some work for him a few years back and he's always had his nose out of joint because Schuyler never invited him to Casa Gran and now this comes when he's away. He'll be furious."

Still reeling from the invitation, I thought aloud, "But why me?"

Casa Gran was a Palm Beach showplace on a par with Mar-a-Lago. It was built by Harry's grandmother in the 1930s for a reputed ten million bucks– depression bucks, that is. Multiply it by at least ten to arrive at today's price tag. Grandma Schuyler's father came by way of Detroit and mother via Chicago. It was said that no American could start their car or roast a weenie without giving Dolly Schuyler a buck.

In her prime, Dolly was a friendly competitor of Marjorie Merriweather Post, and it was said that she employed three complete serving staffs, on eight-hour shifts, to cater to the needs of Casa Gran's residents and guests. If one had a yen for a ham sandwich and beer, or a steak dinner, at three in the morning, all one had to do was ring the kitchen. It was also said, sotto voce, that other needs were thoughtfully catered to at Casa Gran.

After the Big War, Dolly's son and his wife set out to best Scott and Zelda. They succeeded with the purchase of their own beach cottage on famous Gin Lane in Southampton, Long Island's famed watering hole. "Thirty-six rooms and ocean vu," as the summer rental ads tout. The lane's name says much about summertime in Southampton.

I didn't need our research librarian to give me details on the life and loves of Dolly's grandson, Harry III. Both were written in headlines from the time he was slapped with a paternity suit when he was a junior at St. Paul's. Yes, kids, the prep school. After Dartmouth, where he excelled at Winter Carnival, he took a flat in New York and welcomed the age of Aquarius with long hair, funny cigarettes, and substances that sounded like the components of alphabet soup.

Always ahead of his time, Harry married a supermodel before there was such a thing as a supermodel. She gave him a son and a divorce after one year, leaving Harry the boy and taking a good chunk of his fortune to France, where she became the companion of a French film star.

After that there came the movie star, the hatcheck girl who wanted to be a movie star, and the tennis pro who wanted to be the fourth Mrs. Harry Schuyler. The twist came with Harry's son who was so far from a chip off the ol' block he could be a genuine mutation. Shy, conservative, and scholarly, he had graduated from Harvard with honors, went on for a Ph.D., and continued for his M.D. According to Lolly Spindrift, Harry IV had been invited to join the staff of the prestigious Rockefeller Institute in New York and was about to announce his engagement to a young lady from a good family, who was herself an M.D.

"Why me?" I repeated.

"I imagine he's being polite," Mrs. Trelawney said. "I called as soon as this came and told Mr. Schuyler's secretary that your parents were away and I would have to tender their regrets. He said he hoped the young Mr. McNally could attend."

It was becoming very clear that the young Mr. McNally was the sought-after guest and his parents a smoke screen.

If my father knew this, his one eyebrow would reach for his hairline before he acquiesced with pleasure. If this wasn't an indirect appeal to Discreet Inquiries, I would cancel my plans for Bianca Courtney. No, I take that back. Even I can be wrong– sometimes.

But why? Young Harry was Snow White in pants and Harry the elder had become a paragon of virtue since his son's rise to prominence. To learn the answer was what made my job so titillating. There's a little bit of scandal-monger in the best of us and a little bit of voyeurism in the rest of us. But take heart, it's said one cannot become a saint until one acknowledges one's sins.

"Isn't Casa Gran usually wrapped in mothballs for the summer with Schuyler shifting to Southampton for the season?"

"That's what I always thought," Mrs. Trelawney answered, "but these days who knows? No one pays any attention to seasons anymore, or anything else for that matter. It's a scandal."

Mrs. Trelawney was beginning to sound like her boss, who subscribed to the London *Times* in order to keep pace with the Court Circular. At breakfast he will tell us the Duchess of Kent is confined to her bed with a cold, and mother will say, "It's going around, dear."

But I love my parents as well as Mrs. Trelawney, who has helped me out of many a jam as well as let me know when I was heading for one. Our verbal sparring keeps her from getting too bossy and me from becoming too cocksure.

If I wasn't already in debt to Lolly, I would see what he could tell me about Schuyler's impromptu cocktail party, but I couldn't afford to feed the scribe on a steady basis. "Did you tell his secretary I would attend?"

"Naturally. And please remember, Archy, you're representing the firm."

"Meaning?"

"Informal means no tie, not Halloween garb. I'm sure you own a nice summer suit. And not that salmon-colored concoction."

"Yes, ma'am. I swim in it and I shall wear it to Casa Gran, without the top."

I WOULD THINK about Casa Gran, the Sabrina Wright imbroglio, and Lolly Spindrift tomorrow, if the planet Earth was still in her orbit and if Archy was still bumming a ride thereon. To assure that I would remain a passenger on that speck in the Milky Way, I would have to attend to Binky Watrous ASAP.

I headed for the mailroom which, incidently, was four times the square footage of my work space. Binky was surprised to see me. "That's the perfect look, Binky, my boy. Save it for your housewarming."

"You don't think my eyes are too wide open, Archy?"

"Not at all, laddie. The wider the better. You're playing to the balcony, remember."

"I think I'll get there a few minutes late to be sure I'm the last to arrive."

Heaven forbid he should get there before a toaster, a corkscrew, or a potato peeler. "I know it's not necessary, but I want to remind you not to breathe a word to Connie, or anyone else, about the Bianca Courtney investigation. The first rule of detective work is to keep your mouth shut and your eyes open."

"I know that, Archy. You can trust me."

Having made the point, I rubbed his face in it. "It's true,

Connie is a friend, but you say something to a friend and that friend passes it on to a friend who is a friend of the guy we're stalking. Discreet, Binky, is the cornerstone of our business. Don't tell anyone about Bianca's suspicions or that I've met with her and may be acting on her behalf."

Looking as if he were taking the oath of allegiance to the French Foreign Legion, he promised, "I won't say a word to anyone. I won't even tell Connie that you know Bianca."

"Fine, Binky. I'm sure I didn't have to remind you, so forgive the presumption. Enjoy your party."

One down and a zillion to go.

Bianca was delighted to hear from me. "Archy," she exclaimed, "I just got off with Antony Gilbert. I told him I wanted to stop by tomorrow to pick up some things I had left in my room, but I didn't tell him you would be with me. I thought the element of surprise would work to our advantage."

The young have such rich imaginations. But, come to think of it, so do the old. The only thing that might surprise Gilbert was not seeing Bianca alone, as I'm sure he was hoping would be the case. The grieving widower would not take kindly to Archy. I hoped to talk Bianca out of the visit this evening.

"Could we get together later to discuss the situation, Bianca? I like to know as much as I can about the people involved before I tackle a case. What you gave me this afternoon was rather sketchy."

"Why, yes, Archy. Would you like to come here?"

"How about I come by and take you out to dinner?" Did I detect a moment's hesitation? "If you'd rather not . . . "

"Oh no. I would," she assured me, and I believed her because I wanted to believe her. "Where would we go? I only ask so I'll know what to wear. Binky told me about your club. Would we be going there?"

Only if you want to see me strangled with a royal-blue bath towel. "Do you like shore dinners?" I asked.

"I do, Archy."

"Then let's go to Charley's Crab. There's a lovely ocean view from the bar and the crab cakes are so good you could eat the plate they come on."

"Fine. Is seven okay?"

"Perfect, Bianca. See you later."

"And thanks again, Archy."

"*Por nada, señorita.*"

Two down.

WHAT A LONG and arduous day it had been. I had been followed by a stretch limo and ended up in its backseat with Richard Cranston spilling his guts— and what a startling revelation it was. I'd had to listen to Bianca's life story over coffee, then lunch with Al Rogoff to learn that Bianca's cause was hopeless. Fending off Lolly Spindrift and promising to wine and dine him at Acquario— would ultimately break the bank. I had told Lolly I would call Sabrina Wright and had no intention of doing any such thing. Then the strange and totally surprising invitation to Casa Gran, which led to setting up Connie and Binky to clear my way into the Palm Court without being seen. And, finally, securing a date with Bianca Courtney.

When I got home, I was too tired to swim and opted for a warm bath, which I do when I need to meditate on the slings and arrows of life in the fast lane.

The Ford wagon was in its berth but the kitchen was empty. Ursi and Jamie, therefore, were in their quarters over the garage. Hobo stuck his nose out of his castle and withdrew almost instantly. Is his abode air-conditioned?

Once in my sanctuary I undressed, drew my tub, and added a dollop of scented oil to the warm water– Mountain Pine. One comes out smelling a little like a Christmas tree, but is that bad?

I floated the rubber duckies Connie had given me as a gag– hint, hint, you are immature– then eased myself into the aromatic brew where one's troubles are supposed to melt away and exquisite rapture enfolds the senses. Well, that's what it says on the bottle of Mountain Pine. This was not to be my experience. The rubber duckies reminded me of Connie and my inability to make a commitment to her. *For the likes of such as me, mine's a fine, fine life.* Is it? There are times, like when I'm soaking in a hot tub, that I'm just not sure.

Not too long ago, when Connie had caught me carousing with a young lady, she told me she had considered hiring a hit man and having me blown away. Believe me, with Connie's Cuban cousins by the dozens, this is no idle threat. Lucky for me she reconsidered and decided instead to honor our open relationship by accepting a date with my friend, Ferdy Attenborough. I was shocked to learn that Ferdy had asked her for a date, but having preached the virtues of an open relationship for so many years, I could only say I was glad and hoped she had a good time.

That night, alone, my one small marc was almost more than I could handle. My bed became a carousel which spun in counterpoint to my leaky ceiling. I'm sure Ferdy Attenborough, riding a broomstick, went flying by with a mocking grin on his dumb face. If she did or did not go out with Ferdy, I will never know, because I never asked and Connie never told. Henceforth, Ferdy appeared uncomfortable in my presence, or was I imagining it? One night at the Pelican I ran into him in the men's room. He ran out saying he had made a mistake. Really? Had he intended to use the ladies' room?

After that I was especially attentive to Consuela Garcia and she showed her appreciation in many ways both public and private. This taught me that what is good for the gander is not good for the goose and I am a chauvinist— A. Gide notwithstanding.

I climbed out of the tub and patted myself dry, removing the moisture and leaving behind the scent of Christmas in July. I wrapped myself in one of my favorite kimonos, the one picturing Jack and Jill tiptoeing through the tulips.

I sat at the desk, removed the top from my Mont Blanc, and recorded both the interview with Richard Cranston and the antics of Gillian and Zack. I ended by saying the omens were ominous and, as Ursi had once written on her shopping list, *The Tide is out and there is no Joy.* With this I closed the case of "The Man That Got Away" one mo' time.

SIXTEEN

"I'LL JUST GO powder my nose. Won't be a minute."

That exit line could account for at least a dozen chores milady was on her way to performing while her gentleman caller cooled his heels. When he took her home, if all went well, she would excuse herself with, "I'll just slip into something comfortable." Or did that happen only in the movies?

I was cooling my heels in Bianca Courtney's parlor on cement blocks, sipping a white wine that had never been within a mile of a cork. It was dreadful. Bianca did not keep hard liquor in the house, owing, no doubt, to her mother's caution, "Candy is dandy, but liquor is quicker."

I reflected sadly upon why I was sitting in a railroad car decorated in buttons and bows, boxed in by Al Rogoff's sleeper and Binky Watrous's caboose. Final answer: pure lust. Bianca's idea of decor was to bring the outside inside. Every piece of fabric had a flower motif, many with birds and bees and butterflies, all on the wing. I would happily trade the wine for an antihistamine nasal spray.

Bianca had greeted me dressed in peach linen slacks and a blouse just a shade lighter. The blouse was of a material so gossamer that as she moved, one caught glimpses of her bra. I found this distracting. The outfit, accessorized with a pair of finely crafted leather sandals and a tiny matching baguette bag, bespoke not only a casual chic, but expensive taste. If these trappings were due to the largesse of the late Lilian Ashman Gilbert, I could see why Bianca was incensed at the lady's passing, but not a reason to point a finger at poor Mr. Gilbert.

Seeing her peach ensemble, I was glad I had avoided pastels for the occasion and had chosen instead white jeans with a button fly and a boat-neck cotton pullover from JHG in navy. I thought it befitting for a shore dinner, and besides, it made me feel like Gene Kelly dancing with Jerry the mouse. Knowing when to compete and when to withdraw, my T-shirt was not visible beneath the pullover.

Upon returning, Bianca had added a lightweight pashmina wrap to her costume, but not a discernable trace of powder to her pretty nose. "I'm ready, but we can wait if you want to finish your wine," she said.

"No, no," I protested. "Let's go. Our reservation is for eight and they do get testy. It's a popular joint. I'll just leave this in the kitchen." Where it might discourage night crawlers, and I did not mean Binky and Al. When the summer sun sets, Florida vibrates with the pitty-pat of many-footed creatures of the night.

I had parked in Binky's space– was there no limit to

my brass?– and once again lucked out with Al Rogoff's carport empty. He was at work today, so he was most likely at some highbrow offering this evening, incognito. Last winter Al attended the Jacques Thibaud String Trio at Dreyfoos Hall in the Kravis Center and was in ecstasy for weeks. Tweeny does not understand why Al refuses all invitations to enjoy an evening at her digs viewing wrestling or the Roller Derby on her mammoth TV. "I pay the cable company extra to get those channels," she tells Al, who is not sympathetic.

It was a refreshingly cool evening, the sky cloudy and dark. "The top is down," Bianca cleverly noted. "It looks like rain."

I opened the door for her and sang, *"Last night we met, and I dream of you yet, with the wind and the rain in your hair."*

She giggled. "What's that?"

"An old song."

"How old?" she insisted.

I got in the driver's seat and started the engine. "How old are you, Bianca?"

"Twenty-two."

I shifted and got us free of Binky's space and onto the road leading out of the Palm Court. "Let's say the song is older than you but younger than King Tut."

"How old are you, Archy?"

"Older than you but younger than King Tut."

"Binky told me how old you are," she said, laughing. It was such a pleasant sound. Like a child poking fun at a doting uncle. Should I have worn a black mustache and a cape instead of bells and boat neck? I must do something about my cravings. Was there a twelve-step program? I would ask Dr. Gussie.

Her laugh was charming, but her question was disconcerting. If Binky had disclosed my age, why did she ask? Was she testing my integrity? Was she clever or obtuse? Was I on a fool's errand? How wide the ocean? How deep the sea? Questions, questions. "Binky lies," I said.

"But he's cute. Do you know he does birdcalls?"

Blessed mother of Sam Spade, did that boy really do his pathetic birdcalls for her? But why not? He does them for anyone forced to listen. "Yes," I said. "I do know. His loony bird is remarkably accurate."

"Oh, Archy," she scolded, and rested her head on my shoulder.

Her perfume was potent and top-of-the-line. Her hair, moving gently in the breeze, wafted over my right ear. I was an excellent driver, even one-handed . . .

"Binky told me you have a steady girl," she said matter-of-factly, as if commenting on the price of gowns at Martha Phillips on The Esplanade.

And I had foolishly spared Binky's life this very afternoon. Did he do nothing over his Chinese takeout with Bianca but talk about me and imitate birds? "Binky has a big mouth, and as I said a few moments ago, he lies. I see someone more often than I see others, that is true, but she is not my so-called steady and we have an open relationship. Why only recently she was out with Ferdy Attenborough, a good friend of mine. They had a delightful time."

"That's nice. Did you tell her you were taking me to dinner tonight?"

Clever or obtuse? Something told me to keep both hands on the steering wheel as prescribed by law. "I didn't because I do not have to report to her on my whereabouts. In fact, she is dining with Binky at the Pelican as we speak." And I was up to my chin in cow dip.

"Is that why we're going to Charley's Crab?"

"There's a gun in the glove compartment, dear; would you pass it to me? I promise to stop before I shoot myself in the foot again."

"Oh, relax, Archy," she said, putting her hand on my knee. How that gesture was supposed to relax me I'll never know. All it did was cause a muscle spasm that sent the speedometer up ten notches. "I was involved in an open relationship for two years."

"When was that?"

"At college. He played basketball. He was a mile high and an inch wide. I like the type."

I sucked in my tummy and almost keeled over. "What happened?" I asked.

"He had an open relationship with six other girls."

"Surely not six?"

"Six, Archy. Tall and thin gives 'em endurance, like on the court. When we all found out about each other, we had a meeting and drew straws. I lost."

"Who won?"

"Virginia Miles. She was tall and thin."

"I must say your generation is casual about these things. I remember poor Tim Hicks, who was tall and thin and engaged in multiple open relationships in our freshman days at Yale. When the ladies compared notes, they formed a vigilante group to liberate Tim from his pants. It was the day Tim had mislaid his clean laundry, and he was running about with nothing under his jeans but Tim."

Bianca laughed that laugh and squeezed my knee. If she kept that up, we would qualify for the Daytona 500. We had reached Ocean Boulevard and I turned south.

"What happened to Tim?" she wanted to know.

"As I recall, he was bombarded with invitations from

women as far south as Miami and as far north as the Canadian border."

"Oh, Archy!"

Was she blushing? I fear not. But my knee was.

At Charley's Crab we had time for a drink at the bar, which offers an ocean view. The sky was remarkably clear over the horizon, cutting a sliver of blue across a dark sea. The prevailing cloud cover might pass before it rained on my parade. There were a few couples at the bar and several diners circling the salad bar. "What's your pleasure?" I asked my date.

"What are you having?"

This told me she wasn't a drinker and afraid of ordering the wrong thing. I would bet my authentic NY Yankees baseball cap that the preference at the U of Miami was for Alabama Slammers or a cup of grain-alcohol punch dipped from a trash can. Drawing straws? Wait till I told Mrs. Trelawney that one.

I ordered two apple martinis. "Trust me. You'll like it."

"I do trust you, Archy. To pin the goods on Antony Gilbert."

She persisted like a locomotive at full steam and Antony Gilbert was tied to the tracks. The only thing I was going to take a pin to was her balloon. I promised Binky I would let her down gently, but why should I keep a promise to someone who said nasty things behind my back? Like my age.

The bartender put our drinks before us and I raised mine to her. We touched glasses and sipped. "Hummm, this is good," she said.

"You didn't tell me Gilbert was returning the barbell from the recycling bin where it had been used as a paperweight, and the housekeeper confirmed his explanation."

She didn't like this one iota and let me know it. "Who told you that?"

"Sergeant Al Rogoff of the PBPD," I said.

"You told him you were acting on my behalf?" She spoke as if I had betrayed a confidence.

"Calm down, missy. I am not acting on your behalf, because I don't think you have a case. You told me what you suspected and I agreed to meet with Gilbert. That's all. But you didn't level with me, and so I feel no obligation to bother the guy."

She was seething and drinking much too fast, neither of which helped her cause. Did she look this way the day she lost her basketball player? "I thought you asked me out to discuss the case. You like to get particulars, or did I misunderstand?"

Clever or obtuse? Definitely clever. "It was an excuse to have dinner with a pretty girl, okay? I'm not ashamed of it. And stop gulping that drink; it's supposed to be enjoyed."

"I'm so mad I could spit," she said. "Why did you go running to Al Rogoff?"

This was going from bad to badder in leaps and bounds. A few stools away, a couple was looking at us and so was the bartender. That's all I needed– to get bounced out of Charley's Crab and onto the police blotter with a pretty girl in tow. How do I get into these situations? Easy. I work very hard at it. About this time Connie would be giving Binky his towels and Priscilla would be handing over her cutting block. Would I be missed?

Coming back to the present, I told Bianca, "I went to Al because I'm a professional. I don't compete with the police, I work with them. I wanted to know what ground they had covered in their investigation of Mrs. Gilbert's death so I would not waste my time reinventing the wheel.

Doesn't that make sense?" Fearing she would say it didn't, I went on to tell her how foolish it was of her to ask the police to dust for prints on the barbell. "It's Gilbert's home. His prints should be all over the place, and he didn't deny carrying the barbell back to where it belonged."

Looking contrite, she made a hopeless gesture with her shoulders. "I know it was foolish, but I was desperate. He had everything worked out so perfectly I was grasping at straws."

Grasping straws was definitely not the poor child's forte. "What did he have worked out? He was at breakfast and she was taking her swim. Sounds like the usual morning routine."

"Oh no," she cried. "It wasn't. Both the housekeeper and I were out of the house."

"Where were you, Bianca?"

"At Publix, shopping with the housekeeper."

"Did you usually accompany her shopping?"

"No." She was so thrilled to be making a point, her cheeks flushed and her hands waved in the air as she spoke. "No, never. But that morning Lilian asked me to go with Louisa, the housekeeper, because she wanted me to pick up fresh cut flowers for the dinner table that night. She always said I had an eye for flowers, and friends were coming."

I didn't see the point and I told her so. "What did Gilbert have to do with this?"

As if exasperated by my inability to see what was perfectly clear to her, she sighed and said, "Tony must have told her to get me out of the house that morning."

"But why?" I could have throttled her.

With a quick glance from right to left she told me, "They sometimes swam together in the nude– at Tony's instigation, of course, and poor Lilian couldn't resist. He must have suggested it that morning and I was gotten rid of."

I wasn't put off by the thought of a woman Lilian Ashman Gilbert's age doing the backstroke in the buff. Lady Cynthia Horowitz, Connie's boss, has been known to do the Australian crawl in her birthday suit and Lady C admits to celebrating seventy of those anniversaries. As with Hollywood folk, I add five years. Although Lady C has a face that could stop Big Ben, her figure has been, shall we say, an inspiration to many.

"By your own admission, Bianca, it wasn't unusual for the two to cavort like Adam and Eve prior to sampling the apple tart."

"But never in the morning," she declared.

"Yeah, and never on Sunday." The captain was beckoning. I told the bartender to transfer the tab to our dinner bill and left a few bucks on the bar. "I'm starved," I said, taking Bianca's arm.

"Are you going to come with me tomorrow, Archy?"

"We'll discuss it after dinner."

Did I happen to mention that Charley's Crab features "cozy, tucked-away dining areas"? No? It must have slipped my mind.

"This is cozy," Bianca said, as if she had read the ad.

"And tucked away to boot," I pointed out. "Let's not order another drink and have a nice white with dinner." I asked the captain for the wine list.

"I didn't think you liked wine," Bianca said. "You hardly touched the glass I gave you."

"Because it was appalling, dear. But hang on to it. In a few days it will be perfect for a vinaigrette."

With a deadpan delivery, Bianca said, "Binky brought it last night when he came to dinner."

Our cozy, tucked-away dining area pulsated with silence. Then Bianca laughed so loud I feared the captain would withhold the wine list. "Oh, Archy, you step in doo-doo every time out. Wait till I tell Binky."

"No. I will tell Binky. The boy is a menace to himself and others. Now hush while I concentrate." I was torn between a white Burgundy, a Graves, and a Taminer. I went with the Burgundy. "Would you like to share a seafood pasta pagliara to start?"

"It sounds yummy. What is it?"

"Egg pasta. Paglia is Italian for hay. There is a dish called paglia e fieno, straw and hay, which is egg-and-spinach noodles. *Delizioso.*"

"You know a lot about food, Archy."

"A hobby and a huge capacity to enjoy all life has to offer. Here's our wine, tell me what you think."

The waiter had me inspect the label before he removed the cork from the bottle. I nodded because one is supposed to nod when shown you're getting what you asked for. After removing the cork he poured my libation. I sipped, pursed my lips, and nodded my approval. In all my years of dining out in the better chop houses from Palm Beach to New Haven, I have never seen anyone sip, grimace, and request another vintage.

He poured Bianca's before refilling my glass. Civilized customs are so time-consuming. When accompanying a lady into the backseat of a car, do you know she should plop right by the door, forcing her knight to crawl over her legs to plop beside her?

"This is good," Bianca said, "but I wouldn't have minded another apple martini."

"One should not drink them with dinner. It simply ain't done." If nothing else, I would teach her a few things before the night came to a close. As it turned out, she had a few lessons of her own to impart.

Our pasta arrived looking good enough to eat. "Will it leave room for the crab cakes?" Bianca wondered.

"And a few claws, I'm sure."

I must say she had a healthy appetite and with good reason. The pasta was *molto delizioso*. She forgot about her vendetta against Antony Gilbert long enough for us to enjoy polite conversation over our meal. In the seesaw between clever and obtuse, I will say that Bianca Courtney was a little bit of both. Like the very young, she knew a little bit about a lot of things and a whole lot about nothing.

She was remarkably naive about her former employer's desire to marry an obvious gigolo. "How could she do it?" And blasé regarding her brother. "Ken is gay but very well adjusted to his sexual orientation. I guess he's getting it on with his new roommate in New York." The young think they have an exclusive copyright on sex.

Her major was computer science and her minor was, of all things, psychology.

"What did you intend to do with the computer science?" I questioned.

"I intended to marry someone young, cute, and very rich. If it didn't happen, I could teach."

Ask a stupid question . . .

To do justice to the crab cakes and claws, we limited ourselves at the salad bar to the basic greens– crisp iceberg, leafy spinach, romaine, Bibb, arugula, and radicchio for color. We both avoided the vinaigrette dressing. One of the joys of summer is freshly picked tomatoes, which we enjoyed, sliced, with nothing but sea salt, cracked pepper, some torn fresh basil, and a tiny drizzle of olive oil. I ordered a second bottle of wine, and although I imbibed more than my share, Bianca wasn't far behind.

"Are you trying to get me drunk, Archy?"

"But of course. Omar recommended a loaf of bread, a jug of wine, and thou."

"Good for Omar. Art thou dessert?"

"I thought the crème caramel if you don't mind. It goes down so much easier than your sass."

She began to laugh. "Oh, come on. I'm just having some fun with you. You got me here under false pretenses and now you're wondering what you're going to do with me. You don't want to go back to my place where your red car will stick out like a neon calling card, and you wouldn't dare take me to a motel because I wouldn't go. Checkmate."

She was a barrel of laughs, all at my expense. "What do you suggest, Ms. Courtney?

"Have the crème caramel, Archy, and we'll take a walk on the beach. Then you can drop me off– real fast."

"He who makes love on the beach knows the meaning of true grit."

"Archy, that one is older than you."

"But younger than King Tut."

THE CLOUDS WERE dispersing to uncover small patches of stars, but the moon remained hidden. The steady sound of the surf and the distant sound of cars moving north and south on the A1A are the heartbeat of Palm Beach. With a beautiful woman in your arms, it takes on the tremor of a rhapsody.

"Do you kiss on a first date, Bianca?"

"Only when I'm asked."

She was warm, tender, yielding, and doing the most amazing things with her hands. "Did you learn that in college?"

"No, high school. Oh, buttons. How quaint. Will you come with me to meet Tony tomorrow?"

"You little devil, you have me by my compromising position."

"That's the idea. Yes or no, Archy?"

What's a Discreet Inquirer to do? "Yes. Yes, yes, yes."

SEVENTEEN

As YOU MAY have guessed, I awoke late the following morning and Ursi surprised me with one of my breakfast favorites, kippers and scrambled eggs.

"Everyone is talking about Sabrina Wright and her daughter, Archy. Have you heard about it?" Ursi asked as she poured my coffee.

"I've heard something, Ursi. What are people saying?"

"It seems Sabrina Wright's daughter, Gillian, and her boyfriend are down here looking up old society news stories at the library. Well, Mrs. Marsden over at Lady Cynthia's says that Lady C thinks the daughter and her boyfriend must be looking for someone from these parts who was on the social scene some years back. And Hanna Ventura told Lady Cynthia that Sabrina adopted the girl, Gillian, as a single parent and raised her in the lap of luxury. Mrs. Ventura read about it in *Vanity Fair,* and she thinks the girl is looking for her true mother who may be someone we all know. There could be a scandal brewing, Archy, as we speak."

Dear Hanna didn't know how close she was to the truth. But with that kind of talk going around and the only other parent one could have was the father, Appleton and Cranston must be quivering in their limos.

In the interest of learning what other rumors were making the rounds, I queried, "So what else have you heard, Ursi?"

Jamie, as always, sipped his coffee while reading the morning paper and listening to every word. They say N. Bonaparte, né Buonaparte, could also read and listen at the same time, and look what they did to him. Would Jamie one day be exiled to Fisherman's Island in Lake Worth?

"The girl's boyfriend," Ursi continued on pouring a cup for herself, "is a newspaper reporter, and he's going to write about the investigation. You know, many adopted people now go in search of their natural parents. It's exciting. But if the girl's natural mother put her up for adoption and signed away all rights, she wouldn't know the girl had been taken in by a famous author. Won't she be surprised, Archy?"

"That's one way of putting it," I said with a thoughtful nod.

Here Ursi confided, "Mrs. Marsden was wondering if Lady C is the natural mother. You know she's had so many husbands and a few on the side, if you'll excuse the expression."

"You're excused."

"So Sabrina Wright didn't come down here to stop her daughter from eloping, as she told you, Archy. She came to either help or hinder the girl's search. That's what Mr. Anderson told Simone."

"Simone, Ursi?"

"She's the Andersons' upstairs girl," Ursi said.

As noted, when you get enough people taking potshots at the same target, someone is bound to hit the bull's-eye. The only saving grace was that no one would know whose arrow had hit the mark. Apropos of nothing, did Mrs. Anderson know her husband kept Simone upstairs?

I stood, looking rather fit in a crisp cord suit from Chipp, pale green (I believe it is now known as celadon) button-down shirt with open collar, and loafers. Must I say no socks? Socks with loafers in Palm Beach in July is just not done, like diamond tiaras at lunch or pinky rings on gentlemen. "I have to be on my way," I told the couple.

"Don't forget the folks will be home in a few days," she reminded me. "Doesn't the time fly?"

I would be happy and relieved to have the lord and lady of our manor back. I especially missed Mother and at this juncture would even welcome the advice and consent of Father regarding the unenviable positions of Thomas Appleton and Richard Cranston. Or did I just long to retaliate and drop a few names over cocktails? And I had not forgotten my invitation to Casa Gran this evening. Oh, Prescott will be green with envy, tugging on his mustache and sending his one eyebrow toward the ceiling.

Jamie followed me out to our driveway, and surmising he had something to add to the morning gossip, I paved the way with, "What do you hear, Jamie?" I asked because Jamie pioneered in *don't ask, don't tell* politics.

"Bit of a flap over at the Cranstons' is what I hear." With Jamie, that could mean anything from a collapsed soufflé to murder.

"Any details?" I encouraged.

"Seems Mr. Cranston sent his regrets to an invitation from the White House. Big social event. Dinner for fifty and then some guy was going to play the cello for the guests. Mrs. Cranston was furious and let him know it as well as everyone else in the house. She got so testy, Cook almost quit."

This misbegotten affair was taking its toll on the natives. One got the feeling that everyone on the island was holding their breath, waiting for the other shoe to drop. The most disturbing fact to those concerned must be that there was nothing they could do about it, and frustration is a dangerous humor. Blow the whistle and the jig's up. Keeping quiet could get the same result. Sabrina, the paradigm of bargain makers, was the only one in a position to stop Gillian from her inane prying, but was having no success, it seemed. But did Sabrina truly want to stop her?

"Anyone know why Cranston turned down his old fraternity brother?"

Hobo joined us to eavesdrop. Jamie slipped him a treat and Hobo retreated back to his home. "Seems he doesn't want to leave Palm Beach at the moment, is what the staff hears. Why, they don't know."

Neither does poor Mrs. Cranston, which accounted for her rage. With three unmarried daughters, she couldn't afford to turn down invitations where eligible bachelors roamed the range like bison. Ursi's info was secondhand hearsay, while Jamie's was straight-to-the-point fact. He wouldn't think anything else was worth opening his mouth for. I slipped him a *pourboire* along with a thank-you and hopped in my Miata.

As I headed for the Palm Court, I speculated upon how much longer this farce could go on before something gave. But what or who would give was the question. Did Appleton call Sabrina? Did Cranston? If so, had she agreed to see them? And what could she say other than she was sorry she told Gillian as much as she had and promise to stop her– their?– daughter from causing any more talk than she already had? Could Sabrina do it twice, without cracking a smile? She could. But would it be enough? I was tempted to call her, but remained unyielding in my resolve to mind my own business and let the chips fall where they may, as long as they didn't land on poor Archy's head.

Why was I going to the Palm Court? Because little Miss Buttons and Bows had twisted my– er– arm until I agreed to see Antony Gilbert. I must say the girl was as subtle as a rattlesnake and just as mesmerizing. The younger generation is a many-splendored thing, let me tell you. Children in adult garb, they are both vampiric and satyric. I should have sent her packing last night with a sound reprimand. I did not because I wanted to see just how far she would go to attain her goal. Not all the way, but not all that bad either. Did the end justify the means? Well, I'm on my way to do her bidding.

No stretch limos on my tail this morning, but Al Rogoff's car was in its bay. Binky, of course, was at work. If Al didn't happen to be looking out his window, I'm sure Mrs. Brewster across the way would ring him up to announce that the red car was back without the stretch limo.

Bianca was out her door before I had a chance to close the Miata's ignition. She came running to the car wearing white shorts and a man's pink dress shirt with the sleeves rolled up and the tails hanging out. She had her hair pulled back and tied with a white satin ribbon and a U of Miami baseball cap on her head and sneakers on her feet. She looked so good she should be illegal.

"Do you think that's the proper attire for our mission?" I asked as she got into the car.

"Relax, Archy, I dressed down to throw Tony off the scent. You know, casual. Hi, bye, in, out. Let him guess what we're doing." She pulled the baseball cap on tighter as we picked up speed.

"Don't worry, he'll know what we're doing there. I'm sure you didn't hide your displeasure at the police for not carting him off in handcuffs. I hope he lets us in. He doesn't have to, you know."

"He'll let us in. He likes Lolitas, which is really why I got myself gussied up like Betty Cheerleader."

Her candor was amazing. "Did you enjoy our dinner date?" I questioned.

"Sure. Especially the dessert," she answered.

"You mean the crème caramel?"

"If that's what they're calling it these days."

"You are a vixen, missy, and I should take you over my knee." I reconsidered in a split second and cautioned, "And don't you dare say what you're thinking."

She laughed. "Oh, poor Archy. We had some fun last night and he's on a guilt trip. Forget it. I have."

That was unsettling. "I have a cocktail party this evening . . ."

"How jolly."

"I repeat. I must attend a cocktail party this evening. Business, you know. But we could meet for dinner after. Say about eight."

"Only if you take me to the Pelican Club."

"I would rather not, Bianca."

"Why, are you ashamed of me?"

"You know that's not true. I was thinking of something a little more upscale, like Chez Jean-Pierre. Cassoulet, fresh Dover sole . . . "

"Crème caramel," came her sharp tongue. Then, unable to contain herself, she laughed that child's laugh to let me know it was all a tease. "I am going to the Pelican tonight, Archy."

"Not with me, you're not," I said.

"I know that, silly. I'm going with Binky. He called this morning and invited me."

"Binky?" I exploded.

"Yes. What's wrong with that? We're going to look over his loot and then go to dinner. He's a very nice guy, Archy, and he likes me."

"I know he does, Bianca. Don't trifle with him, please. He hurts easily."

"So do I, Archy."

ZAP! I had been put in my place and I didn't like it– but it was where I belonged. In a corner with the dunce cap on my pointed head. I had deluded myself into thinking she had fallen for the McNally charm. Think again, Archy. She had been the seductress, going only as far as needed to get her way. If she was looking for romance, she wanted to find it with someone who didn't plan each date as if it were a mission impossible.

Could you blame her? If you have lost a boyfriend, both parents, and a magnanimous employer before you've hit the quarter-century mark, you build up your defenses and become very suspicious of someone like me and my microwave oven.

"This will not be Jean-Pierre's lucky night," I conceded.

"If you take your lady to the Pelican, we could make it a foursome."

I would rather stick pins in my eyes.

She directed me to the Gilbert residence, which was on the Intercoastal down toward South Palm Beach. A pink one-story villa, it lacked only matching flamingos on the lawn. It screamed two million, give or take. The planting was old even if the money was new. The front door looked like the entrance to a harem den in an old Maria Montez movie. No one answered our ring. Good. We could go home.

"He must have fired Louisa," Bianca said. "Let's go 'round back."

A flagstone path led along the side of the house and to the rear yard. It was a long walk, but pleasant, thanks to the carefully landscaped shrubbery, palms, and royal poincianas. We heard the splash of a diver, an eerie sound considering why we were there, before we turned the bend and came upon the rear patio and pool. The diver was now swimming, and a man I believed to be Antony Gilbert was seated at a wrought-iron and glass table in a white terry robe, balancing a cup and saucer in one hand and a cigarette in the other. It was a typical late-morning Palm Beach scene.

At the sight of Bianca and me, he put down his coffee, rose, and came toward us. "Bianca, my dear. What a pleasure. It's been too long."

The British accent wasn't bad as far as phony British accents go, and Antony Gilbert wasn't bad if you liked the phony British accent type. I could see him in a third-rate touring company of Noel Coward's *Private Lives*. I have identified and studied two types of the male species who inhabit South Florida in packs I call *The Fringe Set*. You know the type– the guys who are perpetually on the outside, hoping to get in.

First we have the Papa Hemingways. They are especially prevalent in the Keys. Bulky, past their prime, with grizzled beards and fishing caps, they drink only rum and sport a single golden earring and a ponytail. They lust after busty women in bikinis and are usually impotent.

Then there are the Cary Grants. Clean-cut, tall, slim, British accent of dubious origin, charming, and witty. They lust after rich women and are usually bisexual. I have already told you what side Tony Gilbert bats for.

"Hello, Tony," Bianca said, all smiles. "This is my friend Archy McNally. He gave me a ride. You know how I hate to drive."

Gilbert and I shook. "A pleasure, Archy. If I may?"

"You may, Tony."

The swimmer did laps, and if my eyes didn't deceive me, I would say it was a she in the pool. A long, slim, yet curvaceous she. Tony had certainly settled in since his loss.

In keeping with taking Gilbert by surprise, Bianca blurted, "Is Louisa not here?"

"No," Gilbert said. "I'm afraid Louisa has left us. She was made an offer she couldn't refuse and didn't. I do the best I can, which is not very good, so if you have a dust allergy, Bianca dear, I suggest you keep out of the house."

"No allergies, Tony, so I'll just run in and take a peek at my old room. I'm missing a charm bracelet I think I left in the top dresser drawer. Won't be a minute, Archy."

It was as painful as listening to amateurs putting on a Passion play. We watched her until she slid open the glass door and entered the house. Gilbert put out his cigarette in an ashtray and turned to me.

"The drawers in her old room are all empty. She knows that. I know that. And you know that. Correct, Archy?"

I don't like having people pointing at the egg on my face, but who could blame the guy? "She's young and foolish," was the best I could offer by way of an excuse.

"Young, but not foolish, and she loves to drive. Would you care to sit? She may be hours. It's a big house, full of drawers."

I sat. "I did try to discourage her from coming," I said. "But she's very headstrong as I imagine you know."

"It isn't very pleasant being hounded by someone who thinks you're guilty of murder." Taking a pack of cigarettes from the pocket of his robe, he offered me one before lighting up.

"No, thanks. I quit. I think."

"Bully for you." He sat and blew smoke in the air. "How did you get involved with little Bianca, may I ask?"

I told him the truth without going into too much detail, like revealing my profession. "And I did try to discourage the visit."

"I know she's at that trailer court. Did she tell you I invited her to stay here until she found work elsewhere?" Before I answered, he hurried on. "Let me tell you something, Archy. I'm a man past his prime who's been to the rodeo and back, as they say. I've been an actor, a bartender, a maitre d', and a hustler, without much success at any of the above. I hooked on to the brass ring a few times, but it always slipped away for one reason or another.

"Then along came Lilian Ashman, the answer to a working boy's prayer. Did I love her? You know I didn't and so does our Bianca, I'm sure. Did she love me? I'm sure she did. And you know what, mister? I made her happy. She paid the price and I gave value for her money. I'm very good at that. When I learned about her will, did I try to get her to change it? Is the pope Catholic? However, I am not as headstrong as dear Bianca, so didn't push the issue. Finesse is my long suit.

"Lilian wasn't that old, so I didn't have to worry. I was a willing captive in a pink Palm Beach villa and thought I was set for life. Then Lilian dove into the pool."

The present occupant of the pool now climbed out of it like Aphrodite emerging from her shell and walked majestically toward us. She was six feet high, barefoot, remember, and wearing a thong bottom and a bra top that covered only the essentials. Her hair, red and dripping wet, was pulled away from her face and fell down her back almost to her waist.

I rose on unsteady feet. "Please, don't get up," she called, extending a wet hand.

"This is Babette." Gilbert introduced us. "She holds a bronze medal in the backstroke and free-form for the French. Babette was born in Algiers."

"The Kasbah," Babette pinpointed her hometown. "My mother sold favors, my father was a steady customer."

"Hush," Gilbert chided her. "You must excuse her, Archy, she likes to shock. Actually, her mother was a schoolteacher and her father was in the diplomatic corps. This is Archy McNally, Babs; he's a friend of Bianca's. She's inside examining our drawers– furniture, that is."

"Naughty girl," Babette said. "She wants to send poor Tony to the pen. May I have your robe, darling?"

"Sorry, but there's nothing but me beneath it," Gilbert told her.

"So?" Babette said with a shrug, "We're all friends, no, Mr. McNally?"

"Sorry, Babette, but we've just met," I said. I couldn't

take my eyes off her and she reveled in the attention. No wonder Louisa had left. She must have gone off screaming. The place was a zoo.

"Run along, Babs, and go dry off," Gilbert advised. "I haven't finished with Mr. McNally."

"I run, but not with pleasure. Mr. McNally is cute. Do you swim, Mr. McNally?"

"Two miles every day, in the Atlantic. We don't have a pool."

"Do you like to do it on your back, Mr. McNally?"

"Will you get out of here," Gilbert insisted.

Babette giggled, an incongruous sound owing to her amazing proportions. She, too, disappeared behind the sliding glass door, looking as alluring from aft as from fore.

"I met her in Vegas," Gilbert told me. "She worked the blackjack table where not even the most dedicated gambler could keep count. I saw a visiting fireman ask for a pull with two kings showing."

"Is she staying with you?" I asked.

"Where else? Babette came to comfort me as soon as she heard of my loss. And a loss it was, Archy. I may be able to keep the house, which is doubtful at this time, but I couldn't afford the upkeep, naturally."

"It should net you a good sum," I remarked, my mind on other things. Algiers in July? Why not? It would broaden my horizons, among other things. I had been too long in Palm Beach pent, as the poet would say.

Gilbert was laughing and I feared I had missed the joke. "This pink palazzo, my friend, is mortgaged to the hilt. The rich don't pay cash for anything and a huge mortgage has many tax advantages. Now tell me why I would want to murder my benefactress?"

I had to admit it. "You wouldn't."

"Tell that to the lady who's auditioning for the role of chief witness for the prosecution— and here she comes."

I sincerely hoped Bianca would not come rushing at us, waving a charm bracelet and shouting . . .

Bianca came rushing at us waving a charm bracelet and shouting, "I found it. I found it."

Death, where is thy sting?

"Get her out of here, mister, and don't come back," our charming host said by way of a fond farewell.

BACK IN MY car I read her the riot act. "That was the dumbest display I have ever seen in my life. You are loony, Bianca, with a capital *L*."

"Oh," she pouted, "what difference does it make? He knows what we're after."

"As of this moment *we* are not after anything and I suggest *you* stop playing Miss Marple and go find a job. The end."

Undaunted, she went right on. "Did you see the woman he's living with? I met her upstairs. I think she's a dominatrix."

This was too much. "Can it, Bianca."

"Okay. So, what did you think of Tony?"

"I think he's sleazy and a leech who never did an honest day's work in life, and he would sell his soul to the devil for a buck, only he can't because even on a slow day hell won't have him."

"So . . . "

"So nothing. It doesn't make him a guy who would murder to no advantage. He's no dummy, Bianca, and he wouldn't bite the hand that feeds unless he's got a key to the candy store. It's against his religion. His wife's death has left him penniless. Now get off his case– and mine."

"Never," Bianca cried. "Never."

Good grief, she sounded just like Gillian Wright.

EIGHTEEN

CASA GRAN.

There was a panel truck parked near the main gate bearing the logo of a local security service and two guards on duty. These were clearly not Schuyler's regular sentries, so they must have been hired for the occasion. More proof that he had interrupted his summer holiday in Southampton on short notice to put together a cocktail party in July. It made no sense, but then Harry Schuyler always had more dollars than sense.

The car in front of my Miata was being stopped at the gate, and as I came to a halt behind it, I noticed it carried a bumper sticker that read TROY APPLETON, in a blaze of red, white, and blue. It was a harbinger to which I paid scant attention. What was left of my mind after a morning with Bianca Courtney was focused on the Sabrina Wright mess and the Kasbah– the ridiculous and the sublime. Or did I get that backward?

The car ahead moved on and I moved up just as another car lined up behind me. For a quickie reception, someone had done a good job of rallying the freeloaders. But then who would turn down an invitation to Casa Gran? The guard looked into the car, and satisfied that I wasn't carrying an arsenal, waved me through the gate. No name check? This shindig was about as exclusive as a BYOB hop at the Feela Betta Thigh sorority house. Many are called and many more show up. Prescott would not have been pleased.

Thanks to Mrs. Trelawney, I had gotten into a blue suit to represent McNally & Son. For a touch of color I wore it with a tie of vermilion silk. That worked so well I placed a matching hankie in my breast pocket. Humming "I've Got To Be Me," I hastened to Casa Gran at the appointed hour.

It was a good mile drive from the gate to the house on a gracefully winding road. The flora, reputed to be in the care of fifty gardeners under the supervision of a landscape architect, was breathtaking, to say the least. After the final curve, Casa Gran appeared like a shimmering mirage rising out of the sea.

An amber marble palace sitting on twenty oceanfront acres with a spa and pool in the basement, another indoor pool on the second floor, another on the roof, and one out back, it also boasted tennis courts, both clay and grass courts, croquet, squash, and a baseball diamond for the kiddies. So much for the recreational facilities. The serious business of living was conducted in quarters larger than life.

Like playing follow-the-leader, I pulled up to the porte cochère, where one of several car jockeys opened the Miata's door and handed me a numbered ticket as I got out.

Up the stairs to a grand portal guarded by a guy in a tux who pointed thataway while intoning, "Cocktails in the solarium, sir." I was on a marble terrace, wider than many country roads, which appeared to girdle the entire house. There was now a group of us, couples and singles, on the march.

Where the terrace angled to follow the Casa Gran's contours, the ocean came into view and my fellow travelers and I joined the party that spilled out of the solarium and onto the promenade. Waiters proffered trays of champagne and canapés, music came from nowhere, and the early evening air was alive with the tinkle of glasses and the hum of conversation. The sky over the Atlantic was growing dark and tiny white lights in trees and shrubs began to twinkle like diamonds. Hey, who knows, maybe they were diamonds.

The solarium and terrace were separated by a series of glass doors that created a wall when all were closed and a multitude of entrances when all were open, as they were for the party. I made my way through the pretty people, and entering a vast room full of more pretty people, I found myself at a political caucus for State Senator Troy Appleton. For this I got a *by-hand* invitation? No way. There was something rotten in Casa Gran; that's why Archy was sent for. I say this with pride, not scorn.

Troy Appleton and his wife stood in the center of the room receiving Harry Schuyler's guests. Troy looked like Flash Gordon, all golden and smiling a million bucks worth of caps. His wife wore a chic ice-blue Paris frock that was so perfectly understated it told the world she had not only borrowed Jackie O's hair, she had also latched on to Monsieur Givenchy. If Troy made it to Washington, she would have to find herself an American couturier. I wondered if she thought Troy's aspirations worth the compromise.

Next to the smiling couple was Troy's dad, Thomas Appleton. Our eyes locked on each other from across the room, and poor Tom reacted as if he'd just seen a ghost. He actually blinked before he forced himself to break the visual contact. Tom Appleton was not happy to see me, therefore he had not insisted on my presence. I got in line, grabbing a dollop of caviar on a sliver of toast from a passing waiter. It was the real thing.

"Hello. Glad you could make it." Troy Appleton greeted me with a smile that must by now be hurting his face, and a handshake that attested to his prowess on a polo pony.

"I'm Archy McNally."

"Nice to know you, Archy. May I present my wife, Virginia."

Virginia gave me her hand, which was small and soft and warm. We touched fingers. "How do you do," Virginia said. "I like your tie and pocket square, Mr. McNally. So original."

"Thank you, ma'am. You are most kind."

"And my father, Tom Appleton," Troy continued his introductions.

Tom and I shook hands. "How nice to meet you, sir," I said as if I had never laid eyes on the man before this moment.

Looking relieved, Tom said, "Same here, I'm sure. Please help yourself to a drink. If champagne is not your thing, there's a proper bar someplace in this mausoleum."

"I will. Best of luck to you, Troy. You have my vote."

"Well," he said modestly, "it hasn't come to that yet. We're still testing the waters."

Was this a fund-raiser? Was I expected to write a check? Sorry, pal, I spent it all on a microwave oven and dinner for two at Charley's Crab. And the idea of giving this crowd money was obscene.

"Jump in," I counseled. "He who hesitates is lost."

"I'll remember that," Troy said as he stuck his hand out to the guy behind me. "Hello. Glad you could make it."

The music came from two lovely ladies playing piano and flute. I made my way to where they were giving away the hard stuff and ordered a vodka martini with a twist. There were three bartenders in black tie to serve what looked like a stag line at the makeshift bar. When I turned to go in search of caviar and other edibles, I found my way blocked by a man in blazer and ascot.

"Archy McNally?" My host asked.

Harry Schuyler looked like his own grandpa. The years had not been kind, but why should they have been? He had drained every ounce of life out of each one, leaving nothing in reserve. Life on Ocean Boulevard and Gin Lane had taken their toll. His hair was thinning, his face was lined, and he stooped in the manner of old men far too thin for their height.

"It is, sir. Thank you for the invitation."

He was holding a glass filled with sparkling water. Were it spiked, it was with something of the colorless variety. "Your father handled some business for me a while back," Schuyler said. "I understand he's out of town."

"On a cruise with Mother. Not the best time of year to sail in the Caribbean, but it's the only time he can get away. He will be disappointed to have missed the party."

"Nice of you to say so, but I doubt it's true. This is not my affair, as you can plainly see. It's a fund-raiser for young Troy– by the way, you don't have to ante up just because you came."

"I have no intention of doing so, sir."

"Smart boy. As I was saying, it's not my gathering, not at all. Tommy Appleton called me up north and asked if he could use Casa Gran for the happening. The old ark has a certain cachet, as I'm sure you know, and it's been used for far less worthy causes. Tommy and I were at Saint Paul's together, so what the hell.

"As it turned out it worked to my advantage. I wanted an excuse to get back here without people wondering why, and this was my ticket." He concluded by taking a long swig of his drink.

I sipped mine. It was one hell of a martini. The bartenders must have been told to pour liberally to get the folks in a giving mood. "Then you invited me so we could meet accidently on purpose."

"You don't waste words or time, Mr. McNally, and that's just what I want. When doing business, I am a man of few words and presently I am very short of time. I've heard good things about you and they are justified." He took another swig.

"I'm at your service, Mr. Schuyler," I volunteered.

"Have you seen our roof garden?" he asked.

"Only in *Town and Country* and *Architectural Digest*. This is my first visit to Casa Gran."

"Is that a martini you've got there?"

"It is, sir."

He flagged the bartender and ordered another. "Don't rush. I'll leave mine, which is just designer water, and carry your spare. Now follow me."

He led me out of the solarium and into a room twice as big with a vaulted ceiling trimmed in gold leaf. It was furnished with a resplendent array of Queen Anne and Chippendale pieces of museum quality, as the merchants along Antique Row in West Palm describe their wares. "The Grand Salon of Casa Gran," Schuyler lectured, sounding like a tour guide. "The proportions and ceiling are exact replicas of the great room in Catherine's Palace at Tsarskoye Selo. Nana Dolly was mad for the Romanovs. They say the furniture rivals Winterthur."

It was stunning, and about as warm and inviting as an igloo. Where did Nana Dolly kick off her shoes and kick up her heels? He opened another door, and for a change, we stepped into a small room. It was the elevator. A press of the button and we rose. The panel indicated four levels: B, 1, 2, 3. We entered on 1 and ascended to 3. Schuyler opened the door, stepped out ahead of me, and magically lit up the scene. Did I say ascended? Right to heaven.

The pool, lit in a rainbow of colors, was the centerpiece. Surrounding it were more reminders of the landscape architect and his minions. Flowering trees, indigenous shrubs, and formal mini-gardens all theatrically illuminated. Replicas of Greek and Italian sculptures in marble looked down at us from their pedestals, most notably *David,* whose appendage was more in keeping with the gigantic original than this far smaller reproduction. Seeing my gaze, Schuyler remarked, "Nana Dolly had a sense of humor."

It was now dark, the sky had turned on its own twinklers, and floodlights highlighted the beach below us and the eternal motion of the surf. The party had now spread out to the sandy terrain. "There are no words," I said. "There really are no words."

Indicating a marble bench, Schuyler sat and I joined him. "I grew up here and it still impresses me. Drink up,

Mr. McNally, or I'll devour your spare and hasten my end."

That was the second time he had alluded to his poor health. "You can't take the hooch, sir?"

"Oh, I can take it all right, but it would only beg the inevitable, and there is something I want to do before I depart this mortal coil." He waved my spare across his princely domain. "Like attend my son's wedding in September.

"I have about six months to live, Mr. McNally. A year at the most. It seems my liver isn't in the best of shape. I'm in no condition to withstand a transplant, should one become available, which is just as well. I would only mistreat that one, too. So, time is of the essence, son."

"For what, Mr. Schuyler?"

"For stopping Sabrina Wright's daughter from adding an addendum to my obit."

Surely I had heard wrong. The height and heady atmosphere must have clogged my ears. "I beg your pardon, Mr. Schuyler. You said . . . "

"I told you I was a man of few words and believed you were, too. I know Sabrina came down here and hired you. I got wind of it in Southampton the day after Spindrift ran his blind item."

That blind item. Would it never rest in peace? "She did hire me, sir, for one day. She is no longer a client, nor are we in touch. Can I know your interest in Sabrina Wright and her daughter?"

Ignoring my question, he bragged, "My son is a fine young man and he's going to be a great research scientist, though God knows how he got that way coming from Linda and me. The boy is about to marry a lovely young lady in the same profession. Thanks to him I have been on the straight and narrow for several years and I intend to stay that way until they plant me. I will not have their wedding sullied by another scandal about his old man. I will not."

His voice shook and his hands trembled. I finished my martini and reached for my spare before it became a puddle. "Please don't excite yourself, sir. I'm sure it won't help your liver, or your situation, whatever that may be. Sabrina Wright hired me to find her husband who came down here looking for her daughter. It's a little confusing, I know, but it's the truth. I found him, or rather he found me, and that was the end of my association with Ms. Wright."

"I don't believe you," he stated.

"You may believe what you wish, Mr. Schuyler, but that's the truth."

"As far as it goes, I'm sure." He put down my empty glass and ran a hand through what was left of his hair. The guy was in a bad way and so was Archy. What was going on here?

"The girl and her friend, a reporter they say, are snooping around old newspaper stories." Schuyler repeated the scuttlebutt I had gotten from Ursi over my kippers and eggs. "Social items, if the gossips are right. There are those who believe she's looking for her natural mother. Thanks to some magazine article, the world knows Sabrina adopted the girl."

"I know this," I admitted cautiously.

"It's all bull because Sabrina is her natural mother. I know that for a fact," he ranted. "So who is the girl looking for? Her father, who else? And why is she looking here? Because someone gave her a lead and the only person who could give her a lead was her mother."

Here's where I came in, I thought, but it wasn't a film

and I couldn't leave. I told myself this wasn't happening and didn't believe me. I drank from my spare. "What is your interest in this, sir?" I held my breath and waited.

"I told you I don't have the luxury of time, so I'll come right to the point. I'm the girl's father."

My flabber was ruptured. My synapses ceased to synapse. Another contender had just entered the ring. Thirty years ago Sabrina Wright had come down to Ft. Lauderdale for spring break and had screwed Tom, Dick, and Harry– literally as well as figuratively. What a remarkable woman.

The sounds of the night floated upward like incense rising from the High Priest's censer– the rumble of the surf, the peal of genteel laughter, the strains of cocktail music. Perhaps, if I counted to ten backward, I would wake up in my garret repeating, *There is no place like home, there is no place like* . . .

"Did you hear me, Mr. McNally?"

"I think you said you are Gillian's father."

"You think right."

He told me the story of the young, the bad, and the beautiful on spring break in Ft. Lauderdale three decades ago. It loses its punch the third time around. Fourth, if you included the lady's version. I wasn't listening. I was thinking of Tom downstairs, wondering what the hell I was doing here. Had he seen Harry leading me out of the solarium? These old school chums were completely unaware that they were competing for the same title along with Dickey Cranston.

Schuyler ended with, "Can you help me?"

"Help you? How?"

"Get Sabrina to pack up, go home, and take her daughter and the reporter with her."

"Why me, Mr. Schuyler?"

"Because you know her. She contacted you for whatever reason the moment she got here. Who else but you?"

"Trust me," I said. "Sabrina wants to do exactly as you wish."

"So you do know more than you're saying," he charged.

"I do, sir, but I could not reveal what I know until I knew what you knew. Client confidentiality."

"Good. I'm a client and don't you forget it. If you breathe a word of this, I'll kill you and if you think I'm joking, try me. All I could get is life or the chair, ain't that a laugh?"

Yes, it was very funny, indeed. There were now three men in Palm Beach poised to do me in, and let us not forget dear Consuela and her long knife should she learn of my coitus interruptus episode outside Charley's Crab. Who says you can never be too popular?

I read Schuyler my set piece. The one I deliver to all of Gillian's fathers. "So you see, sir, Sabrina came down here purposely to stop Gillian from learning the truth."

"Why the hell did she tell the girl she wasn't really adopted? It was a fool thing to do. I paid her a fortune to forget she ever knew me. I had survived one paternity suit and didn't want to face another. My father would have killed me," Schuyler griped.

I was trying to calculate how much Sabrina had walked off with— three times. "But she didn't name anyone," I reminded him. "She didn't break the bargain."

"And she told you," he fumed.

"But she didn't name names. If you hadn't . . . "

"Okay," he said, not liking the implication. "I had no choice. I need someone to talk to Sabrina and tell me what's going on. I want to know how close the girl is getting, and I'm hiring you for the job."

"Why don't you call Sabrina?" I suggested.

"I did."

"And?"

"She agreed to meet with me."

So Harry had called. Again I wondered if Tom and Dick had, too. "So why do you need me, Mr. Schuyler?"

"Quite frankly, because I don't trust her. I want a spy in her camp."

"I'm not in her camp, sir."

"You have entry, Mr. McNally."

I said I was going to keep out of this, but thanks to that chance I took when I told Ursi and Jamie about my meeting with Sabrina, everyone in town knew the author and I had a working relationship. Of course, the most problematic folks on my list were the three kings she had bilked out of a fortune. I took a chance and looked at the hand I drew. Three kings, a queen, and yrs. truly, the joker.

Right there I decided it would be in my best interest to join the game and declare jokers wild. I would call Sabrina. First, to warn her of just how desperate her three old paramours were and to tell her to get them off my back. Also, I wanted to hear what the lady had to say in her defense. Plenty, I was sure. I would also bill Harry for my time and perhaps Tom and Dick, too. I had nothing to lose but my life.

"I'll see what I can do, Mr. Schuyler," I told him, not without some misgivings.

"I wish I could say that makes me feel better, but it doesn't," he said with a show of no confidence. "In my condition I guess I never will."

"I'm sorry about your poor health, sir."

"So am I," he said, standing. "Shall we go below? You look like you could use a drink."

We were both carrying empty cocktail glasses as we walked to the elevator. Mine and mine. Just before Schuyler put out the lights I thought I saw *David* wink at me. Cheeky guy.

The party was in full swing. We deposited our empties on the bar, but before I could get a refill, there was a stir of excitement in the crowded room at the arrival of two new guests.

"Oh, it's Dickey Cranston and Ginny," Schuyler said. "He was at Saint Paul's with Tommy and me. Good of him to come. He and Troy are not on the same team. Different parties, you know. Would you like to meet him?"

"I don't think so, sir. I'd rather scram before they pass the alms plate."

"Nonsense, it'll only take a minute. Dickey is going to be an ambassador or something. Big deal."

Schuyler dragged me into the lion's den and at the sight of me, Dickey Cranston almost keeled over. I hate having this effect on people; it bruises the ego. The crowd made way for Harry Schuyler as they must have all his life, and we had no trouble penetrating the groupies surrounding Cranston. Schuyler made the introduction, and Cranston shook my hand like I was Typhoid Mary. Suzanne was at the moment showing off her Chanel suit to Virginia Appleton.

"Pleased to meet you," Cranston lied. "Are you a political enthusiast, Mr. McNally?"

"No, sir. My father was the invited guest and I'm here in his place."

"That's right," Schuyler mumbled. "Prescott McNally did some work for me a while back and I may need his help again."

Unable to resist, Tom Appleton left his son, the

Givenchy, and the Chanel to join us. "Good of you to come, Dickey," he said to Cranston while looking at me. "I guess we can't count on your vote. What's your party affiliation, Mr. McNally?"

My para- was so -noid I wanted only to run out of the room and into the ocean, never to return. I was at Casa Gran, surrounded by three social-register heavyweights, all giving me the fisheye like the motel clerk who knows damn well you're not Mr. and Mrs. Smith. Looking at them side by side was like playing the old shell game. Which one contained the pea? These three fools all believed they did.

"I'm an independent, sir," I told him. "But I promised your son my vote and I will keep it."

"Mr. McNally is my guest, Tommy," Schuyler explained. "Lawyer business."

"I didn't know you were a lawyer, Mr. McNally," Appleton said.

"I'm not, but my father is," I answered. This was followed by an oppressive pause. Appleton and Cranston glared at me. Schuyler looked wistfully at the passing trays of champagne. I smiled in search of sympathy and got skunked for my efforts. It was time for Archy to do the right thing and get out of these guys' lives while I still had mine.

"I must be going, gentlemen. It's been a pleasure. Best of luck to your son, Mr. Appleton, and to you, Mr. Cranston, on your appointment." To Harry Schuyler I said, "I'll be in touch."

None of them offered a parting hand.

NINETEEN

I COULD FEEL their eyes boring into my back as I made my exit. These three not-so-wise guys had broken the cardinal rule of survival: *When in doubt, keep your mouth shut.* Upon reading that now infamous blind item in Lolly's column, they panicked and blabbed. Trouble was, they blabbed to me which made me as inconvenient as Sabrina and her daughter. Schuyler thought he was speaking metaphorically when he placed me in Sabrina's camp, but the statement was more fact than fancy. That I had been shanghaied made no difference to the enemy.

I rationalized that if any of these three former classmates were going to take drastic action to keep their secret a secret, they would have to do it with their own hand. Out of necessity a hit man would have to go the way of his vic-

tim, and then you're dealing with a box of facial tissues–
pull out one and up pops another.

Of the three, which would be the most likely to act foolishly? My vote went to Cranston. He had the most to lose,
and like all ambitious men, I believed he could be ruthless
when it came to getting what he wanted. That day in his
limo, he had referred to Sabrina being as reliable as a campaign promise. This told you something about his political
integrity. And he had a temper. "Don't ever get wise with
me. You tell me what I want to know or . . . " I never did
hear the end of that threat but I have a lively imagination.

Then we have Schuyler, sickly but determined to go to
his grave as pure as when he came into this world. He was
the only one to openly declare he would kill to keep the
secret. Kill me, that is. And by his own admission he had
nothing to lose if pushed to the limit. "All I could get is
life or the chair. Ain't that a laugh?"

Appleton was the mildest mannered of the three, but I
could hear him telling me, "I will go to any length to protect myself and my family from scandal." Nor could I forget the look he gave me when I horned in on his son's
fifteen minutes. Like they say, *If looks could kill* . . .

Due to all of the above, I had completely forgotten that
Binky and Bianca were dining at the Pelican that evening.
Imagine my surprise when I walked in and saw the pair
seated at my corner table. It being the start of the weekend, the Pelican was crowded and noisy, but Binky spotted me the moment I walked into the bar area. Too late to
run. He and Bianca waved. I waved back and skirted their
table in favor of the bar. "Good evening, Mr. Pettibone.
What can you give me to make me forget that there's got
to be a morning after?"

"They say a good martini can do the trick."

"Very perceptive, Mr. Pettibone. It's what I've been drinking and Father told me never to change intoxicants in midstream. I'll have the vodka variety, straight up with a twist."

"You look like you've had a tough night, Archy," Simon Pettibone observed.

"I've had better, Mr. Pettibone. I've had better."

Priscilla came up to the bar to place an order and couldn't wait to tell me, "Binky is here with his new girl. She's a doll."

"So I noticed. What are they drinking?"

"Binky is on beer, as usual, and Bianca is drinking rum and Coke."

My stomach lurched. "What are they eating?" I also had to know.

"Special tonight is crab cakes, but Bianca said they tend to give her gas."

How infuriating. The girl was impudent. Tonight she wore a lovely cream cashmere cardigan over a lilac blouse. Was she telling Binky about our visit with Tony Gilbert? Pray she doesn't describe Babette. Binky has a weak heart.

"They're having the braised veal chops," Priscilla said.

My stomach mellowed. "Do you think Leroy could put a little something together for me to nibble right here?" I asked.

"We discourage eating at the bar," she told me.

"Says who?"

"The Board, that's who," Priscilla snapped.

Let me say here that I am not on the Pelican's Board. I am a member of the more prestigious Founders' Committee. As the Pelican Club was established as a gentlemen's lodge, the Founders are all hart– pun intended. Later, we made the mistake of admitting women. Connie, like Eve, was the first on the scene. Thereafter I could no longer escort whom I pleased to the club without chancing running into Connie.

Please note: Were it not for that unfortunate decision, *I* would be sharing the braised veal chops with Bianca– and a robust Bordeaux from the Médoc region– not Binky Watrous. Gas? The nerve of that child.

When Mr. Pettibone placed my drink before me, I complained, "Priscilla refuses to serve this starving gentleman at the bar, Mr. Pettibone."

"Oh, we can make an exception, Pris," he kindly said to his daughter. "Archy is tucked away in the corner here and no one will notice."

"No one will notice?" Priscilla echoed. "That tie-and-hankie combo makes him look like a traffic light. And that's the biggest pocket square I have ever seen– you could have a picnic on it." Having critiqued my attire, Priscilla picked up her tray and departed.

Reggie Winetroub took up the slack. "Glad I caught you, Archy." Reggie looked a bit under the weather. He has been known to go from lunchtails to cocktails without taking a work break. "Founders' meeting next week. Very important that you be there. We're considering establishing a new charity under the auspices of our 'Just Say Yes' reserve fund."

"Interesting, Reggie. What do you have in mind?"

"We want to support those we feel have been overlooked, badly neglected, and often maligned."

"Right on, Reggie. Who did you come up with?"

"Unwed fathers."

I couldn't think of a more overlooked, neglected, and

maligned group in our United States. "Good choice," I encouraged. "What services would we provide?"

"A hideaway is what I have in mind," Reggie said. You
had to hand it to him. When he focused in on a project, he
left no stone unturned. "Someplace in the desert perhaps,"
Reggie mused, "where the men can relax and get away
from the haranguing of irate females and lawyers. I was
thinking of Nevada where bordellos are legal. You know,
for the boys' night out."

"Reggie, you are a genius, but you might consider Algiers, too."

"Really, Archy? Why?"

"I'll tell you at the meeting."

"How boss," Reggie chuckled. "See you later. I have to
get back to my table, if I can find it."

"I hope he was kidding," Mr. Pettibone offered in
passing.

"I'm afraid not, Mr. Pettibone. You find the new charity
unworthy?"

"Heavens no, Archy. I'm opposed to Nevada. Too hot
regardless of the amenities. I would suggest Arizona where
one can go south of the border for rest and relaxation."

Mr. Pettibone has tarried too long at the Pelican Club.

Priscilla returned. "Leroy can put together a burger
with cottage fries and a tossed salad."

"Tell Leroy I will marry him if he doesn't forget the
pickle spears."

I lowered my voice and dipped my head. "Tell me, are
the happy couple enjoying their date?"

"I think so," Priscilla said. "She keeps saying, 'Oh,
Binky, how you make me laugh.' "

This was worse than I had imagined. The girl was a
menace. Poor Binky would forsake his Victoria's Secret

catalogues for reality's lash. I should make a citizen's arrest, drag her off to a hallowed shelter, and pray for the redemption of her soul. "Oh, Lord, make her a good girl– *but not immediately.*"

Why do I harbor such thoughts? My precarious position between Sabrina Wright and her three angry adversaries had me on edge and imminent danger activates the adrenal gland, unleashing the steroidal hormone known as adrenaline. In animals this remarkable substance triggers the fight-or-flight instinct. Perhaps due to a missing gene, in Archy it triggers only the flight half. That's why I felt compelled to run off to the Kasbah– with Bianca Courtney. Steroidal hormones will do it all the time. Clearly, I am a victim of genetic imbalance.

"We gave Binky his gifts last night," Priscilla announced as if I didn't know. "Connie said she hopes her bridal shower is as successful as Binky's housewarming, hint, hint."

"Tell Connie that Archy hopes his application for the priesthood is looked upon favorably, hint, hint."

With a nod toward my corner table, Priscilla predicted, "With the way things are progressing there, you may be giving Binky a bachelor party before the year is out. They ordered one chocolate mousse for dessert, with two spoons. Cozy, no?" Priscilla picked up her order and fled.

With that, my evening reached its nadir. Remembering that there was always one step further down you could go, I clung to the promise of one of Leroy's hamburgers, which are a gourmand's delight, proving that the best things in life are not free. At the Pelican Club they start at fourteen ninety-five and advance rapidly. I would have Mr. Pettibone pull a dark lager to go with the repast. Why, I was feeling better already.

There were two couples at the bar waiting for tables, and after seeing to their needs, Mr. Pettibone approached me and asked, "Have you seen your policeman friend, Archy?"

"Not since we lunched here the other day. Are you in need of the law?"

"Thankfully, no, but Pris told us that you told him the Henry Peavey story and he said he would run the name through the police files. I was wondering if he'd turned up anything."

With all that had been going on since Sabrina, Bianca, and Babette had entered my life, I had forgotten all about cousin Lyle and Henry Peavey. "If he had, I'm sure he would have called me," I told Mr. Pettibone. "But I will check with Al and get back to you the soonest. I take it Mrs. Pettibone has heard nothing from California."

"Not a word, Archy, and it's on her mind constantly. She's running up a phone bill with Lyle's daughter and giving me no rest. Probably all nonsense, anyway. Lyle never did have much on the ball, as I recall. The man is a modern-day alchemist, his tools being lottery tickets and football pools. He doesn't have an Oval Office so he works around an oval track."

"Don't count him out, Mr. P; he may be on to something this time."

A couple of new arrivals stepped up to the bar and Mr. Pettibone hastened to greet them. In parting, he called over his shoulder, "All I want from him is the cost of the long-distance calls. Keep in touch, Archy."

"I will, Mr. Pettibone," I promised.

Now Binky and his date were departing, and although I avoided looking their way, they came bounding up to me on their way out. "Pleasant meal?" I inquired civilly.

"Great," Bianca said. "I can't wait to come back."

"No need for an antacid, I assume."

"Not tonight," she beamed. "We're going home to cata-logue Binky's gifts."

"That's right, Archy; remember you told me to keep a detailed list for reciprocation. Bianca is going to help me. I got fourteen in all."

"Sixteen, if you count Priscilla's and Connie's," Bianca reminded him. "Where is Connie tonight, Archy?"

Oh, she was a piece of work, little Ms. Buttons and Bows. "I am not Connie's keeper," I answered, "and here comes my humble meal, so if you will excuse me, I will bid you both happy cataloguing."

"We're having waffles for breakfast," Binky said loud enough for everyone at the bar to hear. "Bianca is going to show me how to use my new waffle iron." He was besot-ted. If, at that very moment, Mr. Pettibone had not put my meal before me, I would have made my citizen's arrest to save the boy from both debauchery and indigestion. This is what comes of getting your own pad while still a youth. Why, Binky was just ten years past his teens. Bianca said she was twenty-two but with witches, who knows?

" 'Night, Archy," Bianca called and toddled off.

The moment she was out of earshot, Binky poked me in the ribs and whispered, "Don't come knocking when the trailer is rocking."

Oh, please.

DIĒS SĀTURNĪ, OR Saturn's day, but there was no rest for Archy. I awoke to the sound of a drip, drip, drip, and knew it was a rainy Saturday morn. Good for the mer-chants on Worth Avenue, bad for the bikini watchers on the beach. I showered vigorously, hot, cold, hot, cold; shampooed my hair and wrapped myself in my hooded white terry robe. Last night, after returning from the Pelican Club, I added an addendum to the last two addenda in my journal, bringing it up to date. First, "The Man That Got Away," second, "The Man That Wouldn't Go Away," third, "And Baby Makes Five."

After recording in detail my visit to Casa Gran, I had written that Appleton, Cranston, and Schuyler would not rest easy until Sabrina and her daughter departed Palm Beach and disappeared from their lives. In the gray light of a rainy morning, I added that this would be only a temporary reprieve, at best. When Sabrina had confided to Gillian the circumstances of her birth, she had opened the closet door, exposing the skeleton. It was only a matter of time before someone fleshed out the bones and added a face.

The men would never rest easy until those who could identify Mr. Bones were silenced. Namely, Sabrina and Archy. The kooky part was that neither one of us could make a positive ID. Was it time the men knew this?

I went down to breakfast in shorts and polo shirt. "Do we own a waffle iron?" I asked Ursi.

"I know there's one someplace, but if that's what you're craving this morning, Archy, I don't have the batter."

"No, Ursi. I was just wondering. For some reason I woke up with waffles on my mind. Must have been something I ate last night."

Seeing as the mater and pater were due to dock tomorrow, I thought it politic not to mention the number of martinis followed by several dark lagers I had also ingested last night. Before getting into my chariot, I had tested my driving capabilities by reciting aloud:

Amidst the mists and coldest frosts,
with stoutest wrists and loudest boasts,
he thrusts his fists against the posts
and still insists he sees the ghost.

Needless to say, I did not miss a beat, flub a word, or wet my chin, therefore I was not hors de combat. I also drew an admiring crowd in the parking lot and remember hearing Reggie Winetroub call out, "How boss."

Ursi served me a glass of fresh-squeezed orange juice and tempted me with, "A cheddar cheese omelet is what I had in mind, Archy, with a helping of chilled honeydew to get you started. Just ripened and sweet as sugar, this one is."

"I'm in your hands," I surrendered. "Anything new to report on our visiting novelist and her brood?"

"They say she was at the Club Colette last night with her husband and daughter and her daughter's beau. They say she looked like a million bucks."

"They" was Ursi's version of "a reliable source" and Club Colette was Palm Beach's version of New York's El Morocco in the golden days of cafe society. Sabrina didn't seem to have any qualms about parading her troops on grounds where an Appleton, a Cranston, or a Schuyler might very well be sampling the bill of fare at the next table, but then restraint was not Ms. Wright's forte. It was time to sit down with the lady and shout in her native tongue, "Enough already."

"A million bucks? In this town, Ursi, that makes her an also-ran."

"They say her daughter is very plain," Ursi gossiped while serving my honeydew.

"Her mother casts a long shadow, Ursi. It must be hard for the girl to find her place in the sun."

Slicing a thick slab of cheddar and breaking eggs, Ursi sighed, "Poor thing. I hope she finds her true mother."

The trouble was, she had. Ascertaining that Ursi had nothing new to report on the comings and goings of Sabrina Wright and Co., I inquired after Jamie to divert her from asking me questions regarding the affair I was loath to answer. I learned that, in anticipation of picking up the seafarers in Ft. Lauderdale tomorrow, he had taken Father's Lexus to the car wash for a bit of sprucing up. With the rain now falling, Ursi feared it would all be in vain.

"If they give it a good coat of wax," I said, "it will keep its shine. What time are they docking?"

"Noon, and I'll be so glad to see them. I miss your mother, Archy."

"Not more than I do, I'm sure." The seigneur was also missed, but as he discouraged overt signs of affection, you wouldn't hear it from us. Like children unattended for too long, we would all be pleased to get back to the familiar and comforting routine of life with Father, and I had much to report to his nibs.

"Would you like a toasted bagel?" Ursi asked, expertly flipping the cheddar omelet in its pan.

"I think not," I declined. "One piece of rye toast for me. I'm watching my diet."

"Dry or buttered?"

Dry rye toast was indistinguishable from cardboard. "Buttered, please. This honeydew is good," I complimented, "and make it two slices of rye toast, Ursi, both buttered."

Back in my room, and far from Ursi's gaze, I lit an English Oval and inhaled deeply. My first and last of the day– barring unforeseen circumstances that would cause me to seek solace from the winsome weed. Speaking of which, I dialed The Breakers and asked for Mr. Silvester's suite.

Sabrina picked up after one ring. Did she monitor all incoming calls personally? I believe she did, because there was no telling when she would be assailed by an irate voice from the past imploring her to scram.

"Archy McNally here."

After a long pause, she welcomed me with, "I thought we had concluded our business, Mr. McNally."

"So did I, Ms. Wright, but circumstances require that we meet again one rainy Saturday afternoon. May I suggest the Leopard Lounge at the Chesterfield, say high noon?"

"You may suggest it, Mr. McNally, and you may go to the Leopard Lounge some rainy Saturday at high noon, but I won't be there. Now if you'll excuse me . . . "

"Don't hang up, Ms. Wright. This is important. Every Tom, Dick, and Harry in town is talking about Gillian's hankering for knowledge of things past. Did you hear me? Every Tom, Dick, and Harry."

We shared another poignant moment of silence.

She came back on the line with, "You are a snooping bastard, Mr. McNally."

"And you are a liar, a cheat, and a con artist, Ms. Wright."

She must have liked that because she laughed. "Seeing as we understand each other, I will meet you at the Leopard Lounge, but make it a little later. Only mad dogs and Archy McNally go out in the noonday sun."

"It's raining out there, in case you haven't noticed."

"I know it is, but I never let reality come between me and a good line. It's the secret of my success. One o'clock, give or take, Mr. McNally, and now I must run, a marvelous young man is coming to do my hair. He's all the rage down here, and it's rumored he was discovered by Virginia Cranston. I just love sharing with Ginny Cranston, Mr. McNally– I just love it."

She rang off with a titter and had me grinning like a schoolboy. Sabrina Wright, you may be a liar, a cheat, and a con artist, but you are irresistible. However, I would suggest she temper her arrogance with caution. The boys of summer were not in a frolicking mood– but Archy was. I called Connie to see what we could get up to on a rainy Saturday night.

"Archy," Connie cried, "I was just on my way out."

"Not working today, are you?"

"No. I'm driving down to Miami to see my cousin. She just had a baby."

That was strange, I thought, and said as much. "Another? Didn't she have one a few weeks ago?"

"That was my cousin on the Garcia side," Connie said. "This is a Mendez cousin, on my mother's side. She had a boy."

"How many cousins do you have, Connie?"

"Well, my father was one of nine and my mother has three brothers and three sisters, so I have . . . "

"I'm sorry I asked," I broke in. Connie could not only name them all, but tell you their birthdays as well. "Will you be back in time for dinner?"

"No way, Archy. I'm having dinner with my cousins. They're all coming to see the new baby."

"Both sides?" I exclaimed.

"No, only the Mendez cousins. Would you like to come, Archy? You know you're always welcome."

"Thank you, Connie, but I'll pass." Being jostled by two dozen Cubans on a buffet line was not my idea of a romantic evening. "I'll call you tomorrow."

If at first you don't succeed, try and try again. Why not? I dialed Bianca Courtney.

"Archy here. How were the waffles?"

"Oh, Archy. A disaster. We never had them."

This was encouraging. "Do tell, Bianca."

"Well," she said, "we bought a packaged batter and had to mix in eggs and milk. That was okay because Binky now has an electric mixer. It came with a bowl. We heated the iron and poured in the batter, but we must have put in too much, because it began to ooze out. Binky went to wipe it up and burned his hand. I went ballistic and pulled the plug, only I yanked too hard and sent the waffle iron smack into Binky's groin. Oh, Archy, it was horrible. Binky was covered with batter and the iron landed on his foot."

"Are you telling me you killed Binky?"

"No. No. I stuck his hand in cold water and ran to get Sergeant Rogoff."

"You went to get Al?" I gasped. "Good Lord, what for?"

"He's a cop, isn't he? I figured he would know how to treat burns, and someone had to get the glop off Binky. It was in an awkward place, if you know what I mean."

I suddenly remembered that the only job Binky had never held was that of short-order cook. The gods were kind to that boy, in spite of it all. "Did Al help?" I asked.

"Yes. And Mrs. Brewster from across the street. She saw me running for Al and came right over. She put butter on Binky's hand."

One hoped that was the only place she put the butter. "A little salt and pepper and you could have had Binky for breakfast."

"We're all going to Patty's Pancake Palace for breakfast. Sergeant Rogoff is driving."

The episode gave new meaning to the term *trailer trash,* and Ma Perkins's Pancake Palace had to be a pit stop for semis. I must remember to tell Binky not to go snoozing when the waffle iron is oozing.

"You certainly had a morning, Bianca. Would you like to step out with me tonight? A movie, perhaps? Dinner? A midnight stroll on the beach?"

"No, thanks, Archy. I'm seeing Brandon tonight."

"And just who is Brandon?" I demanded.

"The basketball player. Remember? A mile high and an inch wide. He's driving up from Coral Gables just to see me."

"What happened to the girl who pulled the winning straw?"

"That was over ages ago. I have to go, Archy, Sergeant Rogoff is beeping for us."

If at first you don't succeed . . .

I went back downstairs and asked Ursi, "What are you doing tonight, Ursi?"

"Nothing much, Archy. Just getting ready for the home-coming. Are you going out?"

"No, Ursi, I am not. I've decided to stay home and thought we might celebrate our last evening alone. If you prepare the feast, I'll raid the master's wine cellar."

"Fine, and how good of you to give up a Saturday night, Archy."

"My pleasure, Ursi. My pleasure."

TWENTY

THE LEOPARD LOUNGE afforded me a chance to don khakis and a safari jacket I had purchased from Abercrombie & Fitch before they broke camp on Madison Avenue. I eschewed my pith helmet on the grounds that the jacket said it all and wore instead a more serviceable waterproof tan porkpie.

Sabrina came dressed as a celebrity incognito. Kerchief, enormous dark glasses, and a Burberry trench. Consequently, she was instantly recognized by the lounge lizards. "Did you expect to shoot a leopard, Mr. McNally?" she said as she joined me.

In spite of the flippancy, it was clear that the events of the past week had left their mark on the lady. She wore no makeup. Her mouth was drawn, her flawless complexion pallid, and when she removed the glasses, I could detect fine lines around those dark eyes, which seemed to have lost their luster. Gone, too, were the theatrical trappings that had so impressed me at our first meeting. The Pink Lady became a Bloody Mary and the exotic black-tipped cigarette was replaced with a Marlboro, *sans* the foot-long onyx holder.

The lady was here on business and she lost no time in getting down to the nitty-gritty. "So you know," she said when we were served our tomato and vodka.

"More than I care to," I answered.

"This mess is a result of my hiring you, isn't it?"

"I beg your pardon, Ms. Wright, but this mess is a result of you baring your soul to your daughter and her determination to come down here looking for her father."

"But had I not contacted you, no one would know what Gillian is up to."

I didn't like the accusation and set the record straight. "The wheels were set in motion before I met you. The day before, to be exact. That line in Lolly Spindrift's column saying you were down here looking for the man that got away was the catalyst. I even suspected you of giving Lolly the lead."

She inhaled deeply and when she exhaled I sneaked a whiff and checked one of the many safari jacket pockets for my English Ovals. I had left them at home. Her Marlboros lay on the table like a temptress in church, but like a good acolyte, I ignored them.

"Me?" she cried. "Why would I do such a foolish thing?"

"I honestly don't know. It just seemed to me that everything that could go wrong went wrong from the moment you got here. I was looking for the director and your name came up. Who else knew you had arrived at this hotel when you did and asked for your husband?"

"My travel agent in New York knew when I was arriving, and so did everyone at the hotel who saw me arrive and heard me ask for Mr. Silvester. Let me assure you, I did not make that call. I came down here to prevent what is happening, not encourage it." Venting her frustration, she extinguished her cigarette with a series of rapid jabs at the ashtray. "The last time we spoke, I asked you why Tom Appleton had thought to call you and you refused to tell me. Will you now?"

"First, tell me how you knew it was Appleton. I never mentioned his name."

With an annoying wave of her hand, she said, "Because he was the first to call me and he told me he had just spoken to you."

"Have they all contacted you?" I asked.

"Yes."

"And have you seen them?"

"Two down and one to go."

"Which one?" I prompted.

"None of your business, Mr. McNally."

I had talked to Harry Schuyler last night. He admitted calling Sabrina and said she had agreed to meet him. I suddenly realized the ambiguity of the disclosure. It could mean they had yet to meet or had already done so. I had never thought to ask him so now I could not name the single holdout by the process of elimination. Sabrina made no mention of Harry's physical condition, and I did not volunteer the information. The guy had a right to confide or not to confide in whom he pleased.

So who was it? On that rainy afternoon in the trendy Leopard Lounge it was all a silly guessing game and one I was weary of playing.

"Okay," I said. "I had no idea how to go about finding

your husband, so I passed the word around that I was working on your behalf to locate your daughter. I said you wanted to prevent Gillian from eloping with a guy you had no use for. I figured anyone who knew anything about Gillian or Silvester might get in touch with me."

"And they did, didn't they?" she laughed. Amazing, but the lady never lost her sense of humor. It was an enviable trait.

"First there was the item in Lolly's column which had all your former flames believing you were after them. When I got into the picture, they contacted me to find out if it was true."

"The fools," she uttered with contempt.

"Yes, weren't they? But they were very frightened, Ms. Wright, and they still are. I told them as much as I knew because there was no reason not to, but I made a point of saying you were here to stop Gillian and that you were determined to keep your half of the bargain. But I must say, Ms. Wright, by the time I got to Harry, I was astounded. I trust there are no more."

"Thank you for speaking on my behalf, Mr. McNally, and there are no more, take my word for it."

The waiter was suddenly hovering over us, and not until then did I notice Sabrina had made short work of her drink. "We'll have two more," I ordered.

Sabrina picked up the pack of cigarettes and offered one to me. I refused, but only after a moment's hesitation. I struck a match and held it for her. "They are very desperate men, Ms. Wright."

"And thirty years ago I was a very desperate young girl from Brooklyn who came down here on spring break looking for a rich husband. Are you shocked?"

"Hardly. This town is full of young women, and young

men, aiming for the same thing. Most of them, like you, miss the mark."

"Miss? I don't know about that, Mr. McNally. Three shots in the dark and one direct hit ain't bad where I come from." She let out that throaty laugh and what could I do but join in? Sabrina Wright might be down, but she wasn't out.

"I'll admit I spread myself rather thin, but when you get the nod from an Appleton, a Cranston, and a Schuyler, you don't say no. And how those boys flaunted their pedigree and their wealth. Me, me, me, my, my, my, and I, I, I, was the extent of their conversation, but as Larry Hart said, *horizontally speaking, they were at their very best.* Would you believe it was once around the block for each of them?"

"I believe you, Ms. Wright, because there's an ancient Chinese saying that reminds us that it takes many nails to construct a crib, and one screw to fill it."

The waiter brought our seconds, and Sabrina saluted my retort. "I must remember that one," she said. "Well, they all made plans to see me again in New York, and each called when he got there. By then I knew I was in the family way, as we used to say in Brooklyn, and passed on the news to my ardent suitors, who suddenly went limp at the news. Pardon the pun."

"Did you know who the father was?"

She shook her head. "No. How could I? And I still don't, nor do I care to know. Those bastards all told me they could arrange for a doctor, all expenses paid, and a few bucks for my trouble. I told them it was against my religion. One by one they said I could do as I pleased, but they wanted no part of their own child. They made it very clear that I wasn't the kind nice young men married. And that, Mr. McNally, was their undoing. I owed them nothing, and they owed me an apology which I proceeded to extract in the only words they understood– cold cash."

She went on to explain how she had cunningly plotted her revenge, dealing with each of the men individually without their ever knowing they were part of a trio.

"These are smart guys," I said, "with family lawyers by the dozens. How did you manage it?"

She sipped and puffed before answering with a smile. "I showed them my birth certificate, Mr. McNally."

"You did what?"

"Can't you guess? The spring break was in April. I was eighteen in September of that year. I believe it's called statutory rape and my heroes had no desire to join the ranks of Charlie Chaplin and Errol Flynn. Oh, the boys did go running to the family lawyers, and I got my apology, in spades. The end."

What a story, and what a woman. "But it's not the end," I said. "When men like these make a deal, especially one that puts them on the paying end, they don't like being crossed. I spoke to all of them and I didn't like what they had to say. They are angry with you for telling Gillian the truth."

"Only a part of the truth," she insisted.

"Enough to get the wind up. What did you tell them, may I ask?"

Another cigarette, hardly smoked, bit the dust. "I told them to go climb the family tree and leave the daughter they wanted to terminate to me. That's what I told them."

And that's what I had feared. "Easy, Ms. Wright. I don't like these guys any more than you do, but they are not to be trifled with. They will go to any length to prevent this mess from going public, and they all have good reasons for doing so. Zack Ward's occupation, by the way, makes them very nervous."

My caution had her fuming, which put color on her alabaster cheeks. "I know all about their political expectations and their lovely children. In thirty years, they haven't changed one iota. Still worried about the family name. Sill crying, me, me, me, my, my, my, and I, I, I. The nerve. The unmitigated nerve.

"Docile Tom runs to New York every chance he gets. You know why, Mr. McNally? Because he keeps a young lady in a smart apartment on Central Park South. She's younger than his son. When Dick disappears for a few weeks *on business* he's at a posh rehab spa, drying out. Harry couldn't marry me, but he ended up tying the knot with a lesbian, a nympho, and a tramp. Don't trifle with them? I'll step all over them, Mr. McNally."

I again advised restraint. "It makes no sense to bait them. Concentrate on getting Gillian and Zack out of Palm Beach no wiser than when they arrived. Harry's son will be married in a few months, Troy Appleton will know his political future by then, and Cranston will get his appointment. It will take the heat off everyone for a spell and perhaps calmer heads will prevail."

"Don't think I'm not trying to do just that. I told you I had offered Zack an interview if he could talk Gillian into giving up the search and going home. He's very interested. I even took them all out the other evening for a start."

"So I heard. The Club Colette."

"Does nothing in this town go unnoticed, Mr. McNally?"

"No, ma'am. The spring break trio will know about this meeting before it's over."

She shrugged as if it made no difference at this point. "I

am so tired," she moaned. "I have spent all my life planning and plotting and scheming and working at that damn
word processor until my eyes cross to keep my family living in luxury, and what do I get in return? Crap, that's
what. Ungrateful pups. Now I have to give an interview to
a tabloid I wouldn't use to wipe my feet on to get Gillian to
do what I ask. I am tired, Mr. McNally. Very, very tired."

"Perhaps if you treated them with a little more respect
and understanding," I ventured warily, "they would respond in kind."

She gave me a vacant stare and spoke as if by rote. "Understanding, you say? Gillian falls in love with any man
who looks at her twice. It's clear what they're after. Her
legacy. Do you think I enjoy playing the party pooper?
Well, I don't, but I must. Robert is always short of cash
and long on places to go, like expensive men's boutiques,
cocktail parties, and topless bars. I am the guy who keeps
the show on the road and the actors from bumping into the
scenery. Now if you don't mind, doctor, I will get up off
the couch and head home. I'm seeing one of Gillian's fathers tonight. The last of the Mohegans."

With Sabrina Wright, if at first you don't succeed, give
up. I reached for her cigarettes and helped myself to one. I
deserved it. "Do you know, Ms. Wright, you are named after an ancient Roman river?"

"Funny, I thought I was named after an Audrey Hepburn movie."

"*Au contraire*. Before there was Audrey Hepburn there
was the river Severn."

FOR MY LAST dinner with Ursi and Jamie in the family
kitchen, I took more care with my attire than I had been

doing since being orphaned. Casual elegance was the goal. Too formal would put a damper on the party and too relaxed would be rude. Taupe gabardine slacks, a plummy silk jacket over a blue chambray shirt, and black patent-leather gentleman's pumps. A look in the glass confirmed that a picture is worth a thousand words.

I was delighted to see that Ursi and Jamie had also taken extra care with their apparel, although both would deny that they had done any such thing. Jamie was in summer flannels with a matching jacket, and I could see a print dress beneath Ursi's apron.

We greeted each other a bit sheepishly before I went into the den and returned with three martinis on a tray. Ursi giggled, Jamie nodded appreciatively, and Archy passed out the silver bullets. "To us," I toasted. One sip and we were laughing at our own maladroit behavior. Reverting to business as usual, we plunged into gossip, the homecoming, and Ursi's feast.

For our last supper, so to speak, Ursi had prepared and now served what I have long considered to be the quintessence of gastronomic delights. A Caesar salad, à la Ursi–only the tenderest inner leaves of the romaine lettuce– steak *au poivre,* garlic mashed potatoes, stuffed mushrooms, and tiny green peas in butter.

The steaks had been rubbed with crushed peppercorns, wrapped in paper, and left for hours, allowing the meat to absorb all the peppery flavor. Minutes before serving them, Ursi sautéed the prime cuts in a mixture of hot oil and butter until they were charred on the outside and succulently rare within.

When the steaks were removed from the pan, Ursi quickly added butter, shallots, and cognac to the remaining juices to create a sauce for the banquet. Sumptuous is an understatement and you could cut Ursi's steak *au poivre* with a fork.

I kept my promise and poured a fine Bordeaux St.-Émilion, remembering to thank Father for leaving me the key to the wine cellar. Dessert was a strawberry chantilly with Bavarian cream.

Leave home? Sure. When elephants roost in trees.

TWENTY-ONE

THE PHONE WOKE me. Trouble. I knew by the insistent urgency of the ring, which was as jarring as chalk on a blackboard. Besides, no one in Palm Beach would dream of calling on Sunday before noon.

When I heard Al Rogoff's voice, I honestly thought Binky had mangled himself with his new electric mixer. "Sorry to wake you, Archy," Al began.

"Not at all, Al. I was just dressing for church."

"You still working for Sabrina Wright?" he asked.

"No. We formally terminated our working relationship yesterday. Why?"

"Someone terminated the lady last night."

I was in my pajama tops, the only half I ever wear, and felt an icy draft attack my lower extremities. "Come again, Al."

"You heard me," he said.

"Where? When?"

"In her rented car. Last night about ten, as far as we can determine."

I jumped on that. "Her car? An accident?"

"No, Archy. Someone put a bullet in her head."

Amazing how calmly Al Rogoff could deliver such news. It must go with the territory. Murder always got me where I lived, and come to think of it, it got the victim in the same place. Sabrina gone. Still half awake, I wondered if I was dreaming the whole thing. Like the guy who's stopped for passing a red light and telling the officer, "I saw it, sir, but I did not perceive it." I heard it but I hadn't as yet grasped it. I could see her face; laughing, seething, cajoling. I visualized her dictating to those she professed to love and ruled like a despot. I heard her telling the three contenders to "go climb the family tree." Brash, brazen, and foolish Sabrina. Did her sense of humor fail her in the end, or did she enrage her assailant with, "Do you expect to shoot a leopard, Mr. . . . "

"The Palace is in an uproar," I heard Al say. "A visiting celebrity gunned down on our turf. The press is here from Miami, Tallahassee, and Atlanta. We hear the boys from New York have touched down in Fort Lauderdale and the rest are arriving at any airport in the state they could book a flight to without having to wait more than five minutes to board."

"Where are you now, Al?"

"In my car on the cell phone. I just got off duty. This call is a warning, Archy. You're going to be questioned, you know that."

I knew it. I also know I could narrow the investigation down to three names, all of which would make headlines in every capital of the western world and especially in our very own. I stood there, bottomless, shivering at the thought of the awesome power I possessed. Until yesterday Sabrina and I held the fate of those three men in the palm of our hands. Now there was only one hand left holding the bag.

I had to think, and I needed the time in which to do it. Time was at a premium, and right now I couldn't parse a sentence in a first-grade reader. "Al, this is important. I need to know the facts. Can we rendezvous in our office in an hour? I won't keep you long and then you can go home and get some sleep."

"Don't worry about me, Archy. I got a few hours off to shower and change my socks. All hands on deck until further notice. You're on in one hour and don't dawdle over your wardrobe. Come as you are."

"If I did, Al, you'd arrest me."

"Cute, Archy, cute."

I put the phone down and it rang immediately. I didn't have the time but I couldn't afford not to know who wanted me. "Archy here."

"Lolly here. Have you heard?"

"I've heard, Lolly, but I don't have time to discuss it. Maybe later."

"Every network reported it and CNN is carrying it as a news-breaking story. There goes my exclusive," he moaned.

A thousand-watt bulb exploded in my head. "Ain't it a bitch, Lol? She had agreed to meet with you tonight in her suite at The Breakers."

"I believe you, Archy, because deep down I'm in love with you. I have a penchant for losers."

"It's nice to be loved, Lol. Now I have to go."

"Any idea who done it, and why? They say it's linked to her daughter's raking up the past. I heard the police are going to commandeer all the old newspapers she was thumbing through as soon as the library opens tomorrow morning. I imagine they'll want to question all the newspaper editors she called and you, too, I'm sure."

The big three were hearing the same rumors— and quaking. Did the fool who did it realize he had cut off his nose? Did the other two think a kind benefactor had interceded on their behalf? Or was it a conspiracy? Could the old school buddies have sat down at Casa Gran after the guests had left and exchanged notes? Was I losing it? I was.

"I know as much about this as you do, Lol, but if I hear anything you'll be the first to know. Now I have to go."

I hung up before he could respond. I showered, brushing my pearlies under the spray to save time, shaved, nicked my chin, doused my face with witch hazel, and got into a pair of briefs, jeans, last night's chambray shirt, and sneakers.

The phone rang. "Archy here, and I can't talk."

"Have you heard?" It was Connie. "It's all over the TV. The local station has a camera outside the police station. I saw Al Rogoff coming out. What do you know?"

"No time now, Connie. I have to meet Al in twenty minutes. I'll be in touch. Will you be at home?"

"Only if a beautiful knight in shiny armor doesn't carry me off to Camelot."

"Fine. You'll be home."

In the kitchen Ursi was all atwitter as Jamie calmly perused his morning paper. Not even Walt Disney could animate the guy.

"I've heard, Ursi, so don't ask. I haven't got the time." She handed me a glass of juice which I downed gratefully, and I poured myself a cuppa, adding only milk.

"It's on the radio and the TV, Archy, but the newspaper doesn't have it as yet." On cue, Jamie raised the morning paper to show me the headline and confirm his wife's words. "It happened late last night, they say. What a tragedy. As I was saying to Jamie just the other day, Archy, this town isn't what it used to be. Time was when we never locked a door. Now you can't go for a drive without fearing for your life. They say her next book was going to be an exposé about an old Palm Beach family, that's why she was done in. Her daughter and the boyfriend were doing the research, everyone knows that."

Strange the things that pop up in one's head when under stress. The rumors making the rounds of our island had me thinking of a line from Browning's "My Last Duchess"– *Here you miss, / Or there exceed the mark.* The execution of Sabrina Wright brought to mind the cruel duke's response to his wife's effervescent charm– *I gave commands; Then all smiles stopped . . .*

"Are you going to Fort Lauderdale dressed like that, Archy?"

"Sorry, Ursi, but I'm not coming with you and Jamie. I have to go out now and will get back here to see the folks as soon as I can. Make my excuses."

"It's about the murder," Ursi stated.

"Don't say anything in front of Mother, Ursi," I warned her. "You know how she worries."

"I'll have a word with your father," Jamie said.

Ursi and I looked at him askance.

AL ROGOFF AND I maintain a mobile office in the parking lot of the Publix supermarket on Sunset Avenue. It's convenient, discreet, and you can't beat the rent. Our location is as far from the madding crowd as one can get, and our bays depend on space availability. Same church, different pews, but it works and what works is good.

As more people sleep in than go to Publix on Sunday morning, I got a spot next to Al and joined him in his car. He was in need of a shave and a few hours' sleep. For a change, Al wasn't chomping on a cigar, but the aroma of those past pervaded his car's interior like a pool hall on a busy night.

"You're ten minutes late," Al griped as I climbed in. "I gotta be back at the station in two hours."

"Sorry, Al, but I'm still reeling from the news."

"It never fails, Archy. You get a case and we get a body. Do me a favor and retire."

I lit an English Oval, and for reasons known only to Al Rogoff, he immediately rolled down the window on the driver's side. "Start that rumor and I'll be forced to retire," I said. "What can you tell me, Al?"

"How about, what can you tell me? Everyone knows that Archy McNally was in the lady's employ."

"You first, Al," I said in a bid for time. How much could I tell Al at this point? Very little. If Al and I were business partners in fighting villainy, I was committing an act of malversation– which itself is a felony.

Al pulled a notebook out of his bulging back pocket and began to thumb through it. He was one of the shrewdest of Palm Beach's finest. Never relying on memory, he always took notes in his own form of shorthand that resembled the writing on Cleopatra's Needle, but I have known prosecuting attorneys to rely on their definitude, making Al one of the most sought-after trial witnesses and the bane of defense counselors.

Sabrina Wright went for a drive last night in her rented car shortly after eight. Her husband said this was not unusual. She enjoyed going for a drive by herself after dinner, saying it not only helped her relax but the time alone was conducive to concocting plots for her novels. In the short time she had been in Palm Beach, she had found driving along the ocean with a sky full of stars overhead especially influential when it came to weaving romances.

Since being at The Breakers, Sabrina had gone on such an outing several times before this particular evening, according to her husband, Robert Silvester. (I immediately made that out to be two times. Each time to meet one of the boys. Last night was, in her own words, to meet with the last of the Mohegans. Which one? "Did you expect to shoot a leopard, Mr. . . . ")

When she didn't return by ten, as she usually did, her husband began to worry. He called his stepdaughter, who was in the next suite at The Breakers, to see if Sabrina was with her. She wasn't. The girl, Gillian, then called Zack Ward, who was in an adjoining suite. He had not seen Sabrina since dinner. When Sabrina did not return by midnight, Robert Silvester called the police to report her missing, giving them the make and model of the car she was driving.

Shortly thereafter, an anonymous caller reported an abandoned car on Island Drive at the turnoff to Tarpon Island. Al, cruising in his patrol car, was radioed to check it out.

Anonymous caller? Where had I heard that before? I did not interrupt Al for details.

"I found her," Al concluded solemnly.

"Did you know who she was?" I asked him.

"Not by sight, but by her car. I got an APB on my radio with the car description a short time before I got the order to proceed to Island Drive. Like I said, Archy, you get a case and we get a body."

"I do wish you would stop saying that, Al. It's bad for business."

"We like it when business is off," Al reminded me. "So, what can you tell me?"

A lot, I thought, and I felt like a traitor for not being able to pass it on to Al, but it was early days. Why drag down the team when only one player had run amok? I wasn't doing it for Tom, Dick, or Harry, but for Sabrina. I was the only one who knew her secret and I was going to keep it and uphold her end of the bargain she had made with those ignoble snobs. When the guilty malefactor was caught, and he would be caught, he could say what he pleased, but Sabrina would not have broken her trust.

I took a chance at the start of this case and now I had to take another. I had to go my own way, without the help of Al Rogoff and the police, and lasso the man that got away. I was in possession of all the puzzle's pieces. I could see the solution, but I could not perceive it. As my favorite wit had observed: *To look at a thing is quite different than to see a thing.*

"Sabrina Wright asked me to find her husband," I told Al, and repeated the story I had been passing around since my first meeting with Sabrina. Was the sin of omission a venial or mortal offense?

"It seems to me her daughter was as interested in eloping as I am," Al said. "Why was she snooping around old newspapers and calling editors? Everyone is talking about it because the girl didn't exactly make a secret of what she was doing. What do you know about it?"

I repeated the rumors as told to me by Lolly Spindrift and Ursi.

Al nodded thoughtfully. "It's the theory we're working on," he said. "Sabrina Wright was here to dig up the dirt on one of our old and respected families and write about it. Now I think she gave you that story about her daughter eloping as an excuse for all of them being here."

"Why did her husband pull out of the Chesterfield without telling her where he was going?" I tossed out to muddy the waters.

"Did he?" Al said. "Or was it all part of the ploy and a good excuse to get you in on the game. He gave himself up as soon as his wife had given you enough misinformation to blab all over town."

I didn't take umbrage because I was delighted the police had a plausible theory and I was perceived as a dupe and not a perp. "Have you questioned the daughter, Al?"

He shook his head. "We ain't seen her yet. The husband came to the station house when we notified him, and he described the events that led to him calling us. No one has been grilled so far. We have to know what the girl and her boyfriend were looking for to crack this one, Archy. Someone didn't like the idea of being wrote about by Sabrina Wright."

Wrote about? Catchy, no? Al does not like being corrected, so I let that one pass and wondered instead if Gillian, Silvester, and Zack Ward would tell the police what they were up to? Gillian had said she did not want to go public with her quest. She wanted only a chance to meet with her father in private without casting aspersions on any concerned. I doubt she would talk, and if she didn't, neither would Silvester or Ward. But did the girl think her father had killed Sabrina to maintain his anonymity? If so, would she talk to revenge her mother's death? And if she didn't think her father was involved, what did she think? What did they all think?

"Did the scene-of-the-crime boys find anything?" I

queried. Might as well learn as much as I could now, as I had no intention of meeting with Al again until I, or the police, had solved the murder of Sabrina Wright.

"They think there was a car parked behind Sabrina's rental. We roped off the area and went over every inch of it and that's all we could come up with. But it doesn't mean much. It's a public access road. There are tire tracks all over the place."

I was certain the car behind Sabrina's belonged to whomever she was meeting last night. I was tempted to ask if the tracks indicated a stretch limo. The meeting place told me nothing except that it must have been chosen by the last of her former sweethearts, as Sabrina was a stranger in our town.

"The anonymous call, Al— what's your take on that?"

"Zilch," he said. "A responsible citizen wants to do his duty but he don't want no involvement. We get a dozen calls like that every day, most of 'em about domestic squabbles. The neighbors don't want the wife beater to know who blew the whistle on him. In this case I would guess the caller was someplace she wasn't supposed to be."

"She? It was a woman?"

Al consulted his notes. "As far as the desk sergeant could tell, the caller was a female."

That was interesting. If I recalled correctly, Lolly's anonymous tipster was a man. "Could the caller have known there was a dead body in the car?" I asked Al.

"Not unless she got out and looked in the window. Sabrina Wright was in the driver's seat, but slumped over toward the passenger side. To a passing driver it would look like the car was empty."

"Was she wearing her seat belt?"

Al grinned. "Good catch, Archy, there's hope for you.

No, she wasn't. She must have parked and unbuckled the belt in anticipation of getting out of the car. She was meeting someone."

I tried my best to point out that this was not necessarily true. "It's possible, Al, but not everyone buckles up, so we don't know if she was strapped in or not. She could have stopped because she was lost. Remember, she was new to these parts."

"I ain't buying it," Al said. "I think the family she was researching knew she was after them and called her for a clandestine meeting. Her husband said she'd had a call that morning and went out shortly after noon."

That, of course, was my call. But when I met with Sabrina, she told me she was seeing the last of the Mohegans that evening, so the assignation was set before yesterday. "That was me," I admitted. "I had a drink with her yesterday afternoon."

"Thanks for sharing, but we already know," Al said. "The husband told us she saw you yesterday afternoon."

"Did you think I wasn't going to tell you? That hurts, Al."

"It hurts me, too, Archy, but we have to know where we stand. It's my job."

That made me feel better about holding out on Al. It was my job, too. "Was anything taken?" I wondered aloud.

"This is strictly confidential," Al said. "Her purse was emptied and she was stripped of her jewelry. According to her husband, she wore a diamond and sapphire necklace and matching earrings that night, as well as her engagement and wedding rings, but she wasn't done in for the loot. We ain't got no highway robbers on Island Road."

I littered the Publix parking lot with the butt end of my English Oval, at which point Al reverted to character and reached into his shirt pocket to bring out his adult pacifier. The stub of a chewed-up cigar. "By the way, Archy, even if the husband didn't tell us she met with you yesterday, we would have known."

"Really? How?"

"Rumor was, she was having drinks at the Leopard Lounge with a guy in a safari jacket. So who would wear a safari jacket to the Leopard Lounge but Archy McNally?"

"I have imagination, Al."

"You have a pair, Archy, that's what you have. So what did you and the lady talk about?"

"Off the record?"

"Way off."

I took a deep breath and resisted lighting up again. "You know Lady Cynthia Horowitz, Connie's boss."

"I know her only too well, Archy. What has she got to do with this?"

"Nothing. She's thinking of writing her memoirs and she wanted to meet with Sabrina Wright to get some pointers from a best-selling author. Lady Cynthia heard I was in contact with Sabrina Wright, and she asked Connie if I would put in a word for her. As a favor to Connie I tried, but got no place."

Al took the stub out of his mouth. "When you write your memoirs, Archy, leave me out, okay?"

"Your wish is my command, Sergeant."

"Now scram. I gotta get washed and head back to the Palace."

"Before we part can you tell me what the family was doing while Sabrina went driving under the stars?"

He thumbed his notes once again. "They had dinner downstairs at The Florentine. Bet it cost a week's salary. After, they all went to their own rooms. Sabrina left and

Silvester read. There was a ball game on the TV. Mets from New York, I believe, and Ward wanted to see it but the girl, Gillian, didn't. She stayed in her room and watched a film instead. They didn't get together until Silvester called about his missing wife. Why do you want to know?"

"Curious, that's all. Thanks, Al. Did you enjoy your pancakes yesterday?"

"No. Between your boy and Bianca, the Palm has become a battle zone. Mrs. Brewster thinks the management should keep a nurse on call. I think a nursemaid would be a better idea. I hear Bianca introduced you to Tony Gilbert. What did you think of him?"

"More your type than mine, Al."

"Screw you, Archy. Now vamoose, I gotta go."

I had the car door open before I remembered my promise to Simon Pettibone. "One more thing, Al. Henry Peavey. Anything turn up?"

"Who?"

"Henry Peavey. Mrs. Pettibone's mysterious cousin in California. You said you would see if you could get a line on him."

Al tapped his forehead with one finger. "Sorry, pal. Forgot all about it, and right now I can't say when I'll get to it."

"Get some rest," I told him. "Henry Peavey can wait."

TWENTY-TWO

IT WAS CHRISTMAS in July. For Ursi there was perfume by Chanel. For Jamie, a cardigan sweater in loden cashmere. For Hobo, a leather collar tooled with banana trees. For Archy, a lemon-yellow sports jacket in raw silk.

"Your mother spotted it," Father said, "and insisted it was made for you. I wonder why?"

"And look what I got," Mother exclaimed, holding out her hand to display a lovely tennis bracelet circled with brilliants. "It was very expensive but your father insisted."

"It was her reward for being such a good sailor," Father told us. "I had chronic *mal de mer* while her team won the shuffleboard championship. Mother also managed to win a few hearts. The gentlemen were very attentive and their wives furious."

"Don't believe him," Mother said with a shy smile.

There was no doubt but that the trip was a rousing success, the voyagers returning rested and in good spirits. Mother's florid complexion, which kept us so concerned, had not disappeared, but it was less evident thanks to a very healthy-looking tan. The dispenser of all this largesse had not left himself off the receiving end. Jamie had to unpack as many fancy liqueurs as one could legally purchase at their duty-free ports of call.

Mother inspected her garden and pronounced her begonias alive but little else. "I don't think Martha talked to them," she complained of the woman who had attended the plants. "Oh, she did a good job, but they do enjoy being spoken to. Tomorrow they will know I've returned."

Tomorrow the begonias would be begging for earplugs.

By cocktail time things had calmed down and the McNally family was back to their familiar routine. We gathered in the den where Father poured and stirred and served as Mother smiled approvingly and I raised my glass in a toast. "The best present you brought us is yourselves, back home safe and sound."

"Why, Archy, how lovely," Mother applauded.

"Thank you, Archy," Father said, unbending as far as the Chairman of the Board would ever unbend. "I trust you're not going out tonight, as I'd like to confer with you after dinner."

"I thought as much, sir, and made no plans."

Being on the ship-to-shore with Mrs. Trelawney daily, it was not office matters Father needed to be advised of. Jamie had apparently had a chance to tell him of my involvement with Sabrina Wright. They say thoughts have wings, and ours must have touched down on Mother's shoulder.

"Did you hear about the writer Sabrina Wright?" she

exclaimed. "It was all the talk at breakfast. The ship's newspaper put out a special edition to make the announcement. I can't tell you how many of the ladies had brought her latest book along for leisure reading. What have you heard, Archy?"

We tend to keep the more harrowing aspects of my business from Mother as it only aggravates her hypertension. However, rather than lie to her, which would be undignified, we simply soften the rough edges or omit the more sordid details. In keeping with this edict, I readily admitted, "I met Sabrina Wright shortly after she arrived here."

"Really, Archy? How exciting. Was it at a book signing?"

"I would be more interested in hearing about Binky's housewarming party," Father insisted. "Did he like my gift, and how many more did he receive?"

Always amiable to forgo a celebrity for a friend, Mother started in her chair, "Oh, yes. Mrs. Trelawney told us Binky now has his own apartment. Tell us all about it, Archy."

I regaled them with life at the Palm Court until Ursi announced dinner. It had been a long day for the travelers, who were looking forward to retiring early in a bed not bolted to the floor. With this in mind, the ever-vigilant Ursi presented us with light but satisfying fare, consisting of a crabmeat cocktail with lemon and a tangy red pepper sauce, grilled chicken breasts, chilled sliced beets marinated in vinegar and tossed with diced onions, steamed broccoli florets, and Ursi's own home-baked bread, which has become a staple of her kitchen.

In a celebratory mood, the Squire poured a bottle of Château Lafite, 1950. Mother, as always, stayed with her sauterne. The homecoming meal ended with ice cream and Ursi's almond cookies.

I kissed Mother's velvety cheek before Father escorted

her to bed shortly after dinner. "I missed you so," she whispered to her favorite son. I assured her the feeling was mutual and went into the den to await Father's return. When he joined me, he took his customary seat behind his desk and asked if I would join him in a glass of port. "I would, sir, thank you." I went to the sideboard and poured two glasses of the wine, serving the Gov'nor before perching in a comfortable wing chair.

"To your good health, Archy," he saluted. "It's good to be home." Stroking his mustache, he said, "Wasn't there a book a while back called *Ship of Fools?*"

As the Master is a latter-day Victorian who reads only Dickens, this caught me off guard. But like Jamie Olson, *mon père* is a keen listener and what he hears, he does not forget. "Yes, sir. A much praised novel by Katherine Anne Porter. It was also a very popular film. I take it your holiday is what brings it to mind."

"Yes," he sighed. "There were a few good chaps aboard, but Porter's title has much to say about the majority of our shipmates. However, your mother relaxed and enjoyed it and for that reason I have no regrets and would gladly do it again."

Amazing how devoted he was to his wife of almost half a century. Would I one day sit in that swivel leather chair behind that great oak desk and utter the same sentiment? I think not. I gently swirled my port in the fine crystal glass, savored its aroma, and drank. *For the likes of such as me, mine's a fine, fine life.*

Father opened the side drawer of his desk and brought out his cigars. "Archy?" he said, proffering the box.

"No, thank you, sir." I took out my English Ovals. "I'll have one of these."

Don't be misled by this. Father was anxious to learn my

news, but the rituals must be observed. The after-dinner port, the comments regarding his shipmates that were not meant for feminine ears, the cigar, its tip now being removed with a special scissors, and finally touching flame to stogy before puffing it to life. Did he pretend we sat in a gaslit room filled with furniture adorned with antimacassars? Did he hear the *clop, clop, clop* of horse-drawn carriages on cobblestones echoing through the dense evening fog? Was I Boswell to his Johnson, or was he Watson to my Holmes?

Exhaling a cloud of smoke, he said, "Perhaps Sabrina Wright's death brought to mind the Porter novel. Jamie tells me you were working for the lady?"

"Briefly, sir. If you would indulge me, I think I should tell you all that transpired from the day I met Sabrina Wright to this very morning."

"You have the floor, Archy."

As the story unfolded, Father stroked, tugged, and blinked as his one eyebrow rose and fell with the speed of an express elevator in a busy office building at lunchtime. Each gesture depicted his thoughts more eloquently than the spoken word.

"An Appleton, a Cranston, and a Schuyler," he intoned at the conclusion as if each were a deity, and perhaps, to Prescott McNally, they were. "All three? And the story is true?"

"I see no reason why those involved would lie, sir."

He shook his head as he tugged on his bushy mustache. "And you were at Casa Gran?"

"It was a fund-raiser for Troy Appleton," I said, but it's so seldom I get a chance to impress Father I went into details with, "Harry Schuyler took me to the roof garden where we spoke in private."

Father's eyebrow disappeared into his hairline. "The roof

garden is off-limits when the house is lent for charitable events," he said. "You know I did some work for Schuyler a few years ago. Nothing much, but I was hoping for more."

As I related my meeting with Al Rogoff, I commented, "The police are convinced that Gillian's search is the reason Sabrina was murdered. They think the girl was gathering information on a prominent Palm Beach family for her mother. Zack Ward's involvement with a tabloid only adds fuel to the rumors. Strange how close everyone is to the truth."

Father continued to smoke thoughtfully as I put out my cigarette. The second for today, but it was an exceptional day.

"Would you please pour me another dram, Archy, and help yourself to more if you like." When I had refilled both our glasses the Gov, still nonplussed, ruminated, "An Appleton, a Cranston, and a Schuyler. Remarkable."

Father was never a gossip, but he could not conceal his excitement over this intimate look into the lives of three of the richest men in the country. "Tom Appleton keeps a mistress, Dick Cranston has a drinking problem, and Harry Schuyler is not long for this world," he went on. "Each of them thinks he is the father of Sabrina's daughter, and without even knowing which one is, she beat them all out of a fortune. What an extraordinary woman."

"She was, sir, but not very timid, I'm afraid. She ruled her family like a czarina and harbored a great resentment against those three men in spite of beating them at their own game and continued to goad them when they met again this past week. For all that she was special and, as you said, extraordinary."

"You've seen the daughter. Do her looks give the father away?"

"I'm afraid not, sir. She doesn't resemble her mother either, but then I'm told my sister looks like Mother and I look like an orphan."

"You look like my father," he said with foreboding.

Having seen pictures of Freddy McNally, I was aware of this, but as Father likes to think the stork brought him (directly to Yale, I presume), I am mum on the subject. That I am a constant reminder of the McNally days on the burlesque circuit is a tough rood to tote around Palm Beach, believe me. Being tossed out of *mein papa's* alma mater does not help my cause.

"Who do you think did it, Archy?"

"Cranston. He's the most desperate and the murdering kind. Maybe he had one too many before his meeting with Sabrina."

"I cast my lot with Schuyler. As he said, he has nothing to lose."

Experience told me that the least likely suspect was usually the guy who done it. Sorry, Tom.

"For all her faults," I said, "I would like to see the one who did this pay for his transgression while upholding Sabrina's end of the bargain."

Shaking his head as if to clear it of all I had told him, Father returned to his abstemious self when he said, "I don't think that's possible, Archy."

"Sir?"

He flicked his cigar ash in the tray on his desk and answered, "If Sabrina Wright was killed to prevent her from revealing the name of Gillian's father, you are in danger of meeting the same fate."

"The thought had occurred to me and, apropos of this meeting, so are you."

"No one is aware of this meeting, Archy, but you and I,

and I promise not to tell if you don't." He smiled at his own wit, which was indeed a rarity. "But there's more to this than your imminent danger."

It's rather startling to be prioritized and come in second.

"I speak of our duty to assist the police in apprehending a murderer," he lectured, "especially one who is poised to murder again. You know all the facts and it's your duty to report them to the police and let them proceed from there. You are not capable of hunting down a murderer, especially one who is out to get you first. I don't relish the idea of my son in the role of a moving target."

I did not remind him that I had apprehended a few murderers in my time, with great success, because I thought he might be genuinely worried about me getting in the way of a bullet. "If I go to the police, sir, two innocent men will go down with the guilty one."

"There are no innocent men in this scandal, Archy. There are only rotters and scoundrels who will get what they deserve."

Remember, he was speaking about those he revered— the super-rich landed gentry— but in the age-old battle between justice and privilege, Prescott McNally would always side with the former and lament the errant ways of the latter. Pomposity is Father's style, not his religion.

After a pause— a bit theatrical I thought— he continued, "This is not an order. When I put you in charge of Discreet Inquiries, I did so without reservations. You've proved yourself worthy of that decision many times over and what I suggest now is not a matter of opinion but of law, the law we are all pledged to uphold."

He was right. No question about it, but I could not turn my back on the obligation I believed I owed Sabrina Wright. To this end I pleaded my suit. "I discuss all my

cases with you not because I must, but because I value
your judgment," was how I began. "This case is no exception. When I learned of Sabrina Wright's death this morning, your return was the only light at the end of a long,
dark tunnel. I sought your counsel and you've given it."

"But there's a caveat," he anticipated.

"I want a chance to talk with Appleton, Cranston, and
Schuyler."

"That could be dangerous, Archy," he put in.

"One of them may have killed her, sir, but none of them
are hardened criminals who would murder indiscrimi-
nately. Sabrina didn't know the meaning of tact and may
have driven her adversary over the edge in a moment of
rage."

"He went to meet her with a loaded gun," came the attorney's rebuttal.

"Perhaps to frighten her, but she wasn't the type to
kowtow even when facing a loaded pistol. I'm asking for a
chance to meet with them and I want to see Sabrina's husband and daughter. I want to know what they're thinking
and what they intend to do now that Sabrina is gone. Will
her husband and daughter cooperate with the police? Will
Gillian give up the search and go home? Did they really
believe Sabrina went riding at night to think up romantic
plots? They may possess crucial knowledge but don't realize it because they know only half the facts."

"More like one-third of the facts," Father corrected with
a sardonic air. "What are you asking, Archy?"

"For time, sir. Give me twenty-four hours." I looked at
my watch. Mickey's arms were wide open. Fifteen minutes past nine. "I will go to the police tomorrow evening
regardless of what I turn up between now and then."

Father tugged at his hairy upper lip. Bad sign. Then he

began to stroke it. A reprieve? "I will go along with it, Archy, not because I believe it's right but because I don't wish to live the rest of my life speculating on what might have been."

"Thank you, sir."

He began fingering a leather-bound copy of *Great Expectations* and I knew I was being dismissed. "One moment," he said as I prepared to get out of my chair. "That girl you were telling us about. Binky's neighbor. Did you say her employer met with an accident in her pool? I think I recall reading about it before your mother and I left on our holiday."

"That's correct, sir. Her name is Bianca Courtney and the woman was Lilian Ashman Gilbert." I repeated the story I had told earlier, only now I included the saga of Lilian's marriage and Bianca's suspicions, which I had left out in deference to Mother.

"And he doesn't inherit, you say?"

"No, sir, he does not."

"Interesting. Very interesting."

But I didn't know if he was talking about Tony Gilbert or Pip.

TWENTY-THREE

"YOUR FATHER HAS already left," Ursi informed me when I came down to breakfast.

Good. It was why I had lingered over my ablutions. Ever diligent, I knew Father would want to arrive at the office exceptionally early on his first day back at the helm. Mrs. Trelawney, as always, would be there to greet him when he walked in the door. I was more than a little apprehensive about the day ahead and I did not want to start out with Father's doubts, fears, and cautions ringing in my ears.

"Just scrambled eggs and toast, Ursi, please," I ordered. "It's all I can take this morning."

"I have a lovely fruit cup," Ursi tempted me, "with fresh pineapples and cherries."

Not wanting to offend, I accepted the offer. "But no cream. Just the fruit." The colorful array was cool, refreshing, and delicious, but I missed the cream.

"Jamie has gone to gas up the Ford and your mother is in the greenhouse. She's been there practically since dawn."

I saw Ursi add a splash of milk to the bowl before she started scrambling the eggs. "I have those breakfast sausages you like. Should I put a couple in the skillet?" she asked.

"Why not?" I would start my diet, once more, tomorrow, if I wasn't shot dead before then. If I was, it wouldn't make any difference if I had my eggs with or without the sausages.

Busy at her stove, Ursi prattled, "The murder is the talk of the town, Archy. Everyone is guessing who the family is that poor Sabrina Wright was after. Neither her husband nor daughter has given the police a statement as yet, but when they do, we'll all know who it is."

Curiosity made me ask, "Who are the leading suspects?"

"Harry Schuyler, hands down," Ursi said. "He wasn't called a terrible infant for nothing."

"I believe the expression is *enfant terrible* when you're talking about the very rich. But what could one write about Harry Schuyler that hasn't already seen print?"

"With his kind I imagine what we know only scratches the surface. I think Sabrina Wright had something on him that no one in the world knows."

Out of the mouths of babes, I pondered. "And you think he did her in, Ursi?"

"Him or the one she was after. Her daughter knows who it was. Why, it's like a Sabrina Wright novel without the romance."

My eggs and sausages were placed before me, and forgetting to tell Ursi I wanted dry rye toast, I was handed a generously buttered English muffin. Having been taught to eat what is served without making a fuss, I did just that.

I went to the greenhouse to have a word with Mother before I left. I do this as often as time will allow because I enjoy seeing her in the joyful serenity she derives from administering TLC to her beloved blossoms. The dappled light coming through the tinted glass cast her in a warm glow, and when she looked up at my entrance, I noticed a smudge of brown earth on her perpetually blushing cheek. Her apron was also stained, her hair slightly ruffled, and her smile endearing. It was a picture I would cherish all my life.

"Oh, Archy, your new jacket, and it's a perfect fit. I knew it would be."

I wore the raw-silk yellow jacket with a dark brown shirt and chinos. "I dressed for you this morning, Mother," I said kissing her unsoiled cheek.

"How flattering. And see how much better my begonias look since I've been back. I told them all about our cruise."

They did look rather perky on this lovely Palm Beach summer morning. Blue sky, bright sun, and a refreshing ocean breeze that promised not to forsake us by noon. "Father told me how much you enjoyed it."

She frowned. "Between us, Archy, it wasn't all that wonderful. Too much to eat and too much to do. What they have against only three proper meals a day and a good old lounge chair, I'll never know. But your father needed to get away, and even if he did call the office every day, he managed to relax and unwind a bit, and that made it all worthwhile."

Was this a marriage made in heaven? And how nice to

be a by-product of the union. "He said he had a marvelous time, Mother."

She looked at me wistfully. "What are your plans today, Archy?"

"This and that. Nothing special."

"You will be careful, son, won't you?"

What was this all about? "I'm always careful, Mother. Why the long face?"

"You are involved in the Sabrina Wright murder, aren't you?"

I could not believe that Father had told her and I have never known Ursi or Jamie to trouble Mother with any gossip more malicious than reporting what Palm Beach matron had worn the same dress twice in one season. Seeing my quandary, she said, "Your mother is not as sharp as she used to be, but she's not ready for the recycling bin just yet."

"If they recycled you, Mother, what would you come back as?"

"A begonia, what else?"

"Do your begonias tell tales out of school?"

She brushed back a stray curl and anointed her forehead with yet another smudge. "I saw Jamie whispering to your father when we were waiting for our luggage at the dock. Last night I decided to open up a few topics and see which I would not be allowed to pursue. Sabrina Wright's murder was the obvious choice. Your father couldn't be less interested in Binky's housewarming than I am in growing roses."

I laughed. Long concerned with her short-term memory loss and her torpid interludes, I was more relieved at this sudden burst of astuteness than in her knowing the truth. "Okay, Miss Marple, I did some work for the lady when she arrived in town, and she was alive and well when the job was done. I was not connected to her at the time of her death."

"Will the police want to question you?" she asked.

"I imagine they will, Mother."

"Are you going to help them find the murderer?"

I could honestly answer in the negative because what I intended to do I would do on my own. "I am going to tell the police what I know and leave it to them."

"I'm so glad, Archy."

"So am I, Mother." I gave her another peck on the cheek and made my way out of the greenhouse.

THE STRETCH LIMO got on my tail the moment I pulled onto Ocean Boulevard. I picked up speed and raised my voice in song, *Three blind mice, three blind mice . . .*

I was tempted to lead him to the scene of the crime, but I didn't fancy being CNN's morning newsbreaker. Would the guy shoot me in the bright light of day? No, he would have his driver do it. Taking my time I drove to an outdoor juice bar in Lake Worth. I pulled into the limited parking area and the limo joined me. I did not get out of the Miata. If Dickey Cranston wanted me, he could come and get me. If he sent his driver to invite me in, I would hold my ground.

We played the brinkmanship game for a couple of minutes, which is a long time when you're taking up space in an outdoor juice bar and not lapping up the papaya. I decided to give the future ambassador to the Court of St. James's sixty seconds to make his intentions known, then I would be the man that got away. At the count of thirty the limo door opened, the passenger door that is, and Mohammed came to the mountain.

"What do you know?" he grunted before he was seated.

"I know that Sabrina is dead."

"Thanks. I got the news yesterday, shortly after midnight."

Had he made his first error? "Strange, because it didn't hit the wire services until early yesterday morning."

"Stop playing the clever dick, Archy. Washington never sleeps and I'm never out of touch. What do you know about it?"

"I know I had no reason to murder the woman," I said.

"Implying that I did? Sorry, but I didn't."

Time and space precluded finessing around the bush. "Don't tell me you weren't relieved to hear that the only person who could name Gillian's father was dead."

"You look very much alive to me, Archy," he shot back, pulling a pack of cigarettes from his jacket pocket.

He was correct, as far as the supposition went. With Sabrina gone I was the only person who could name the contenders. What I could not do was crown the champ. Neither could Sabrina, but that didn't prevent her from getting a bullet in her head.

Covering my back, I told him, "I keep a journal, Dickey, and everything that passed between Sabrina Wright, you, and me, has been faithfully recorded. I willed it to Lolly Spindrift."

He lit up. The Miata is not a stretch limo, therefore I was forced to have my first secondhand cigarette of the day. I rolled down my window but Cranston didn't seem to notice. He sucked on the filtered tip like it was the first one he had had in a year and wasn't likely to get another in the near future. His hand was trembling, his forehead was wet and shiny, and his knee had suddenly developed a spastic tic. Was he in the throes of withdrawal or scared out of his gourd?

"I didn't kill Sabrina," he said, "although I would have liked to when last we met. Fame and good fortune only made her more arrogant. And I have no intention of killing you. I've done some foolish things in my life, Archy, but I am not a fool. Killing Sabrina, or you, only draws attention to the problem. It solves nothing.

"With Sabrina alive there was a chance to ride this out. Now, every gossip in town is speculating on what she and her daughter were doing here. Looking for the girl's natural mother? How long before someone trashes that myth? Then who is the girl looking for?"

He wasn't telling me anything I didn't already know. As none of them were idiots, I couldn't understand why one of them had pulled that trigger. It had to have been done in a fit of rage and just because Cranston was stressing the stupidity of the act didn't mean he wasn't the guilty party. As stated, he was no fool.

"What were you doing at Harry's place?" he suddenly asked.

Calling Casa Gran Harry's place was like referring to Buckingham Palace as Lizzy's pad. "He told you I was there in lieu of my father."

"Spare me. Harry doesn't need a lawyer unless he's planning on making a new will which he isn't." He dragged on his cigarette and pulled out a handkerchief to wipe his forehead. "So?"

I pleaded client confidentiality and he attacked. "When I saw you with Harry at Troy's fund-raiser, I remembered that I met Sabrina at a party Harry gave in his hotel suite in Fort Lauderdale that spring thirty years ago. Harry must know her, too."

Puff, puff. Wipe, wipe. "Sabrina hits town and contacts you. Her daughter starts snooping around and the next thing we know Harry Schuyler and I are chummy with Archy McNally. Coincidence?"

It was just what Sabrina had rightly feared. Open a can of worms and there's no stopping them from crawling out. Was Appleton at that party? How long before Cranston would place all three of them in the same hotel suite, at the same time? But it wasn't Gillian who wielded the can opener. It was Lolly Spindrift's blind item that had the three former preppies in a dither. And two anonymous calls? Coincidence?

Avoiding his insinuation, I got down to the nuts and bolts of our second meeting on wheels. "The police are going to question me," I told him.

"And what are you going to tell them?"

"The truth. What else? I often work with the police and screwing them has a boomerang effect. I have to work in this town, unless you have an opening at the Court of St. James's."

He pulled another cigarette from his pack and lit it with the other before tossing it out of the window. I hoped his buddy on Pennsylvania Avenue had more control over his emotions. "If you tell them about Sabrina and me, all you'll be doing is screwing me, my family, and everything I've worked for all my life. I didn't do it and I can prove it. Fingering me would help no one but Sabrina's killer."

"What's your alibi?"

"It happened about ten Saturday night– is that correct?" he said.

I nodded. "Give or take an hour. The M.E. will always give himself an hour either way."

Puff, puff. Wipe, wipe. "At seven that night my sponsor picked me up and we attended an AA meeting in West Palm. It lasted until eight. From there my sponsor, I, and two other persons from the meeting drove to a rehab center to lecture the new recruits. They didn't like what we had to say. We left there at ten and went for pizza and diet Coke. I was driven home just after midnight when my wife told me about the call from Washington and Sabrina's murder."

Silence. I mean, what could I say?

He went on. "If you link me with Sabrina, I will have to give the police my alibi. The world will learn of my problem as well as my boyhood indiscretion. I will most likely lose my appointment and the witnesses will have to be interrogated. My sponsor is a prominent family man. Also with us that night was a schoolteacher and single parent with a child to support. None of us are ashamed of what we are but we do have our pride. You will be rocking many boats for no reason. Give it some thought, buddy."

I was giving it so much thought I couldn't think. Was he bluffing? If I folded and walked away, he wins without showing his hand. If I called him and he laid out a royal flush, I'm a skunk. Excuse the old cliché, but it does say it all– damned if you do and damned if you don't.

"Will you give me the names of your witnesses?" I said.

"No," he responded without hesitation. He appeared to be in control of himself for the first time since entering the car. He looked at his cigarette as if wondering what it was doing in his hand, and it followed its predecessor out the window. Perhaps the truth does set one free– if he was telling the truth. It was a tough confession to make for a man with the conceit of Richard Cranston. Or was he manipulating me? Could I afford to take another chance or had I taken too many already?

"I have to think about it," I finally said.

"Thanks."

"Por nada. May I say I admire your courage and wish you well in your new life?"

He smiled his best press-conference smile, obliterating the impudent snob. Which one was the real Richard Cranston? "My new life in sobriety or in England?"

"Why not both?" I answered.

"Before I go, tell me if Harry is involved in any of this. You know he's dying?"

"And therefore he has *carte blanche* to commit murder. Sorry, but I won't tell you the nature of my business with Harry Schuyler. Last time we met we talked about the sacrosanct nature of client confidentiality. It applies to all clients."

"If you go to the police, you'll be breaking the rule with this client."

"As they say, Dickey, damned if you do and damned if you don't."

"You missed your calling, Archy, you should have gone into politics."

ON THE DRIVE back to the McNally Building, I regretted that time did not allow me to present Father with the perplexity of Cranston's alibi. Would Justice tip her scale in favor of the law or compassion for those brave souls striving to make a new life for themselves and trying to help others along the way? Archy leaned toward compassion, but Archy is a soft touch– and is the guy telling the truth?

Herb gave me the high sign from his post in our underground garage. Today, I did not need Mrs. Trelawney to tell me who had called. On the way to the elevator, I paused long enough to report, "Binky's waffles landed in his lap."

Unconcerned at having presented Binky with a lethal weapon, Herb told me, "Two of Binky's fingers are wrapped in bandages."

"Burns," I said.

"No, Archy. The burns were superficial. Seems he nicked himself on his chopping block. Maybe he should go to a cooking school."

"I think a reform school is the answer. Did he mention his new lady friend?"

"Mention her? He can't stop talking about her. She bandaged his fingers."

Binky Watrous was being buttered and bandaged by his neighbors. How nice. But did he know about the basketball player? I couldn't wait to tell him.

I called Mrs. Trelawney. Mr. Appleton had called and left a number where I could reach him. It was urgent. Al Rogoff had called and said I should contact him regarding setting up an appointment to meet with the lieutenant in charge of the Sabrina Wright case. Nothing from Harry Schuyler.

Appleton picked up on the first ring. "Archy? Thank goodness. Where have you been?"

"Working, Tom. Some of us do, you know."

"I must see you. You know why, I'm sure. Where can we meet privately?"

"The PB Institute of Contemporary Art?"

"They're closed on Monday," he said.

I thought a moment, then asked, "Do you know where L'Encantada is now located?"

"Who doesn't?" Appleton said.

"Meet me at the site in thirty minutes. It's still a tourist attraction and we'll pretend to be one of the gawkers."

"Fine. I'm on my way."

L'Encantada is an Addison Mizner mansion that has become one of the wonders of Palm Beach. Built in Manalapan in the roaring twenties, it was destined for demolition last winter when the daughter of a local real-estate investor attended a party in the doomed house and begged her father to save it. Recently divorced and wanting to please his little girl with a grand gesture, he bought the mansion for millions and spent even more millions to have it floated to a new site on Seaspray Avenue and South Ocean Boulevard.

Yes, I said, floated. Like Caesar's Gaul, the twenty-room house was divided into three parts, and each section, one weighing in at four hundred twenty tons, was hoisted on rollers and pulled with cables along the beach and into the ocean, where they were mounted on barges for the short trip north, where the process was reversed and the house put back together on its new lot. Watching the house come ashore was last winter's most popular spectator sport. In these parts, the gesture has become the standard by which all devoted fathers will be judged.

Sofia Richmond called before I left my office. "I hear you lost a client," was her opener.

"You win some and you lose some. What do you hear?"

"It would be easier to tell you what I haven't heard. Sabrina was after one of our elite. Her daughter was doing the legwork and pretending to be looking for her natural mother. Sabrina is her natural mother and the girl's father is Prince Philip, Porfirio Rubirosa (remember him?), and Frank Sinatra."

"All three?" I exclaimed.

"No, Archy. One must choose. I understand the ladies who lunch have gotten up a pool."

"And who are you putting your money on?"

"Archy McNally, of course. I'm betting he knows all the answers."

Smart lady, my Sofia. Very smart. "Put a fiver on Porfirio, Sofia, they say he had . . . "

"Careful, Archy, this call may be monitored for quality purposes. Did you see Lolly's obit this morning? He links her with every big name in pants, including you."

"Me?" I would kill Lolly Spindrift.

" 'When Sabrina Wright arrived in Palm Beach just a week ago, the first person she contacted was our own most eligible bachelor, and my dear friend, Archy McNally. Stay tuned to these pages for all the latest developments on the popular author's murder,' unquote."

The little twerp. Implying that I was going to tell all for him to pass on to his readers. "Wishful thinking," I said aloud.

"I thought so," Sofia said. "How much can you tell me?"

"Today, nothing. Tomorrow, the world. Now I have to go, Sofia. I'll catch you later."

"That's the story of my life," she sighed audibly. "Take care, Archy. Someone out there didn't like Sabrina and Lolly has made you her confidant."

I wanted to tell her that everyone had made me their confidant and Lolly had nothing to do with it. I rang off with a promise of taking her to lunch before the week was out.

AS PREDICTED, THERE were a few cars parked near the newly planted stucco and tile Mizner dream cottage. I saw Appleton get out of his BMW convertible and, after parking, joined him on the street. Given the venue, it was a perfectly natural place to congregate and chat. Thomas Appleton, however, was anything but natural, unless hysteria is your bag.

"What the hell happened?" he stage whispered as I approached.

We were far enough from the two couples who had stopped to see what the tide had dragged in to speak without being heard. "Someone murdered Sabrina, that's what happened. Any ideas who did it?"

His Santa jowls glowed. "If you think I did, forget it. It must have been a lunatic."

"Did you meet with her last week?"

"Yes, and she was a perfect bitch. She told me not to worry and to bug off, thank you. She said she would take care of her daughter."

"But someone took care of her instead, didn't they?"

"I tell you, it wasn't me." He kept a stealthy eye on the tourists. "Have the police questioned you?"

"Not yet, but I got a call today to contact them."

"And what will you tell them?"

Each time I met with these three guys was like being in a hit show on Broadway. One had to play the same scene again and again. Thirty years ago Sabrina must have felt the same way, but being the star she had been well paid for her trouble. "I'm going to tell them what I know. I have no choice."

He was practically doing a tap dance on Seaspray Avenue. "You do have a choice. I spoke to you in confidence and you have no right to betray that trust."

"A woman has been brutally slain and I have every right to tell the police what I know."

"When you saw me at Troy's gathering you pretended not to know me. Why can't we keep it that way?"

"I just told you," I said, "there's been a murder and that changes everything."

"And why did Harry want to see you? I find it very strange that a few days after our meeting, you get a call from Harry."

"I find it very strange that a man who has nothing to hide is afraid of being questioned by the police."

The tourists went back in their cars, leaving Tom Appleton and me alone on the street. He was biting his lower lip so hard I thought it would bleed. "Damn it, I do have something to hide, but not what you think.

"I didn't want to do this," he ranted, "but I see I have to. I went to New York for the weekend and stayed with a friend. I got back this morning. I took a commercial line and the stewardess will vouch for me. I'm a regular commuter. Then we have the doorman at the apartment building where I was a guest and the staff at Le Cirque where I dined Saturday night. For reasons which are none of your business I do not wish to implicate my New York friend in this mess. You can go to the police and tell them I'm Gillian Wright's father and then you can go to the devil."

Well, ain't that a boot in the buttocks?

TWENTY-FOUR

THAT EITHER DICK Cranston or Tom Appleton had employed a hired gun to do the job for them was too insane to be worth a precious moment of my time. Only the one who was to meet Sabrina that night knew where to find her and both Cranston and Appleton had scheduled other appointments which they had both dutifully kept. That left Harry-come-lately. The guy who was up north when Sabrina hit town, the guy who was the last to meet with Sabrina, and the guy who had nothing to lose by committing murder.

Harry Schuyler was also the only one not eager to confer face-to-face with Archy this morning. What was he waiting for?

After being told where to go by Tom Appleton, I heeded him not and went to The Breakers instead. The television vans and their crews were being kept a good distance from the exclusive grounds. Their presence told me that Silvester and Gillian had not left the compound. The reporters on the grounds and in the lobby tried to look like paying customers and failed miserably. The hacks from New York were in dark suits and their colleagues from California sported designer jeans and polo shirts emblazoned with a variety of circus animals.

I marched up to the desk and asked them to ring Robert Silvester's room.

"Sorry, sir. Mr. Silvester is not taking calls or seeing visitors."

"If you ring him and say Archy McNally wants to see him, I think he will acquiesce."

The clerk started and gave me the wide eye. "Mr. McNally? Yes, sir. I'll ring Mr. Silvester's suite."

There were times, like now, when a mention in Lolly's column went a long way in awing restaurateurs and hotel clerks. Unfortunately for Sabrina Wright, Lolly's glib notice was the prelude to the end of her life. Either way, it was a chilling indication of the power of the press. The clerk told me Mr. Silvester would see me and gave me the suite number, which I already knew. With a thank-you, I headed for the elevators.

They were all there– Silvester, Gillian, and Zack Ward– exhibiting signs of repressed hysteria aggravated by a good dose of cabin fever. Silvester looked angry, Gillian looked as if she had been crying, and Zack Ward stood slightly apart from the pair looking as embarrassed as a stranger who had intruded upon a family squabble. Gillian was done up in a rather smart beige linen suit featuring a knee-length skirt and a mock turtleneck in white knit. Her hair had been cut short and shaped like a snug cap about her head. Could she have been made over by Virginia Cranston's hairstylist? If so, he had made her look remarkably like her mother.

"I'm glad you're here, Mr. McNally," Silvester said. "I've been calling your office all morning."

"I've been out," I answered, then quickly added, "My sympathies to both of you."

"Thank you," Silvester said.

"My father didn't do it, Mr. McNally," Gillian cried.

Out of patience, Silvester reproached her. "Let's discuss this with Mr. McNally like rational people."

"We have been discussing it for two days and my answer is still no," the girl ranted. Ward went to her and took her hand.

Ignoring them, Silvester turned to me, "Have you spoken to the police?"

"No. I wanted to speak to you and Ms. Wright before I saw them."

"Thank you, and we wanted to talk to you," Silvester said. "We have to report to the police station in an hour and we'll have to face the press before we do and make a statement"– here he glared at Zack Ward– "although some of us have already been talking to the press . . . ad nauseam."

"It's my job," Ward said, not concealing his defiance. "And all I've reported are the known facts. I haven't told them anything else."

"You've told them you're on the inside," Silvester charged, "holding the distressed daughter's hand, when not even the man from the *New York Times* has been able to get near her."

"But he didn't tell them my father did it," Gillian said, "as you want to do."

It was clear this screaming match had been going on since the murder, and the bone of contention was becoming clearer with each salvo. Joining Cranston and Appleton, Silvester asked me, "What are you going to tell the police, Mr. McNally?"

"The truth, and nothing but."

"No," Gillian screamed. "No, no, no."

"Jill, shut up and listen to reason," Silvester all but shouted. "We, and Mr. McNally, have no choice. We must tell them the truth."

Gillian reprised her mantra. "My father didn't do it."

Playing the arbitrator, I offered, "If you would all calm down a moment, maybe we can work this out to everyone's satisfaction." It was pure swagger, but it did get their attention. "Rob, why don't you tell me what's been happening here this past week. I mean what was Sabrina doing— we all know what Jill and Zack were up to."

Silvester told me in detail that Sabrina had been nervous, edgy, and short-tempered with all of them since they had settled into The Breakers. She had pleaded with Gillian to give up her search and return to New York. She had promised Ward an exclusive for his rag if he could talk Gillian into returning home.

"She saw Gillian's father three times," Silvester said.

"You're just guessing," Gillian interrupted.

"One at a time," I reminded the girl. To Silvester, I said, "An informant told me that you told the police Sabrina went driving at night for creative inspiration."

"When they found her, I got the call," Silvester started to explain. "I went to the station house and Jill stayed here with Zack. They asked me what Sabrina was doing out alone at that hour and I didn't want to tell them until I had talked to Jill, so I made up that story."

"There," the girl pounced, "you wanted my permission to tell them and I won't give it to you, so why don't we stick to your original story? My father didn't do it."

"Do you know who your father is?" I asked her.

"You know I don't," she said.

"Then you don't know what he is capable of doing or what circumstances might have driven him to the limit," I stated, beginning to feel empathy with Robert Silvester.

On the brink of more tears, she sobbed, "It's too horrible to be true."

The clever reporter looked at me and asked, "Do you know who her father is, Mr. McNally?"

One of the few perks of the situation made it possible for me to answer honestly in the negative.

Determined to finish his story, Silvester was saying, "Sabrina received three calls last week. She went out at night after each one of them. I asked her where she was going, but she refused to tell me. I had no doubt that it was to meet Jill's father."

"How could he know what was going on?" Gillian said.

"Really," I answered for Silvester. "Between Lolly's gossip column and your snooping around the library and calling newspaper editors, he would have to be deaf, dumb, and blind not to know."

"I think," Silvester said, "that Sabrina tried to assure him that she would keep his secret and that she would take Jill home. Zack's profession had also become common knowledge because Zack can't refrain from showing people his press card. You can imagine how Mr. Anonymous felt about that."

"I show my card when I have to," Ward said. If Gillian wasn't clinging to his hand, I believe he would have hauled off and hit Silvester.

Unperturbed, Silvester continued, "Sabrina was not a diplomat, and I think the guy lost patience in their last meeting."

It was clear they all believed only one man was involved. Would I have to tell the police differently, naming all three? How would Gillian react to that? Silvester? Zack Ward would love it. Would the men be forced to give a blood sample? Would the doctor go on national television holding an envelope and emote, "And the winner is . . . "

But now that Cranston and Appleton were in the clear, did I have to name them? Couldn't I just cut to Harry Schuyler? I didn't know. But either choice would result in a betrayal of Sabrina's bargain.

"Lost patience," Gillian ridiculed. "Lost patience and took mother's jewelry and money? It was a common thief. We would only be helping the murderer if we force the police to look elsewhere."

"How would the police find your father?" Ward asked, as usual making the most sense. "If we couldn't find him, how will they?"

"That's not the point," she answered. "If we confess everything to the police, the media will have a field day with it and my father will think that we are accusing him. That I believe he's guilty. He would never agree to meet with me."

"Which he has no intention of doing anyway, Jill." Silvester seemed to take great pleasure in reminding his stepdaughter of her father's reluctance to come forward. "I think that should be perfectly clear to you by now. We have to tell the police what we know." Silvester looked at his watch. "The time has come to go down and face those reporters."

My steroidal hormones were telling me the time had

come to beat a hasty retreat. I began to withdraw slowly, shortening the distance between my back and the door.

"What do you suggest we tell the press, Mr. McNally?"

"No comment," I suggested.

"Would you like to come to the police station with us?" Silvester invited.

"No, thanks. I have my car."

"What will you tell the police?" Gillian called.

I had reached the door and opened it before replying, "The truth."

"No," she moaned. "No, no, no."

I WENT DIRECTLY to an accommodation phone and dialed Al Rogoff. If he was there, I vowed to have no more than one cigarette a day for the next year.

"Palm Beach Police, Sergeant Rogoff speaking."

And I learned firsthand the peril of answered prayers. "Al, it's Archy."

"Archy, where have you been? Sabrina Wright's family is on the way here and the lieutenant wants to speak to you before he sees them."

"Indulge me, Al, and refresh my memory. You told me no one knew that Sabrina had been relieved of her cash and her baubles. Does no one include her husband, Robert Silvester?"

"Yeah. We didn't tell him nothing. He told us what she was wearing and he made a brief statement. That would be about three o'clock Sunday morning."

"Could he have seen the jewelry missing when he saw the body?"

"He didn't see it," Al said. "The body went straight to the morgue. We knew who it was because of the car and the photo on her driver's license, which was in her purse. The formal ID and grilling is set for today. How come you're asking about them gems? We got a screwy call from some cheap rag up north this morning. They wanted to know if we could give them an estimate of the value of the missing jewelry. The lieutenant blew a fuse. So who leaked it?"

"Zack Ward. Sabrina's daughter's boyfriend. He works for that cheap rag."

"So how does he know?"

"The murderers told him, Al."

That got his attention. "You said 'murderers,' Archy?"

"That's right. The plural of murderer."

"I don't need no English lesson, pal. You on the level?"

"Trust me with this one," I said. "The only people other than the police and this ignoramus investigator who knew that the money and jewels were missing are the people who took them. Gillian Wright knows because she told me so and Silvester didn't seem a bit surprised by the fact. When they get to the Palace, Al, separate them posthaste."

"You telling us how to run the show, Archy?"

"I think Zack Ward is a patsy. But he can tell you who told him about the missing loot and I can corroborate."

It was to Al's professional credit that he took my news calmly, silently digesting the facts before acting upon them. "Good," he said, "the lieutenant will still want to see you."

"I'll be there, pal."

Inspired by a flash of diabolical naughtiness I was unable to resist, I dialed Arnold Turnbolt. Arnold is secretary to Mrs. John Fairhurst, a PB matron on all the "A" lists.

Arnie doubles as Mrs. Fairhurst's private "walker," a labor of love for which he is compensated by a tailor-made tux in which to strut about the best homes on the island.

Arnie is also a film buff nonpareil with an impressive collection of movie memorabilia, like old movie-house showcase stills and the official wedding photo of Alice Faye and Tony Martin, whose marriage was so brief neither party seemed to remember it in later years. When the actress Debbie Reynolds visited PB to speak at the Mary Rubloff YWCA Harmony House luncheon, she saw Arnie's collection and tried to snare a few items for her movie museum. If anyone could help me, it was Arnie.

"Fairhurst residence," Arnie announced.

"Archy McNally here."

"Archy, how are you? Long time no see."

"Busy days, Arnie."

"Sabrina Wright," he said. "What a scandal. According to Lolly you were her main man. What do you know?"

"No time now, Arnie. I'm calling to ask if you have a mock statue of Oscar."

"You mean the Academy Award Oscar? No, but I wish I did. When an actress, who shall be nameless, pawned hers, I tried to get it out of hock, but the ghouls with deep pockets got there first. Why do you need one?"

"I want to present it to a young lady," I confessed. "She just gave the performance of her life and I thought it would be a nice gesture."

"Is she Hollywood bound?" Arnie asked.

"No. In fact, she's on her way to twenty-five years to life without parole."

"You know the nicest people, Archy."

"It's my star quality that attracts 'em. Thanks, anyway, Arnie, and if you drop in at the Pelican tomorrow night, I'll stand you a drink for your trouble."

"You got a date, Mr. McNally."

TWENTY-FIVE

WANTING TO GIVE the police and their suspects time to get acquainted, I lunched before driving to the station house. My gourmet meal consisted of two slices of pizza topped with pepperoni and washed down with a bottle of commercial beer. This gave me time to reflect on the events of the past week and the circumstances that had shaped them. In that week a life had been snuffed out and two others would pay the piper with theirs. But the real story went back thirty years. An unwanted pregnancy resulting in an overbearing mother and a virago wife. Sabrina Wright had ruled her kingdom like a tyrant and there would be those who said she got what she deserved. Not this observer. Daughter and husband were not indentured servants. They could have walked away but refused to leave all that moola and privilege behind. Oppression was their excuse, greed their motive.

At the end of every case, you look back and rue all the stupid mistakes you made from the start. You gather information, draw conclusions, and drive merrily up the garden path, never noticing the towline attached to your front fender.

The television vans and the reporters, including Lolly Spindrift, had followed Sabrina's family to the precinct. Lolly waylaid me as soon as I got out of the Miata.

"What's happening, Archy? And remember, you owe me big," he hassled.

"The police will have a statement for the press shortly and I will give you an interview when they do," I promised. I moved past him and the others who now recognized me, thanks to Lolly's reception.

I entered the Palace without my statuette and was immediately grateful for Arnie's inability to provide one when I was greeted by an officer bearing the name tag "Lieutenant Oscar Eberhart." The gods move in mysterious ways, and as Mother often said of life's disappointments, "Everything happens for the best."

"I'm going to overlook Sergeant Rogoff's telling you what you have no business knowing because it's saved us mucho time, trouble, and embarrassment," Oscar said. "If he does it again, it'll cost him his badge."

"Thank you, sir." I tried to sound humble, which was difficult under the circumstances. I did crack the case. "Have they made a statement?"

"The reporter, Ward, told us the husband and the girl told him about the missing jewels and cash. When we confronted them with it, they clammed up. I think the girl will crack, but this Silvester won't budge. He called some big-shot lawyer in New York and the guy is on his way here."

"I can corroborate Ward's story," I said.

"So Rogoff tells me." Oscar didn't seem particularly pleased with my offer. "We're getting a warrant to search their rooms at the hotel. If the jewels Silvester described turn up, we can hold the one who's hiding them until a judge sets bail. The reporter is innocent. He talked, never knowing that he had incriminated the pair. He can go as soon as we've gone over his room, but he'll have to stay in Palm Beach until we issue a formal indictment."

"Can I see Silvester?"

"Ten minutes, but only because he might open up to you. There's a guard in the room with him. If you can get him to talk, the guard will get me."

It was a small room containing a table, four chairs, a uniformed policeman, and Robert Silvester. "Nice try," I said.

He told me what I could go do to myself, which, as we all know, is a physical impossibility.

I sat opposite him. "How long have you and Gillian been plotting to get rid of Sabrina?"

I was again told to do the impossible, so I answered my own question. The two of them must have said, "I could kill her," often enough for the empty threat to become a conspiracy. Perhaps a joke at first, devising means and opportunity, they were suddenly handed both when Sabrina made her confession to the girl. How simple. Gillian goes in search of her father, who is reluctant to come out of hiding, and the man must silence the only person who can finger him.

"I'm sure it was your idea," I said. "Gillian is the actress. You're the writer and director. When you told me she had attended drama school, I should have paid closer attention. I also should have asked you how you managed to find the girl and Zack Ward so soon after arriving in Palm Beach. Now we know the seemingly chance meeting was prearranged.

"Zack Ward, a tabloid reporter, was a dividend sent from heaven. Gillian and Zack came to Palm Beach in search of daddy, and up went the curtain."

They needed an investigator to snoop around and spread the word, and Silvester remembered me. He comes after Gillian, breaks contact with Sabrina, and she comes looking for the both of them. Silvester has already told Sabrina he will elicit my help in finding Gillian, therefore Sabrina contacts me upon arrival.

"It was you who tipped Lolly Spindrift, wasn't it? You told him Sabrina was here looking for a man and that was the match that lit the fuse. How did you know when and where Sabrina arrived? Now it's perfectly clear. Like a dutiful husband you called her travel agent in New York.

"Then Gillian, with the unsuspecting Zack, starts her search with all the fanfare of a marching band. Were you surprised when Sabrina got that first call and went off to meet the man you believed to be Gillian's father?"

Forgetting himself, Silvester said, "I was shocked. I didn't believe Sabrina's story. She was a genius when it came to creating plots."

But not even Sabrina Wright could have created the plot she had lived. Now, thanks to her assassins, and a loyal Archy McNally, her story would never be told and three very lavish floral wreaths, unsigned, would see her to her rest.

If Silvester didn't believe Sabrina's story of Gillian's birth, neither did Gillian. But when the calls came, they didn't stop to wonder that Sabrina was telling the truth. They thought it convenient that their fictional patsy was real, but Gillian had no intention of waiting around to claim her birthright. She and Silvester wanted only to get away as soon as possible and leave it to the police to solve the thirty-year-old mystery.

The first call must have taken them by surprise. They were not ready to make their move. They needed time for the gossip mill to build momentum. The second call was also a surprise, but when Sabrina went out that night, they must have lacked opportunity, perhaps because they couldn't get rid of Ward. Time was running out and just as they were beginning to put what must have been their original plan into operation, the third call came. This time luck was with them. Zack wanted to see the ball game. Lucky for him. If he hadn't, they would have gotten him out of the way if they had to drug him.

"Sabrina left, you and Gillian got in Gillian's rented car and followed her. It was conceivable that the meeting would not take place in a public place and you were right."

But where was Schuyler? If he had kept his date, Silvester and Gillian would have seen him. Did he arrive late to find Sabrina dead?

"It was Gillian's turn to make the anonymous call," I finished. "And because you thought any murderer would try to make it look like a robbery, you took the jewelry and cash. That was stupid, Rob. Very stupid."

Breaking his silence for the second and last time, he said, "The only stupid thing I did was remember your name." Then he turned his back on me.

Outside, I spotted Al Rogoff but we did not communicate. Due to the delicate nature of our business, we find it advantageous to keep our friendship under wraps when in public and especially on Al's home turf. It was absolutely necessary for Al to tell his superior of our last conversation, and Lieutenant Eberhart's reaction, grateful though he was, exemplifies the prudence of this artifice.

I could not see Gillian Wright as she was making a statement. I could imagine her trashing mommy, putting the gun in Silvester's hand, and pleading guilty of being abused by the one and manipulated by the other. If she gave a jury of her peers as good a performance as she had given me this morning, and if she only aided and abetted in the act of matricide, she just might get off with a slap on the wrist. Would she write a book? I must remember to tell her to refrain from mentioning me, as I don't like to be written about.

I did see Zack Ward.

"I'm sitting on the biggest story of the century and I can't get to a phone," he griped.

My, wasn't he concerned for the fate of his sweetheart. When he held Gillian's hand, all he was doing was hanging on to a story. Poor, poor Gillian. "Tell me," I asked him, "did you believe Sabrina's story about a former rich lover in Palm Beach?"

He shrugged. "Yes and no. I was along for the ride. If we struck pay dirt, I had the scoop. If we didn't, I could get an exclusive with Sabrina."

"What did you think when Sabrina got a call from Gillian's father?"

Ward grinned. "Was it Jill's father? Only Rob was so certain. Truth is, I thought Sabrina was getting it on with some young dude. That was her thing, you know, young hunks."

"Silvester didn't mind?"

"Why should he? He had a few bimbos on the side." Tabloid reporters sure do tell it like it is.

Fearing the worst, I said, "Not Gillian, I hope."

"No way. Jill is in love with me," came the modest retort.

"And you never found Daddy Warbucks," I said by way of an exit line.

"But I came up with something interesting," he divulged. "Just about thirty years ago this rich kid named Harry Schuyler gave some wild parties in his hotel suite in Fort Lauderdale during the spring-break craze. The police raided one of them for dope. It was all pot then, remember? All the kids were hauled in and this Schuyler's father posted bail for the lot.

"I'd like to check the Fort Lauderdale police blotter for an account of the raid and see if Sabrina Wright was one of the guests. Good angle for my piece, and who knows where it might lead?"

I knew exactly where it would lead because this is where I came in-- so I left.

"THE HUSBAND DID it," Herb called as I passed him on my way to the elevator. "The daughter made a statement. She was in on it. It's on CNN." Herb keeps a television the size of a postage stamp in his kiosk.

Mrs. Trelawney was about to tell me much the same thing, but I stopped her with, "I was at the police station when the girl talked."

She was most impressed, but for the wrong reason. "You went to the police station in a raw-silk yellow jacket? I'm surprised they didn't arrest you."

"Watch your tongue, Mrs. Trelawney; the mater and pater purchased this handsome coat on their travels. Is the master in his lair?"

"He is and he told me to let him know the moment you arrived."

"The moment has come," I said, and tapped gently on Father's office door.

When I heard, "Come," I entered a time warp.

Father's office could double as a set for a nineteenth-century film, and I have long suspected that a framed photo of Queen Victoria is hastily removed whenever the door opens. For this reason, one must always knock.

"Well," Father said, "you are saved from having to make your momentous decision. I've heard the news."

Taking a chair, I answered, "I am very relieved, sir, but not overjoyed at the outcome."

Father, in a blue suit with vest and regimental tie I do not believe he is authorized to wear, nodded solemnly. "Yes, a terrible business, but I'm glad it's over and you are still with us."

"Thank you, sir."

"Were you instrumental in breaking the case, Archy?"

"Let's say I helped."

"Fine. With the Sabrina Wright murder taking up all the news these past two days, something that should be of interest to you slipped through the cracks."

"What's that, sir?"

"Harry Schuyler has been hospitalized with a stroke."

Astonished, I asked, "When?"

"Saturday night as he was getting dressed to go out. I understand the situation is not life-threatening and that he is expected to make as much of a recovery as possible for a man in his condition."

Kismet, I thought. Was Harry's stroke responsible for Sabrina's death? Had he showed up, would it have deterred her avengers, or would Harry have saved them the trouble? "I'm sorry to hear that," I responded, not sure if I meant it.

In his business-as-usual tone, Father said, "That girl you were telling me about, Bianca Courtney, was it?"

This was a surprise. "That's her name, sir. Why do you ask?"

"You said the woman she worked for left her money to charity and not her husband. Is that correct?"

"It is," I assured him.

"Well, Archy, when I heard this I immediately thought the situation was not what it seemed but wanted to check my facts, which I did first thing this morning, and I was right."

"Right, sir? About what?"

"In the state of Florida, a surviving spouse has a right to claim up to thirty percent of the estate regardless of the designated legatee. Thirty percent of a large fortune amounts to millions of dollars." I would check to see if the husband has contacted a lawyer and begun proceedings.

THAT EVENING, ALONE in my penthouse, I poured myself a marc, lit my first and last English Oval of the day, and made the final entry in my journal regarding the case of "The Man That Got Away." Then I called Al Rogoff at his home. When he picked up I could hear Vivaldi in the background.

"She talked?" I said.

"Talked? Archy, the broad won't shut up. She's coming on as a witness for the prosecution against Silvester."

"Don't worry– when Silvester's lawyer gets here he'll have his say. He's very smart to keep silent till then."

Would Silvester raise the father issue? It could hurt him more than help him, and it was his word against Gillian's. Ward could be the deciding factor, saying they all believed Sabrina had made up the father tale without actually perjuring himself. He could say their search was an excuse to get away from Sabrina. When Sabrina followed them here, it infuriated Gillian, and with a little prodding from Silvester, who has a girl in the woodpile, the infamous deed was conceived. Yes, I think that's how it would play out, with Silvester taking the fall.

"Your boss read me the riot act, Al; sorry about that."

"Screw him, Archy. Between the two of us we have him looking like a hero. I ain't worried."

"I have another lead for you, Al."

"Yeah, what's that?"

"Tony Gilbert," I said.

"I don't want to hear it, Archy."

I told him anyway and, except for Vivaldi, was rewarded with silence. "I would exhume the body and have the forensic boys go over that barbell with a fine-tooth comb."

"Maybe we should contact Gilbert's lawyer first."

"That would help. And, Al, you don't have to tell Oscar Eberhart I fed you this one."

"I'll say it came to me in a dream," Al laughed.

Remembering my invitation to Arnie Turnbolt, I asked, "You free tomorrow night, Al?"

"I pulled a double, so I got twenty-four hours off. Why?"

"Drop in the Pelican and I'll buy you a round." Might as well make it a party.

"I just might, pal. Thanks."

TWENTY-SIX

"THE GIRL IS the victim," Ursi said, handing me a glass of juice. "She came down here to elope with the man she loves and her mother followed her and tried to stop her. The stepfather has a girlfriend and he talked the daughter into the murder, but it was him who pulled the trigger. It's all in the morning paper."

Jamie, at table with his coffee, waved the headline in my face.

Gillian had officially plagiarized my early account of her plight. Could I sue? "I think I'll have your fruit cup, Ursi, coffee and rye toast."

"That's it?" she wondered.

"That's it," I said, determined to drop a few pounds before summer's end. I was feeling the accumulated effects of yesterday's pizza and last night's roast beef extravaganza. Not wishing to rehash Sabrina's murder over my dismal breakfast, I turned to Jamie. "What other news is there, Jamie?"

"They say Troy Appleton is about to announce his candidacy for the Senate," Jamie reported.

"How nice," I observed over my fruit cup.

"Harry Schuyler, who had a stroke, is on the mend and expected to go back to his summer place up north in a week."

"More good news," I said.

"Richard Cranston has been named our ambassador to the Court of St. James's," Jamie rattled off.

"And his wife has a new hairdo," Ursi got in. "Cut very short and layered close to the scalp. Very fetching, they say."

Virginia Cranston will be reaching for a wig when she sees that photo of the accused in today's paper.

I CALLED BIANCA from my office to tell her of Father's brilliant clarification of the late Mrs. Gilbert's will.

"So I was right. He did it," she gloated.

"Easy, Bianca. Easy. This just means the police now have a good reason to open the case. I'm sure they'll want your testimony as they gather the facts."

"I'll leave them a forwarding address," she said.

"What's this?" I asked.

"I'm moving, Archy. I'm going to Coconut Grove with Brandon. He says it's wild down there, like Haight-Ashbury in the sixties."

"Does Binky know this?"

"Sure. He's taking me to the Pelican tonight for a farewell drink. Why don't you come?"

"Oh, I'll be there," I told her, "and so will your other neighbor, Al Rogoff."

"A party!" she said gaily. "My trailer will be up for grabs and Binky is giving Hermioni Rutherford your name as a potential tenant."

Me, Binky, and Al Rogoff living in a row like cabbages? For this Binky Watrous deserved to die. Could I talk him into using his microwave oven for a hair dryer? Yes, that's how I would do it.

"Why don't you call your girl, Archy? I'd like to meet her before I go," Bianca urged.

"She's busy," I said.

"Don't worry. I won't squeal on you."

The girl was out of control. "Okay. Maybe she's not busy."

I MUST SAY we were a happy group that night at the Pelican. Of course Bianca berated Al Rogoff for not believing her, and Connie was on my case for not calling her back last Sunday. But that aside, we ordered our frozen daiquiris, martinis, beers, and one rum and Coke, happily concocted and served by Simon Pettibone; then bent our elbows in a toast to friendship.

The girls looked splendid in jeans and the guys summery in chinos, white ducks, and shorts. The shorts, I'm happy to say, were on Arnie Turnbolt, not Al Rogoff.

Binky, his bandaged fingers reduced to two Band-Aids, spoke of running down to Coconut Grove to check out the scene. Connie and Bianca seemed to hit it off and giggled a lot over very little. Arnie Turnbolt told us he's dating Virginia Cranston's hairdresser. Priscilla, exotic in a black sheath that began well below her neck and ended well above her knees, joined the party between making her appointed rounds. And dear Jasmine Pettibone once again brought around a tray of shrimp for us to nibble on.

"Any news from California?" I asked Mrs. Pettibone.

"Nothing, Archy. Still not a word from my cousin and his daughter is frantic," she told us.

"Sorry I never got around to checking out Henry Peavey," Al apologized. "But I will when I get back to work."

"What's this about Henry Peavey?" Arnie exclaimed.

We all stared at him. "You know who Henry Peavey is?" I asked.

"Of course I know who Henry Peavey is," Arnie said. "Doesn't everyone?"

"Tell us," Mrs. Pettibone begged. "Tell us who he is."

Mr. Pettibone paused in the midst of shaking a dry Manhattan, his hands frozen in midair. Priscilla pretended not to see a diner beckoning for her. Mrs. Pettibone put down her tray of shrimp. Al, Binky, Connie, Bianca, and I all circled around Arnie as he dramatically expounded:

"On the morning of February 2, 1922, the Los Angeles police were summoned to 404 Alvarado Street, Bungalow B. There, they found two executives of Paramount Pictures burning papers in the fireplace, the film star Mabel Normand frantically searching through drawers, unidentified men simply milling around, one of whom had come with a case of bootleg gin– and Hollywood's most popular and talented director, William Desmond Taylor, dead on the living room floor with a bullet hole in his back.

"In the kitchen, Taylor's valet, Henry Peavey, was washing dishes."

To be continued . . .